FOXPRINTS

Other Books by Patrick McGinley

Bogmail

Goosefoot

Foggage

The Trick of the Ga Bolga

FOXPRINTS
by
Patrick McGinley

A
Joan
Kahn
BOOK

ST. MARTIN'S PRESS
NEW YORK

Library of Congress Cataloging in Publication Data

McGinley, Patrick, 1937–
  Foxprints

  I. Title
PR6063.A21787F65   1985   823'.914   85-8362
ISBN 0-312-30216-9

First U. S. Edition

10 9 8 7 6 5 4 3 2 1

To Patrick Whelan

1

THOUGH Martin Reddin was in a hurry to get away, he did not fly to London. Instead he took the morning ferry from Cork. An air hostess, he thought, might easily remember a handsome face, whereas no ship's steward would look twice at him. On the eight-and-a-half-hour crossing he took every precaution, however. He avoided the deck, where sea winds kept people alert; and he avoided the bar, where stout made his garrulous compatriots inquisitive. He got himself a seat in a corner of the darkened television room, and there he sat until they docked at Pembroke, though several times during the voyage he was tempted to go in search of a ham-and-tomato roll.

He was hungry on arrival, so he bought three sandwiches and two cans of orange juice before boarding the train. The sandwiches were little more than an appetiser, but they kept him going till he changed at Swansea. Now the worst was over. In three hours he would be in London, one unremarked and unremarkable man among several million. He was careful to make himself unremarkable. He had shaved off his carefully cultivated beard and put on a cloth cap, an unironed shirt and a second-hand jacket that smelt vaguely of mackerel. He told himself that, apart from the essence of long-dead fish that rose tantalisingly from his cuffs, he might pass for a typical Paddy, returning dourly to England after a month of excessive drinking and talking with the boon companions of his now romanticised youth.

With a pleasurable sense of ceremony renewed, he lit his first pipe in four years, stretched his legs, and coughed as he inhaled. The cough gave him comfort. It would be nice to have a good morning splutter in the bathroom again, to have the satisfaction of cocking a snook at doctors, medical journalists and all men who lived long lives of desperate moderation. A life without drink and tobacco, like the unexamined life, was not worth living. He would not have his first drink yet, though. Barmen were sharp. They too might look at a face and remember it. He would wait till he had put at least five hundred yards between himself and Paddington Station. He looked at his reflection in the window pane and then at a row of lights in the darkness beyond. He was alone in the compartment. He sniffed his cuffs and closed his eyes.

At Newport he was joined by two middle-aged men who flung themselves on the seat like well-filled bags of flour. He barely turned his head but he was in no doubt about their origins. The tall one was mellifluously English, the short one fricatively Scots. It amused him to think that the compartment now accommodated an Englishman, and Irishman and a Scotsman. All they needed was a Welshman to complete the fearsome foursome, to make possible perhaps an intertribal game of whist. Would the Englishman and the Scotsman play the Irishman and the Welshman? Or would they spurn whist and plump for a card game without partners? Pretending to sleep, he listened to their heavy breathing, which seemed to reduce the size of the compartment. It was the breathing of heavy men who had been drinking heavily, and it reminded him of the breathing of bulls in hot weather. The Englishman suddenly stopped breathing and spoke.

"As I was saying, I've seen foxes in action more than once. I'm not an innocent in these matters, I'd have you know."

"You may have seen, but have you observed?" To judge by his speech, the Scotsman was three sheets in the wind, at least one more than the Englishman.

"I've taken the trouble to time them. They take from fifteen minutes to half an hour, and then they remain locked together for another hour, tail to tail, facing in opposite directions."

"There's nothing odd about that. I've often seen Highland sheepdogs in tug of war for longer. What happens is that the vixen's vulva contracts and the dog fox can't withdraw. It's the vulpine equivalent of our vaginismus."

"Our vaginismus! Our cobblers, more like. It's got nothing to do with vaginismus. The real reason is that the fox has a bone in his pile-driver. Unlike yours, his isn't just erectile tissue."

"I beg your pardon!"

"The bone, you may wish to know, is called a baculum or an os penis," the Englishman continued blithely.

"Have you ever got close enough to measure it?" The Scotsman spoke with the confidence of a man who thinks he's being witty.

"I'm afraid not. To tell the truth, I lack the necessary skill in baculometry." The Englishman, who thought he was being wittier, laughed with tipsy delight.

"You need a drink, my friend. You're laughing at your own jokes." The Scotsman struggled to his feet.

Reddin watched them shuffle off to the bar, while the carriage swayed with their unbalanced laughter. He had no idea what to make of them. It was not the kind of laughter, nor was it the kind of conversation, he was accustomed to in Cork.

As Wales gave way to England, he wondered what he should call himself. Martin Reddin's picture would be in the papers tomorrow. He would have to settle for a less conspicuous name. Robert Lydon? Neil Murphy? Jerry Rooney? None seemed as real as Martin Reddin. Then he remembered Charles Keating, who worked with him ten years ago on *The Cork Clarion* before emigrating to Newcastle to restore to happiness his homesick Geordie wife. Reddin had not heard of him since. He was still in Newcastle, maybe, subbing the local rag, unaware that on the highroad to London was his old boon companion who would apply for jobs as Charles Keating, ex-sports writer of *The Cork Clarion*. It would work if he wasn't asked for references and cuttings, but that, he felt, might be a large "if." However, he did not have to stick to his last. If it came to the worst, he would clean windows, paint houses, drive vans, cook fish and chips, or run a Chinese laundry. He was only thirty-six, and he was ready, willing, and moderately able.

At Reading the heavy breathers returned, breathing more heavily. They breathed so heavily in fact that he could no longer get the smell of mackerel from his cuffs.

"The trouble with you Scots is that you don't think stubbornly. With Celts the Socratic method is the only medicine. I'll ask you once more. Who hunts the fox?"

The Scotsman thought deeply.

"The unspeakable, of course." He smiled like a precocious schoolboy.

"Balls, my dear chap. Not unspeakables, not fox hunters, but landowners. Now for the next question. If it wasn't dark night, what would you see through the window?"

"Land."

"Landscape. English landscape," emphasised the Englishman. "And what gives the English landscape its English character?"

"The English weather." The Scotsman managed to make three sibilants out of one.

"Wrong again. What gives the English landscape its English character is the fox—what you would no doubt call the uneatable."

"I beseech you, in the bowels of Christ, think it possible you may be mistaken."

"You may address me as if I were the General Assembly of the Church of Scotland, but I still say we owe the lineaments of the English landscape to the red fox, commonly known as *Vulpes fulva*. The landowners who hunt the fox—sod the City gents who ape them—preserve those features of the landscape which make it English—the coverts, the copses, the hedges without which there would be no fox hunting. Most of those features are agriculturally uneconomic. They are preserved entirely for the convenience of the fox. Pass an Act of Parliament to abolish fox hunting and you transform the English landscape. The hedges created by the Enclosure Acts would vanish within a decade. So would the coverts and the copses, and Reynard would have nowhere to lay his head."

"You forget that he's an opportunist. If you destroy his country seat, like Mr. Deeds he'll come to town."

"He's already arrived." The Englishman laughed triumphantly.

"I've seen the future," the Scotsman shouted, "and the pavements of our hermetically sealed suburbs were fouled not by pyedogs but pyefoxes."

"Then we both know what we must do!"

The Englishman looked the Scotsman in the eye, and the Scotsman's eye lit up with the thrill of it. The Englishman laughed with sterling glee and the Scotsman joined him so enthusiastically that his prawn-pink cheeks shook till they glowed like fox fire on a dark night.

When they had exhausted the fox and the peculiarities of his penis, they turned to Fleet Street, leaving Keating transfixed in incredulous fascination. A moment ago he was certain that he had fallen among aristocrats, but now as he noted the cynical knowingness of their conversation, with which his craft had made him so familiar, he knew that he had come unto his own. They spoke lightly of *The Times, The Guardian, The Financial Times* and *The Daily Telegraph,* but they did not speak at all of *The Express, The Mail, The Mirror* and *The Sun.* Slowly, it dawned on him that he was not in the company of his peers but of his betters, men who read only the quality prints and found even them illiterate. It occurred to him that he could amuse them with the comic absurdities of *The Clarion,* but he knew the dangers of self-advertisement in a situation that called for self-concealment, so he closed his eyes again and listened with growing admiration to the Englishman giving the Scotsman a convincingly erudite lecture on alopecia, or what he called "fox mange," in foxes.

Both of them were already standing as the train drew into Paddington. Keating, who did not have a suitcase, also stood up to find that in his new-found interest in the fox he had forgotten that he was bursting for a pee. He hurried to the toilet already unzipping, and as he passed his compartment re-zipped on the way back, he noticed that the Englishman had forgotten his briefcase. He looked for him in the crowd, but he and his friend had gone. He thought of handing in the case at the barrier, but then it occurred to him that he might be asked to give his name, and anyhow he did not want to attract attention. He thought that never before had he heard such unusual conversation, and it saddened him to think that he might never hear it again. He opened the briefcase out of curiosity. It was almost empty. All it contained was a copy of *The Times* and *The Princess Casamassima,* a long, red-handled knife like a stiletto, and a diary. He put the knife and diary in his pocket— the knife as a weapon of defence and the diary as a souvenir— and with a sense of disbelief walked out into Praed Street.

The next week was one of bafflement for Keating. It was his first time in London, and he found it disappointingly uninviting, full of black men and brown men and young men with their hair dyed red and yellow. Wherever he went, he looked for fresh, young women, but they were all being kissed by black men, brown men and young men in jeans and leather jackets. He felt so out of date that it seemed to him that it might not be so easy to get the poke he'd been looking forward to for the last four years.

In the mornings he read the English newspapers, but none of them, not even *The Sun,* had anything to say about Martin Reddin. In the afternoons he looked at buildings—St. Paul's, Westminster Abbey and the Houses of Parliament—but, though he liked them, he soon discovered that not on stone alone does man live, at least in London. In the evenings he went to the cinema in the hope of meeting some dark-eyed, slender-ankled beauty with a taste for outré sex, but he always came back to his guest house alone to look through the Englishman's diary, which seemed to be his only connection with the sane world of the eminently sane Anglo-Saxons.

The entries were short. They consisted of double-barrelled names such as Weston-George, Chambers-Granby, Crawford-Woodman, and Elliott-Anglesey, cryptic perhaps, but disappointingly prosaic compared with the enthralling conversation about fox mange in foxes. However, one day outside "The Marquis of Anglesey" in Convent Garden he realised that they weren't cryptic at all but plain as a pikestaff; they referred to the Englishman's drinking trysts, nothing more. If he went to all the pubs mentioned, he might eventually catch up with him, but the list of pubs was long and there were several of the same name in London.

Such concerns were luxuries, however. He knew that he had only £5,500 to his name, that he would soon have to think of earning a living, but before he started looking for work he would devote a week to finding an inexpensive and not inconvenient place to dip his wick. The problem was that in sex he was finicky. He was sick of the missionary position, which was the only position that Esther and most Irishwomen would allow, but he had heard from friends who had been to England of the incredible sexual ingenuity of the Anglo-Saxons. He had heard from them too that you could get it off any barmaid in any London pub, but he knew himself better than to take the first that offered. He would insist on certain stipulations regarding height, colour of eyes, condition of teeth and circumference of ankle. Being Irish, he was much preoccupied with the ankle, because most Irishwomen had ankles like tree trunks. To him the correct ankle was as important as the correct accent to an Englishman, because the correct ankle in Ireland is as rare as the correct accent in England.

After a fortnight of walking about London in stunned admiration of the permissive society, he decided that if he was to get what he wanted he would have to pay for it. To pay, even in a capitalist society, was to admit defeat, but he took comfort from the thought that his defeat was due to his aroma, which caused the barmaids he approached to take him for a fishmonger. Now that he had decided to turn punter, he would have to look the part. He would have to make certain sartorial adjustments. He asked a news vendor outside Charing Cross Station where he might buy a dirty raincoat. The news vendor was a kindly sort. He enquired which part of Ireland he came from and told him that the best second-hand macks were sold in Petticoat Lane on Sunday mornings. Keating was delighted. It was Saturday. He had only one day to wait.

On the way back to the guest house he went into St. Martin-in-the-Fields for a rest. He was the only one in the nave and he sat in the back pew and opened the prayer book, finding, as he might have known, not solace but cause for self-accusation. He knelt on a hassock and with his head in his hands recited the most elegant prayer he knew, a prayer for his eleven-year-old daughter whom he would never see again:

> May she be granted beauty and yet not
> Beauty to make a stranger's eye distraught,
> Or hers before a looking-glass, for such,
> Being made beautiful overmuch,
> Consider beauty a sufficient end,
> Lose natural kindness and maybe
> The heart-revealing intimacy
> That chooses right, and never find a friend.

On the way out he spied a notice about a jumble sale in the crypt, which made him think that, with a bit of luck, the journey to Petticoat Lane might not be necessary. It was late in the morning and the best bargains had gone, but after a ten-minute search a charming old lady, breathing churchiness and sanctification, found him a splendid tweed hacking jacket and off-white mack in the correct state of dilapidation. After paying her, he gave her his own second-hand jacket, the one that smelt of mackerel, and she accepted it with Christian good humour, which nevertheless failed to conceal her reluctance. He left St. Martin's in a state of excitement, and on the steps outside put on the raincoat over the hacking jacket, though the morning was warm. Next he put on a pair of spectacles without lenses, which he had bought in a magic shop in Southampton Row the previous day, and set off for Soho, which to judge by his map was only a fox's step away.

Looking, feeling and smelling the part, at least in his own

opinion, he crossed Shaftesbury Avenue into Greek Street. To his surprise, it was full of restaurants, not quite the street for a man who had already breakfasted well. He walked the length of Frith Street, then Dean Street and finally Meard Street, of which he had high hopes, but not one woman turned to look at him. In Wardour Street he saw a man, who was dressed exactly like himself, reading a sex magazine as he went along. Keating was scandalised. That, he thought, was going a bit far. Tearing the arse out of it. Or gilding the lily, as Shakespeare took care not to put it. Now, he himself had a sense of proportion. Reading about sex in Soho was surely like reading about coals in Newcastle, assuming of course that there were coals in Newcastle. Not the kind of thing a level-headed man would do.

"He's obviously English," he told himself. "And unlike the English, we Irish are not promiscuous. We seek not sex but solace, not the infernal grove but the lactiferous breast, not the furry cup of the Nibelungs but the golden apples of the Hesperides. Place an Irishman between two open-legged whores so that he is equidistant from both, and the chances are that he will scrounge a drink and a fag before dying of sexual starvation. We are a spiritual people who love wine and song first and only late in the night, under the influence of both, turn to women.

Having absolved himself of his failure to find coals in Newcastle, and proved at least to himself that the Irish are more spiritual than the Anglo-Saxons, he spied something that made him forget for a moment his weary feet and sexual hunger, a yellow fascia above the traffic on which were inscribed the words "Intrepid Fox." Recalling the Englishman and the Scotsman and imagining a cool pint of English bitter poured by an English rose, he opened the door and went in.

The barmaid was not English, she was Irish; but the bitter, which came from Burton on Trent, tasted cool and nectarine after the heat of the streets. He looked round for a place to sit down, and there in the corner, deep in conversation, were the upright Englishman and the portly Scot. Keating, having found himself a seat at the next table, was pleased to hear that they had not lost their enthusiasm for the fox.

"The best way to tell the dog from the vixen is by the white of his scrotum, as opposed to the white of his eye. But if you can't get close enough for a dekko, you may be lucky enough to see him urinate. That's the giveaway. The dog doesn't squat as low as the vixen. Sometimes he will even stand and risk wetting his legs, especially in a wind."

"I've never seen a fox make water alone," the Scotsman admitted. "But I've seen one scent-marking a vixen. He passed his tail over her shoulder and urinated in a manner to which she was clearly accustomed."

"I once watched a fox scent-marking a stone, and when he had gone I went and sniffed it."

"Pungent?" the Scotsman enquired.

"Very. I think I can tell the smell of their urine, but this, I should say, came from the anal sac."

"I'm off to do a bit of scent-marking myself." The Scotsman got to his feet.

"Another drink?"

"No, I must first do my shopping, but I'll see you in the 'Cheshire Cheese,' if you like, in an hour."

"At two, then."

When the Scotsman came back from the gents, he picked up his paper and left. Keating kept a surreptitious eye on the Englishman, who sat staring at his glass of white wine, meditating perhaps on the fox's supracaudal gland or the seasonal variations in the colour of his pelt.

Whatever engrossed him, Keating could not withhold his admiration. The Englishman was tall and well-proportioned with clear, blue eyes, fairish skin and a closely clipped military moustache that formed a kind of thatched gable over the square end-wall of his chin. His brown hair was thick and straight, combed back from a high, broad forehead that was well defined below by triangular eyebrows reflecting the triangularity of his moustache. Though he must have been nearly sixty, he was extremely handsome, not only in looks but in bearing, so handsome in fact that Keating had to admit that he himself took second place.

He followed the Englishman out into Wardour Street and Shaftesbury Avenue, as he made his towering way towards Charing Cross and the Strand. Once he paused to look in the window of a record shop but for the most part he walked at a pace that was metronomic in its regularity, shoulders back and head above the other less felicitously proportioned heads beneath him. He was wearing a brown hacking jacket and cavalry twills, and though his hacking jacket was well cut, it was no smarter than Keating's—or so Keating told himself as they crossed the eastern boundary of the City of Westminster. When they came to "Ye Olde Cheshire Cheese," the Englishman entered but Keating, for the sake of verisimilitude, remained outside for three or four minutes. He made good use of his time, though. He took off his dirty mack and folded it inside out over his arm, and then he brushed the dust of the pavements from the perforations of his brown leather shoes. His trousers could have done with a press, but he flung back his shoulders and confidently checked the slant of his jacket pockets before going in.

The Englishman was at the bar with another glass of white wine before him. Keating, who saw himself as a quick thinker, asked him if it was drinkable. The Englishman turned and considered Keating and his glass. Then he took a careful sip and said: "No."

Keating ordered a glass of red and for the comfort of the Englishman pronounced it no better than the white. The Englishman was not to be comforted, so Keating tried to elicit his sympathy by confiding that he had come in for a quick one to steady his nerve before seeing the sports editor of *The Sunday Mirror*. This unsolicited piece of information had an extraordinary effect on the Englishman. Wittingly or unwittingly, he clicked his heels, shot his cuffs, and inspected the red handkerchief in his breast pocket. Keating, pretending not to notice, said that he had just arrived from Newcastle on his beam ends, that he was looking for freelance work in Fleet Street, that he was desperate, that any freelance work would do.

"You don't sound Geordie to me. In fact, if I may say so, you sound positively Irish."

"I'm an Irishman who's worked in Newcastle," Keating agreed. "I was sports writer on *The Newcastle Chronicle* for seven years."

The Englishman said that he himself worked on *The Telegraph,* and then asked him why he had come to London and where he was now living.

"I may not be able to put you in the way of work immediately," he said, "but I have a vacancy for an Irishman in my house which might conceivably interest you."

"A vacancy?"

"I share my house with a Scotsman and a Welshman, who are what a certain class of persons call 'paying guests.' As things stand, the Celtic fringe is under-represented. The Scots and the Welsh do their best, I know, but for Celtic excess I believe you've got to go to West Britain. Are you a man of excess?"

"I do my best." Keating could only marvel at the other man's detachment.

"Celts are as necessary to the Anglo-Saxon temperament as is cellulose to the Anglo-Saxon digestion. My father, who was a doctor and knew about the function of cellulose, always said that Celts are the social equivalent of roughage. Without them, your over-refined Anglo-Saxon would die of spiritual constipation. For that reason, I'm sorry I can't offer you a local habitation here and now, but, if you are interested, I should like to meet you on Monday to talk things over. If we hit it off, I might offer you a mock-Tudor roof over your head, a silk shirt on your back and three square meals a day in return for certain services which should not prove too exacting. In other words, you would live comfortably and cheaply until you found a suitable job."

"What are the services?" Keating enquired.

"That is something we shall discuss on Monday. As I already mentioned, before we strike a bargain we must both be satisfied that we can spark off each other."

They arranged to meet in "The Tipperary" at noon on Monday, and Keating went off to meet the sports editor of *The Sunday Mirror,* who was too busy to see him at short notice. He made an appointment for the following Wednesday, and walked along Drury Lane with undiminished self-confidence and a touching faith in the milk of Anglo-Saxon kindness. He felt so pleased with the day's work, particularly with his second-hand hacking jacket, that he went into Horne's in Tottenham Court Road and bought a pair of beige cavalry twills to match.

"Couldn't carouse with Carruthers in those old bags, could you, Keating?" he thought and laughed in Bedford Square on the way back to Gower Street.

Keating arrived at "The Tipperary" at a quarter to twelve but the Englishman was there before him.

"I'm Peter Quilter." He extended his arm.

"Charles Keating."

"Keating? Is that an Irish name?"

"Yes."

"I somehow imagined you might be called O'Brien or

14

O'Shaughnessy, which would go well with MacGeoch, the name of our formidable Scot."

Quilter ordered drinks and came to the point without hesitation.

"What I need is a man of parts, a man who can turn his hand to anything. Are you a good letter writer?"

"I think so. But why does a journalist need a letter writer?"

"There is a fair, but not an overwhelming, amount of correspondence. Lawn mowers, televisions, cookers, washing machines breaking down. Standing orders to be filled in. A serious owner-occupier could spend most of his time writing letters of complaint to manufacturers. Bookkeeping is another asset. Do you do double-entry?"

"I have been known to balance simple accounts. Nothing elaborate. I was treasurer of a golf club once."

"Have you been in the army?"

"Only the FCA."

"What's that? Something to do with chartered accountants?"

"It's Irish for Local Defence Force."

"Doesn't count. I fought in the Western Desert, but I don't mention it."

"I'm afraid I don't remember the War."

"I don't remember the First, but I prefer it to the Second. It comes closer to achieving the unities of time, place and action. Are you married?"

Keating noted a sudden fierceness in the Englishman's eye, and without hesitation decided to say "no."

"Divorced?"

"No, separated. We don't have divorce in Ireland."

"At 'Foxgloves' we're all divorced, all men who can look after themselves. A man, as opposed to a milksop, should be self-sufficient. Are you?"

"My needs are simple. I'm more self-sufficient than most."

"At 'Foxgloves' we're all over-educated."

———

"I have a double first in Old Irish and mathematical phys-
ics."

"A *rara avis*. From an ancient university?"

"Mine was founded in 1592."

"No need to enquire further. There are two types of university: those that were founded in the thirteenth century and
those that weren't. But tell me, am I to call you doctor?"

"I fear not. I started a Ph.D. thesis on why there is no apos-
trophe in *Finnegans Wake,* but I ran out of steam after twenty-
five thousand words."

"I was wrong. *The Sunday Times,* not *The Telegraph,* is the
place for you. You obviously have the knack of saying little at
some length. Do you cook?"

"Cooking is one of my hobbies." Keating felt that he was
winning.

"Are you a creator of *haute cuisine?*"

"I have never had either the equipment or the resources to
create it, but I have often frequented it—in my dreams."

"Before the day is out, you'll have the opportunity you have
dreamt of. But first for a little of the theory. Name two birds
that are best cooked undrawn."

"Woodcock and snipe."

"Very good. If I cooked you a *charlotte russe* and *a charlotte
aux pommes,* which would you say was the real charlotte?"

Quilter looked triumphantly at Keating, and Keating shivered as he saw that the Englishman was not perfect. From a
certain angle, his left eye looked sunken and his right eye
hooded. The sunken eye looked smaller than the hooded eye,
perhaps because it seemed farther away, and it also looked odd
because you could see the complete eyelid that covered it. Keating lost his concentration and asked Quilter to repeat the
question. As he repeated it, a strange thing happened. The
sunken eye grew until it was the exact replica of the hooded
eye, thus giving Keating the correct answer.

"Both are equally real." He smiled omnisciently.

"Right so far," the Englishman conceded. "Now tell me which is served hot and which cold."

"The *russe* is served cold, the other hot."

"Correct again. But listen to this. If I asked you to sauce a capon, would you prepare Sauce Hollandaise or Sauce Polonaise?"

Keating deliberated with all the subtlety of a privy counsellor. He looked at the right eye, now once again cucullated; then he looked at the left which had receded like a magic island in Celtic mythology, but no answer came from either. The barmaid picked up a carving knife and Keating remembered the answer.

"Neither," he said. " 'To sauce a capon' is simply to carve it."

"And if you sauce a capon, what do you do to a goose?"

"Rear it, of course."

"And that," said Quilter, "is precisely what you and I are going to do." But now for a hypothetical question that only intuition will answer. If you were chef in a country house where fox meat was regarded as a delicacy, how would you garnish fox chops?"

"I'd first consult the master of the house as to his preference, and, if he didn't care to divulge it, I'd serve them *à la forestière*."

"An imaginative suggestion. You've passed the theory, now for the practical."

"I shall need a spacious kitchen, a set of non-stick saucepans and a cooker with a timer." Keating tried to discourage him.

"Are you free this afternoon?"

"Yes, as far as I know."

"Come down with me to 'Foxgloves.' That way we'll kill two birds with one stone. You shall have your practical and I shall have lunch."

There was no denying him. They took a Sevenoaks train from Charing Cross and sat in silence until they passed Chislehurst. At the first hint of the countryside, Quilter stretched his legs and breathed more freely.

"Do you intend remarrying?" he asked.

"No, I am happy as I am." Keating could tell what pleased him.

"Life begins with divorce; not, as they say, at forty. Marriage, however, is as necessary as school. In fact, it's a form of schooling, but once over it should never again be entertained. I hope you like 'Foxgloves.' What I need is a major-domo to look after house and garden, but he must be a man I can treat as an equal. I had a houseboy until he drank all my claret. Housekeepers are too nosy, and housemaids are a thing of the past. Moreover, they all expect sex, and waiting for it in their favourite position they develop housemaid's knee."

Quilter's sunken eye expanded while his hooded eye beamed like a lighthouse on a moonless night. Then the hooded eye transmitted half its light to the sunken eye, and Quilter laughed the kind of laugh that can only be laughed by a man whose throat is dry. Keating laughed too, but his laugh was different from Quilter's. While the Englishman's laugh had its history in overheated drawing-rooms, the Irishman's came from bare mountains and salty mud-flats with the honk of winter wild geese overhead. Keating thought of telling Quilter which was the better laugh, but he didn't. Instead he warmed to his benefactor. There was nothing he liked better than the innocence of a man who can laugh at his own jokes, and he had a feeling that there were a lot of innocent men in England.

They got off at Wistwood, and he followed Quilter up the steps to the bridge.

"All Wistwood is divided by the railway into two parts," Quilter said with heavy predictability. "Look east and then look west and tell me what you see."

"Houses of the mock-Tudor variety."

"Can you see any variation within the variety?"

"I know nothing of mock-Tudor but I think I can distinguish it from the Baroque."

"Look at the chimneys. That's where the difference lies, and *vive la différence* is what I say. Chimneys came into their own in Tudor times, when coal began to replace wood in the fireplace. They grew taller and more idiosyncratic, and some of that idiosyncrasy has reached Wistwood East. In the East the chimneys are high and gracile, never squat like the chimneys in the West. In a word, my dear chap, by their chimneys ye shall know them."

"On which side is 'Foxgloves'?"

"On the East side, of course. And don't look surprised."

They walked in silence along a quiet, tree-lined avenue until they came to a house on the corner of Raleigh Way and Essex Ride.

"'Foxgloves.'" Quilter pointed proudly. "Note how it outranks the others. Note the steeper gables and the curved timbers. The close studding, I'd like you to observe, is pure East Anglia."

With a key that was positively medieval in size, Quilter opened the heavy baronial door, telling Keating that at least in Wistwood East an Englishman's home was still his castle. Inside, the hallway was streaked with coloured light from the circular stained-glass window above their heads, and the kitchen beyond was a riot of reflections from polished bronze utensils.

"This is where it all happens." Quilter pointed to the gas cooker. "Though I once had a cook who put too much on the back burner."

He opened the fridge door and peered inside.

"My godfathers, all we have left is eggs, milk and cheese. I was sure we had a pound of sirloin."

"I'll cook you an omelette, then." Keating was pleased that he did not have to tackle steak Béarnaise.

"Can you cook me an omelette without breaking eggs?"

"No." Keating decided to be honest.

"That is the correct answer. But since you insist on breaking eggs, make me a soufflé, a cheese soufflé, *un soufflé au fromage*. I shall put a bottle of plink-plonk in the fridge to chill. You'll find me in the dining-room when you've done."

Keating made what he judged to be the lightest soufflé of his career and placed it before the Englishman, who had fallen asleep over the wide oak table. He tapped the table with the fork, and the Englishman woke and said he had just scored a century in his dream.

"Now pour yourself a glass of wine and sit opposite." He smiled. "All great cooks are voyeurs. Their greatest pleasure is to see their dishes being dispatched. Every good cook deserves a good trencherman in the same way that a good composer deserves a good orchestra."

Trying to ignore the pangs of hunger, Keating waited for the effect of the first forkful. He need not have worried. Quilter raised his glass and toasted "the best soufflé I've tasted since the days of Escoffier at the Savoy."

"The making of a soufflé is an acid test," he pronounced. "Like the writing of a *Times* leader, it requires spiritual preparation. A man who can make an impromptu soufflé is a cook."

Keating drank two glasses of white wine, while Quilter talked about the *bombe Nero,* which in his view was Escoffier's greatest invention. Keating felt jealous of Escoffier and wished that the Englishman would concentrate on his soufflé. He knew that no man can do justice to a soufflé while conjuring up images of flaming ice. At length Quilter ate the last forkful. He sat for a long time looking at Keating, then slowly opened his mouth to break the silence.

"Come live with me and be my chef," he said with all the languor of a sated lover.

"But I'm not a chef, I'm a journalist."

"Then stay till you get a job. I know several Fleet Street editors. I'll do my best for you."

"I could do worse than stay, I suppose."

"It's a bargain, then. I'll give you free board and lodging, in a manner of speaking, till you land a proper job. You can come and go as you please. You'll have no expenses. All you need do is shop and cook and run the house."

"I'll move in tomorrow evening."

As Keating walked back to the station alone, he felt pleased that he had lit on the suburbs. Central London was noisy, dirty and cosmopolitan, overwhelmingly the haunt of graceless youth. The suburbs, from what he could see, were clean, quiet and fast asleep, if not already dead. They were a row of overtended gardens in which anything that looked remotely like a weed was plucked and burnt the moment it raised its head. That suited him. Here he would move among other sleepwalkers until the storm clouds behind him had cleared. He would ask no questions and answer none. He would accept Quilter's hospitality for as long as it suited him, but no longer.

2

IT was already dark when Keating arrived at "Foxgloves" with the suitcase he had bought secondhand that morning. He also bought shirts, socks, underwear, pyjamas and a dressing gown of cotton and polyester patterned with little portcullises which he thought would be acceptable in a house described by the owner as his castle.

"What do you think of the name 'Foxgloves?'" Quilter asked him in the hallway.

"It's unusual, at least in Cork."

"It was called 'The Covert' when I came here. Too obvious, too common, I thought, so I renamed it. To tell the truth, I'd much prefer a converted oasthouse. I could easily find one farther out, but I choose to live here because, as the author of *Vanity Fair* knew so well, the true pleasure of life is to live with one's inferiors."

Quilter then showed him to his room and delivered a brief but informative lecture on the finer points of mock-Tudor décor which, he said, it exemplified. Lastly, he took him across the landing to a door marked "Ooja-cum-Pivvy."

"What do you make of that, Keating?"

"A corruption of 'Ouija-cum-Privy,' perhaps?"

"Not true, but full marks for effort. That's the latrines, the place to which even the C.O. is summoned on occasion. A word of caution, though. You may read behind that door, but you may not gossip. Remember there's a war on. As an officer, I have reason to know of the damage that can be done by latrine rumours."

"I shall bear that in mind." Keating tried to be serious, but he doubted if Quilter was as eccentric as he pretended.

"No need to worry about MacGeoch. As a Scot, he's mean with words, but Garlick, whom you'll meet, is a gossip. He's our Welshman, as I think I've told you, but he isn't really Welsh—he spent a term at an English public school. And while I'm on the subject of your fellow guests, never refer to MacGeoch as 'Kilty' or 'Monsieur le Picte.' He takes exception to all intertribal joshing except what emanates from me. And mind how you pronounce his name. Say it till I hear."

"MacGeoch."

"Excellent. There's nothing he likes better than a well-taken fricative. You have the flair, Keating, you have the flair."

"But it was we Irish who gave the Scots their much-vaunted fricatives!"

"Now, none of that. I shall not have intertribal dissension in my house, especially dissension that has no basis in scholarship. But I mustn't digress. Don't worry about getting breakfast tomorrow. We'll all get our own. Your duties will begin at noon. I shall expect dinner at nine. That will give us time for an early-evening drink. And may I suggest something simple for a start—goulash or bourguignon—until you find your way round the cookhouse."

"I'm tired," Keating pleaded. "I think I'll turn in."

"A final word. You may be woken by a sound in the night. It's Fox knocking over the dustbin lid. When you hear him, just turn over and go back to sleep again. True Wistwoodlanders say at such moments: 'Charles James is in the back garden, all's right with the world.'"

Keating closed his bedroom door and thanked his ancestral gods, not to mention Cuchulainn and Finn MacCool. In pyjamas and portcullised dressing gown, he lay on the side bed and read a poem from his pocket book of Old Irish nature poetry:

> Blackbird, it's well for you,
> Wherever in the thicket be your nest,
> Hermit that sounds no bell,
> Sweet, soft, peaceful is your whistle.

He pronounced aloud the sacred words, but the blackbird, the thicket and the silent bell were in another country. He closed the book, but he couldn't sleep because of the disturbing effect of Quilter's eccentricity. Twice he crossed the landing to the loo, and each time it was empty, surprisingly innocent of the much-feared latrine rumour. The ancient Royal Doulton lavatory bowl was mounted on a block of wood about six inches high, which gave him a feeling of being enthroned, and in the moment of evacuation a sense of remoteness from the common concerns of unaccommodated humanity. In front of the bowl was a music stand with a French magazine showing a daring young woman, trousered but topless, bestowing a fellatious kiss on the erect member of a trouserless sandwichman. On the wall opposite was a shelf with six or seven books, including the collected works of Robert Burns, the *Mabinogion* and, for the benefit of the Englishman, a leather-bound edition of *Alice in Wonderland*. He reminded himself to buy a copy of the *Táin Bó Cuailgne* for the same purpose. He would then remind the others that the eighth-century Ulster epic predated anything of comparable worth that they had to offer.

When he finally slept, he slept soundly and woke late. As he came down the stairs at ten, Quilter was about to leave.

"A word of advice, Keating. If you'll pardon my saying so, you'd better get yourself properly kitted out. You'll need brown brogues, knee-length gumboots and a good dinner jacket."

"It's an odd combination." Keating pretended not to be puzzled.

"Not at all. In Wistwood East we live under the illusion that we're out in the depths of Hampshire."

"I can see how that might account for the brogues and gumboots, but—"

"At 'Foxgloves' we like to think that we live in a country house."

"Hence the dinner jacket?"

"Correct, Keating. You're not a double-first for nothing. And now before I go, I shall impart a final word of advice. If time should lie heavily on your hands in the forenoon, you will find a brass telescope in the upstairs room we call the Arsenal."

"A brass telescope?"

"Mrs. Slim-Bum Gardener across the road spends her mornings in the front garden. I'm told by MacGeoch—note the correct pronunciation—that her arse in slacks is a treat when she stoops. Hence the telescope. It was MacGeoch's idea, not mine. He claims to be able to count the number of shots to the inch in her new herringbone trousers."

"Do you believe him?"

"My own view is that her garden suffers from overweeding."

When Quilter had gone, he made himself coffee and toast and waited patiently for the forenoon, when time would lie heavily on his hands. But soon his patience deserted him. At half-past ten he went up to the Arsenal and sat beside the cannon-like telescope. After twenty minutes Mrs. Gardener came out of the house with a wheelbrace in one hand and a garden trowel in the other. She looked up at the sky, dropped the wheelbrace, and sniffed the heart of an ailing flower, while outside her gate a poodle raised a hind leg against a chestnut tree. Mrs. Gardener looked severe and the owner of the poodle looked into the distance, innocently serene. A second poodle sniffed the dripping bark, and Mrs. Gardener turned her back and furiously ladled the earth at the bottom of her rose bush, as if she were ladling thick soup in a cauldron sunk to the rim in the lawn.

Keating put his left eye to the telescope which he found already focused on the back of her left trouser leg, about fourteen inches above the knee. He tried to count the number of shots to the inch, but the cloth was too fine or the telescope insufficiently powerful. The cloth was a shiny electric blue, taut over the fullness of her buttock, and, as he looked, the barrel of the telescope became an electrode through which the electricity of the material entered the vacuum of his open eye. He straightened quickly and moved backwards, astonished at the force of the erection in the left leg of his cavalry twill trousers. He half-limped to his room and sank onto the edge of the bed, hearing Quilter explode with incredulity: "An erection before lunch? Unheard of at 'Foxgloves.' As I said, you may have a sherry, but not an erection. Like a vintage port, a firm erection should be reserved for after dinner."

To bring down his temperature, he thought of the boyhood deeds of Finn and studied the map of Kent and Sussex on the opposite wall simultaneously. It was a colour map, dotted with pictures of ancient castles: Hever, Dover, Herstmonceux, Rochester, Mereworth, Lewes, Leeds, Deal, Bodiam, Arundel, Saltwood, Scotney. He was interested in castles. He had seen Blarney Castle as a boy and kissed the stone. That was before he began looking twice at girls. He stood up, his trouser leg once again sufficiently commodious to accommodate in comfort his muscular left thigh. Nevertheless, it was a problem postponed, not solved. The telescope may have provided the answer to MacGeoch's problem, but Keating knew that he himself must find relief, not in telescopic observations, but in carnal juxtapositions.

To take his mind off sex, he decided to go shopping. He had no idea where to find the best shops, so he did the sensible thing. He chose a young, prosperous-looking housewife without a pram but with a lilting swing to her hips, and followed her from the butcher's to the baker's to the green grocer's and in each he bought what she bought but in larger quantities, because he judged his family to be larger and greedier than hers.

He walked back on Mrs. Gardener's side of the road, sauntering tourist-like with a carrier-bag in each hand, noting the inscrutability of half-timbered house fronts and the sad curtailment of nature's plenitude in front gardens. To his surprise he found himself looking out for Mrs. Gardener, but now she was nowhere to be seen. As he passed her gate, he looked up her driveway, and there she was, squatting by the flat rear wheel of her red Metro, her elegant left ankle clearly visible below the cuff of her shimmering trouser leg.

"Having trouble?" He smiled evenly, with neither prurience nor machismo.

"The nuts are tighter than they should be." She straightened her springbok back and faced him fully and critically, fair and freckled with hair the colour of wild rose honey. He decided that it had been a mistake to look at her through MacGeoch's telescope.

"Let me have a go." He put down his shopping by the gate and took the proffered wheelbrace from her tender-fingered hand. Pretending that the nuts were tighter than they were in case she happened to be a feminist who would resent any crude show of male strength, he loosened all four and asked for the jack.

27

"Thank you very much, but you've done enough."

"It's no trouble."

"I can do the rest myself. I like doing it. If I didn't, I'd ring the garage."

She spoke pleasantly but firmly, in a voice she might have used to discourage an over-solicitous waiter from giving her a second helping of overcooked broccoli.

He picked up his bags and crossed the road to "Foxgloves," pained by the memory of his telescopic erection of only an hour ago. In his crotch was an unaccustomed calm; in his stomach were the flutterings of a thousand butterflies; about his heart was a cocoon of helpless constriction; and in his mind's eye was the dazzling image of her cut-glass ankle. He looked uncomprehendingly at the two storm lanterns outside the studded door of "Foxgloves," knowing that he had regressed into the shallows of adolescence. He was hopelessly and incurably in love.

He stood by the kitchen window, dicing the beef for the bourguignon, aware of little but nescience, negation, and imperfection. A large bird with black, lustrous plumage came to rest on a chimney pot three houses away. Crow, rook or raven, or a tribrid of ill omen? "The crow flew over the river with a lump of raw liver." To keep himself from thinking, he repeated the sentence aloud three or four times without stumbling. An awkward toad crossed the patio to shelter under the ivied trellis. Warty and brown, it was a stranger in the green of the garden, a visitor from a dead planet, itself perhaps already dead, a visitor who had known adversity but not the sweetness of its uses. The brown croup disappeared and in its place, jutting from under the ivy, a palely transparent ankle took shape before his sceptical eyes.

He put the beef and bacon in the slow cooker and switched it to low. He had decided to go out for the afternoon, to escape from the toad, the ankle and the uncharacteristic feelings he had brought back to "Foxgloves" from across the road. A short train ride would take him into the country. From the window seat he would watch stands of birch and in their transient autumn beauty move through the landscape like Great Birnam wood on its way to Dunsinane. He thought of the map upstairs and then of Dover Castle.

He took a train to Orpington and caught another bound for Dover Priory. He chose an empty first class compartment and lit his pipe. All was peace and rhythmic ease. The smoke curled above his head, the October sun shone on isolated farmhouses, a triangular field of yellow-grey stubble reached upwards towards a thin line of trees in the south. His pipe fell to the floor. He must have fallen asleep, he thought, as he tried unsuccessfully to read the name of a passing station. In his slumber he had been repeating "The lump of raw river overflowed the crow's liver." He wondered if he had been sleepwalking and had changed compartments, because on the seat opposite was a girl with one leg, an empty right boot with a zip standing beside the other leg. He asked himself why she carried an empty boot. Was it to remind her of a leg no longer hers? She was knitting furiously, two plain and two purl, her lips moving in an effort to keep pace with the hammering of the wheels. To take his mind off the empty boot, he began counting the pylons as they passed; and when he looked at her again, she had two legs, her right leg now in the boot that had been empty. She must have had it tucked under her skirt in her plain and purl fury, little knowing that she was more attractive with one leg than two. He moved to an empty compartment and relit his pipe. He would guard his peace of mind against all comers. He would fix his thoughts on the castle, the chalk cliffs and the sea.

He arrived back at half-past seven and put the button mushrooms and onions on top of the meat in the slow cooker. They ate at nine, mainly in silence except for an occasional lighthearted reference to the fox. Quilter sat imperiously at the head of the table with MacGeoch on his right, Garlick on his left, and Keating facing him at the other end.

"If I gave you a book called *The Badger's Wardrobe,* what would you expect to find in it?" he asked Keating when he had poured the coffee.

"A story for children about a badger."

"Not correct. I'm surprised at you, Keating, and you a countryman too. What do you think, Garlick?"

"I'm thinking about the fox."

"You should always address yourself to the subject in hand. But what says our formidable Scot?"

"I agree with our Irish friend. A book for boys of between six and eight."

"Gentlemen, you are all wrong. A badger's wardrobe is his excrement. Like an otter's spraints or a hare's crottels. It's the sort of thing that every true Wistwoodlander should know."

"Why don't we write a book called *The Badger's Wardrobe?*" Garlick wondered. "We could write at one level for suburban boys and at another for the would-be countrymen who are their fathers."

"Too vulgar." Quilter dismissed the idea. "Not a book for the Christmas stocking. But tell me, which of you knows the correct term of art for a fox's faeces?"

Keating felt like laughing, but he could see that MacGeoch was thinking deeply.

"What is it?" Garlick asked.

"Difficult," said the Quilter. "Even I don't know, but the first of you to come up with the correct answer will be given remission from sanitary fatigues and a week's furlough to boot."

At ten they went into the lounge to watch the news and deliberate further on those matters that Quilter considered to be of interest to countrymen, particularly the countrymen of

Wistwood East. Suddenly Keating felt a tightening of the throat muscles. The news reader was saying that a young woman had been strangled on the Dover Priory–Charing Cross train a few hours ago. She joined the 5:35 PM train from Dover at Folkestone, and when it arrived at Charing Cross her body was discovered in a first class compartment in the last carriage. Keating looked at the others to see if they had looked at one another or at him. He thought it best not to let on that he had travelled back to Orpington on the 5:35 from Dover Priory.

He went to bed early but he could not sleep. Shaken and excited, he kept seeing the face of "the woman with one leg," the face of a woman with lustrous black hair like a raven's wing that spiralled inwards to touch the white of her vulnerable neck; and he kept hearing the voice of the news reader, the warm voice of a woman who ate well, repeating deliriously and senselessly, "The lump of raw river overflowed the crow's liver."

At three someone went to the Ooja-cum-Pivvy and stumbled on the landing as he returned. Keating lay on his back and tried to sleep but the image of a vulnerable white neck, a Pre-Raphaelite neck, burnt like tinder behind his eyelids. He went to the loo at four to find a turd of equine proportions in the bowl. He tried to flush it twice but its specific gravity was so great that it would have resisted the river that cleansed the Augean stables. Towards five he slept, and then the alarm woke him at seven-thirty and he disentangled himself sleepily from the bedclothes.

He was wide awake, cooking bacon and eggs, when Quilter came down in his dressing gown.

"We must get things organised, Keating. For too long we've started the day on bacon and eggs at 'Foxgloves.' I want you to ring the changes—grilled kidneys, tomatoes, mushrooms, kippers, and, for MacGeoch's benefit, Arbroath smokies on occasion. But never sausages, because there's no longer such a thing as a good sausage, and anyone who says there is is too young to remember better. Another thing—something you were not to know—I, as C.O., nosh off silver. I'm the only man in Wistwood East with that distinction. The next best scoff off Royal Doulton. Breakfast sets the tone of the day. Everyone should be down by eight-thirty and anyone who isn't can do without. Strict discipline in battle and in bivvy, that's what I always say."

The four of them ate well, especially Quilter who made short work of two eggs and four rashers while not neglecting *The Times* crossword. When Garlick had left, MacGeoch said that he was next to go up the line, that he had an appointment with the Queen's press secretary at eleven. Quilter, who did not seem in the least impressed, looked up from his paper and said to Keating: "Were you surprised the other day when I called the kitchen 'the cookhouse' and the loo 'the latrines'?"

"No."

"You may be innocent of the army, but you're a good cook, Keating. That bourguignon last night wasn't made by one of life's wankers. What I'm telling you is that in a lighthearted way we observe certain military conventions here at 'Foxgloves.' We have a cookhouse, an orderly room, an officers' mess, latrines and the rest. This is not a rest camp. You are now in battalion headquarters, and we, as you may have gathered, are the officers and only gentlemen. I am the Colonel, MacGeoch is the Major and Garlick is the Lance-corporal, the lowest rank of N.C.O. We also have an M.O.—a medical officer—who visits us once a month, sometimes rather unexpectedly but never without gratification. I haven't yet decided on your rank, but from our brief acquaintance I should say that you will be senior to the Lance-corporal. I shall ask you three questions and your rank will depend on your answers. Are you ready?"

"Yes, sir," Keating tried to enter into the spirit of "Foxgloves."

"Which bird do you associate with Martinmas?"

"The goose."

"And which quadruped do you associate with the goose?"

"The fox."

"Correct. Now, if I sent you to the butcher's to buy a young goose, how would you know the right bird from an old age pensioner?"

"I'd feel its underbill. If it bent easily, I'd buy it."

"The best pleasures in life are stolen, and thieves of pleasure make the best company. You, my dear Keating, are a thief of pleasure. I have no hesitation in calling you Captain. I shall inform the others over dinner this evening."

Quilter got to his feet and surveyed the seated Keating from a height.

"What I need is a good adjutant. Do you know what that means?"

"No, sir." Keating got up and faced his Commanding Officer.

"You are to assist me as C.O. in the execution of all details of duty and discipline. Now, let me see you salute."

Keating straightened and saluted with the kind of histrionic exuberance he thought might please the Colonel.

"No, no, Captain. Far too rococo. The English salute is simplicity itself, as befits a salute that saw Agincourt and Waterloo. In bivvy there may be time for falderals; in battle there is not. Have you ever seen Sir Adrian Boult conduct Elgar?"

"No, sir."

He used to conduct with Crippsian economy. That is the way to salute."

"I'll do my best." Keating tried to get the right degree of stiffness into his upper lip.

"I'll tell you one further thing before I go. 'Foxgloves' is an oasis in a desert. Within these walls the ego is triumphant. Outside reigns the superego, creator of anxiety and guilt. The desert has a fascination for many men, which has often proved fatal. Outside the door of this house is sand."

"Is the house itself built on sand?"

"'Foxgloves' is built on rock, but you must not break the spell. You must never import the desert, or what passes for life in it, past this threshold. Here we lead charmed lives, here we fleet the time carelessly as they did in the golden world. What I am saying, Keating, is that if you are a man who follows his nose, you must not let your emotions become your nose. You may lust after another man's wife—you may poke her and bugger her for all I care—but you mustn't love her. You must learn to suck wisdom out of lust as a weasel sucks eggs. Not an easy trick, I do assure you, because lust is circumscribed whereas love is illimitable. So if you succeed in that particular sucking act, you'll do better morally than the man who loves."

"I'll think about that as I cook dinner."

"Another thing, don't let Garlick get you down. He has a mind that reduces and finds fault with everything he touches. He finds fault with Wistwood. But there is nothing wrong with Wistwood that the presence of one or two aristocrats wouldn't put right. If we had even one ancient family, we wouldn't have to spend our time cultivating eccentricity in the hope that the lower-middle class on the other side might mistake us for the real thing."

Quilter laughed and Keating knew that the interview had ended. He watched the other man set off for the station and he wondered if anything really moved him. He always looked grave as he spoke, but in his voice and choice of words was the unmistakable exhilaration of flippancy.

After the confusion of the night, the morning mirrored sanity and clarity. He walked up Raleigh Way, pleased to be among innocent housewives sauntering with shopping baskets, satisfied in the knowledge that their husbands were off their hands for seven hours. He had come to a place of trees. They lined the pavements and hung over porches and front gardens, their still-green leaves dancing in the lively crispness of early autumn. A retired gentleman in a red waistcoat was hammering at a fence; another was washing his already shining car; and further along a young workman on a ladder was burning paint off a window with a blow-lamp, filling the air with keen acridity. A grey squirrel on a gate turned to him with darkly glistening eyes. It was sitting on its haunches, holding a crust to its lips, then it dropped it, brushed its cheek with its forepaw and made off like the clappers along the top of the fence. Keating was filled momentarily with a sense of enchantment. The place he had come to was within half an hour of London, but with the menfolk up to whatever they did in the city it was now as sleepy as a village in West Cork. Here he could come and go without interrogation, because here every man was a sleepwalker, lost, according to the Colonel, in the illusion of rusticity which magnified the dream of high living inside his head.

He bought *The Telegraph,* did his shopping, and sat in the diningroom, because, unlike the sitting-room, it faced the morning sun. The murder was reported on page seven. It was only a paragraph, but it shattered the clarity of the day like a pebble going through a windscreen. The woman was Mrs. Miriam Trek, she lived in Wistwood, and she was found wearing a second-hand fox-fur, not her own. Her husband said that he had never seen her in a fox-fur and that she never bought anything second-hand. Keating had hoped for a picture, but he was disappointed. He went upstairs, took Quilter's knife and diary from his suitcase, and hid them in the ventilator in the loo.

He spent the afternoon in the garden, visited occasionally by cheeky starlings that came to peck at windfalls. It had been a poor year for tomatoes by the look of it. They were no bigger than conkers and still green, though the leaves on the stems were already a sickly yellow. Around him red roofs and smokeless chimneys rose with mathematical regularity, and black-and-white gables made a line of isosceles triangles among the silver birches. It was a world of illusion that changed with the changing light. Neither city nor country, it was too pretty to delight an eye that preferred nature ungelded by landscape architects.

He cooked goulash for dinner and watched them eat. Mac-Geoch and Garlick were gluttons, pigs to the ears in beechmast. Garlick paid him an ambiguous compliment, but he waited for Quilter's judgement because his was the only palate he respected. He waited in vain,

> Like Verdi when, at his worst opera's end . . .
> He looks through all the roaring and the wreaths
> Where sits Rossini patient in his stall.

Though it was only his second day at "Foxgloves," he was already aware of the tensions between the other three and the peculiar piquancy they gave the conversation. Though Mac-Geoch was a sour man, he agreed with nearly everything Quilter said. At dinner he cleared his plate before the others, locked both hands over his wide stomach, and with lower jaw extended watched Garlick like a stoat watching a rabbit. Though he would pronounce the food eatable when it pleased him, he never had a good word to say for the wine.

"Horse piss!" he would hiss, as he poured another glass to a cackle of amusement from Quilter, who would observe that MacGeoch knocked back more horse piss than the rest of them together.

MacGeoch did not seem to mind Quilter's chaffing, but he

would turn puce at the least hint of criticism from Garlick. Garlick was much given to criticism, overt and implied. He was indefatigably disputatious, which displeased Quilter, who preferred men with sufficient intelligence to accept his judgements. It was obvious to Keating that Garlick was the odd man out. He was not what Quilter would call "officer material." He would never rise above the rank of lance-corporal.

In appearance MacGeoch and Garlick were opposites. MacGeoch was red-faced, short and burly with sad, upturned eyes. If he'd had a gentle disposition, he'd have resembled a Saint Bernard without the keg of brandy. But he wasn't gentle. Towards all except Quilter, he was fiery, sharp-tongued and curt. His most uninviting feature were the black vibrissae that protruded like quills from his flared nostrils; and his best were the grizzled side-whiskers which in a more handsome man would have been reminiscent of the nobility of Matthew Arnold's.

Garlick was not in the least like a Saint Bernard. He resembled a wire-haired fox terrier. He was of average height but he looked taller because of the spareness of his frame. His head was his most distinctive feature. It was almost egg-shaped, broad and somewhat flat on the crown with narrow jaws beneath and thin, fastidious lips that curled upwards into a grin of censorious ill-humour. His thick, greying hair was combed back to expose his bony temples and form a triangular jetty above a forehead that was furrowed like the sea. Altogether, he had the look of a mad scientist with a skull that shone through the skin, as if it had been put together hurriedly in a laboratory by another mad scientist.

Of the three, the Scotsman was the most chauvinistic. Apparently a man of wide reading, he could display an enviable mastery of history, philosophy, literature, science, politics and economics when the discussion demanded, a mastery which only confirmed him in his opinion that Robbie Burns was the greatest poet, Sir Walter Scott the greatest novelist, David

Hume the greatest philosopher, Adam Smith the greatest economist, David Livingstone the greatest explorer, James Boswell the greatest biographer, Ramsay MacDonald the greatest prime minister, and Ben Nevis the greatest mountain. Quilter looked kindly on MacGeoch's chauvinism, but when on occasion he would suggest that the English could also boast a great man or two, MacGeoch would declare that "the Scot, wherever he finds himself in England, is bound to rise to the top as oil rises to the top of water."

Keating served the coffee and Quilter suggested that they all drink a glass of port.

"I was thinking last night," he said, "that the life we lead in Wistwood is based on a lie."

"But it's a little lie, not a big one," Garlick prodded.

"What lie do you mean?" the Colonel confronted his Lance-corporal.

"That two and two make five."

"That is not the lie I meant," Quilter said. "Suburban man in his semidetached dreams not of two and two but of rural retreats—country houses, country lanes, arable acres and the MFH shouting "Tally-ho!" on frosty December mornings. He thinks that the fox in his garden is a certain sign of rurality. Little does he know that the urban fox is at least as numerous as his country cousin."

"I went into a butcher's on the other side a few weeks ago," MacGeoch said, "and a woman from the West came in and asked for a bone for the fox. 'How is he today, madam?' the butcher asked, and without batting an eyelid she said, 'Very cunning.' Damn cheek is what I call it."

"Damn lies," said Quilter. "There *are* no foxes on the other side."

"Of course there are," Garlick protested. "I've seen them myself."

"The foxes on the other side are itinerant." Quilter made no attempt to conceal his contempt.

"And what are the foxes on this side, then?" Garlick tried sarcasm.

"Resident, my dear chap, resident."

"I fail to see the reason for the fuss," Keating cut in.

"It's simple," Quilter told him. "The prime status symbol in Wistwood is the fox. A man with a fox in his garden is a man with a stake in the land. The foxes live in the woods. The woods are in Wistwood East. Therefore the houses and gardens of Wistwood East are more desirable than those of Wistwood West."

"Nonsense," said Garlick. "The houses and gardens in the East are bigger. The red fox is a red herring. Even if he didn't exist, Wistwood East would still overshadow Wistwood West."

"You surprise me, Lance-corporal," said the Colonel. "You should read more deeply in the book of snobs. Your sophisticated Eastsider wouldn't dream of saying to a Westsider, 'My house and garden are bigger and more mock-Tudor than yours.' It's simply not done. What can be done is to complain that you can't get a wink of sleep at night because of the yelping of mating foxes in your garden. For those who wish to surpass their neighbours, the fox is the perfect status symbol, and the very fugacity of the symbol gives it a mystique that no Rolls or Bentley can confer. It has gone so far that we try to emulate the fox. We grow more like him every day. The fox is an opportunist. He will eat anything, and so will Wistwood man. Which accounts for the four Indian restaurants on this side of the tracks and the two Chinese take-aways on the other."

"I think it's time we turned the fox to financial account," said the Scotsman.

"It's happening already," said the Englishman. "Yesterday I saw an ad in an estate agent's window offering a 'villa' in our road which supposedly had a fox's earth under the garden shed."

"I was thinking of something else," said MacGeoch. "Only four hundred years ago our Tudor forefathers mixed fox and duck fat, roasted it in a goose, and took it as a cure for paralysis. I was thinking that it might be possible to manufacture similar concoctions today and sell them at a profit to Wistwood man."

"It's an interesting idea," said Quilter.

"Here we are, living in a mock-Tudor suburb," said MacGeoch. "Isn't it altogether fitting that we should seek to cure our ailments with mock-Tudor medicines."

"You're both quite mad," said Garlick.

"We're not the only men who appreciate the fox. I'm sure it hasn't escaped your attention that the murdered woman was found wearing a fox-fur."

"Who put it round her shoulders, a man from Wistwood East or a man from Wistwood West?" MacGeoch demanded.

"You are the authority on that." Garlick got up and left.

When Keating had washed up, he went to his room and read his book of Old Irish poetry for an hour. Snatches of their after-dinner conversation came back to him, and as he mulled them over, he couldn't help thinking that the Englishman was more intelligent than an Englishman deserved to be.

3

ON Thursday morning he travelled up to London for an interview with the sports editor of *The Sunday Mirror*. He walked to the station with Clem Garlick, who told him as they arrived on platform three that he was now in the no-man's-land between East and West, where Eastmen and Westmen stood glumly together looking down the line towards Orpington on Monday mornings when trains were late.

"On these occasions," he said, "they have been known to overcome their mutual suspicions and exchange a word or two of restrained disapproval directed at the common enemy, British Rail."

Keating said nothing. He did not wish to hear about the warring tribes of Wistwood at nine o'clock in the morning. He wanted to enjoy the warm October weather with the sunlight dancing on the polished rails and executing arabesques on the roofs of cars which commonsense told him had been bought not as status symbols but simply as means of conveyance. He was glad when the train came in and he and Garlick, after the manner of commuters, could retire behind their newspapers without giving or taking offence.

The sports editor was forthright. He wanted to see some of

Keating's work but Keating had none to show. He reminded him that he was not the only journalist in search of work; however, he promised to bear him in mind if he should need someone to do a shift at short notice. Though Keating was disappointed, he knew that he still had the inestimable Quilter to pull a string or two. He realised now that he was unlikely to be handed a permanent job on a plate, but if he managed to land some regular freelance work it would at least be a foot in the door.

Quilter was outside the house, looking up at the apex, when he got back.

"I've been surveying the timbering, Keating. Perhaps you could give it a coat of creosote before the weather breaks."

"I shall need a long ladder."

"You'll find one in the garage, and don't spare any expense. There's nothing like half-timbering after a good drink."

"Who owns the tractor?" Keating pointed towards the driveway of the house next door.

"Oh, that belongs to Giles Oxbone, whom we all call 'Farmer Giles.' He takes the illusion of country life to the extreme, as you can see. When he retired from Lloyd's a few years ago, the first thing he did was to buy a tractor. He uses it to mix cement for crazy paving and carry home the shopping. He even drives it to church on Sunday mornings. Needless to say, he's a figure of fun. There are certain illusions you must not harbour, even here in the heartland of illusion. There are illusions that are socially acceptable and illusions that are not."

"In other words, you may buy a bone for the fox, but you mustn't buy a tractor." Keating laughed.

"Yet to me he is more congenial than Michael Jesty at number forty-nine across the road. When Jesty bought his house, it was called Willow Break and he had the nerve to change the name to 'Seven Squared.'"

"Rather insensitive. It shows a blindness to the beauty of 'Two Trees,' 'Tall Trees,' 'Foxgloves,' and 'The Dales.'"

"As you might expect, he's a mathematician. Rumour has it that he has installed a computer in the master bedroom."

Keating left Quilter tapping the barometer in the hallway and retired to the Ooja-cum-Pivvy upstairs. Pleased to be alone, he sat on the loo and read chapter one of *Alice,* but he could not put from his mind the police notice outside Wistwood Station, requesting all who had travelled on the 5:35 from Dover Priory to Charing Cross on October 15 to get in touch with the police immediately. He recalled the woman with "one leg," and he thought it strange that he had not noticed if she'd been knitting a cardigan, a scarf, a pullover, or a pair of mittens.

It was extraordinary how the height of the loo could elevate the thoughts of a man in the act of evacuation. A tiny silverfish passed across the floor, far beneath him, and he thought of God sitting on a throne of cloud creating the universe with a Bang, big to us but not to Him, and he wondered if the silverfish, hearing his thunder, was also moved to think of matters that would remain forever beyond its grasp. And if he broke wind twice, would the silverfish hear and perhaps propagate the Two-Bang Theory as opposed to the Big-Bang Theory among the more gullible of its disciples?

He decided that if he should ever own a house again, it would have a loo at least eighteen inches above the floor. It really was the answer to life's social problem, because from it you could look down on the Warden of All Souls, the Headmasters' Conference, the Wistwood Fox, and the Massey-Ferguson tractor. He broke wind so exhaustively that he wished for a more accurate appreciation of the principles of jet propulsion, and then he realised that all this hot air was—in a mixed-metaphorical sense—buttering no parsnips, that he would still have to take the Dover Priory train to Folkestone in the morning.

Again he chose a first-class compartment, which he filled quickly with delicious pipe smoke. It was a day of dancing sunshine with not a hint of brumous December to come. He thought of last night's moon, a silver denture four days old, and after they pulled out of Tonbridge he got up and went to another compartment where a foxy young woman was reading alone. She was wearing a tartan skirt with a large pin at the side, and he sat opposite her, trying to picture the richness of autumn woods, but as soon as his eye met hers she closed her book and hurriedly left the compartment.

The way she glanced at him reminded him of Esther. The first time he saw her she was looking down at him from a neighing horse in a field outside Wicklow. He was only twenty-two; he still saw life through the gauze of literature; he fell in love with her on the spot. Later, when he told her, she laughed and said that he had fallen in love with her horse or with a fantasy on a horse, but that first day he did not even speak to her. He followed her at a distance round the field until he heard her say to a friend that they would go to the show-jumping in Kilmacanogue the following Saturday. He went to Kilmacanogue but neither she nor her friend turned up.

That summer he went everywhere he thought he might see a girl on a horse, but he never once glimpsed anyone who remotely resembled her. It was almost a year before they met again, and it was a further six months before she consented to go out with him. Whenever they met, she surveyed the top of his head from her horse, but he told himself that it was a horse like any other, that it ate grass and oats and fouled the air when it defecated. Then suddenly the impossible happened. One night in the back row of a cinema she let him kiss her and the following night he put his hand down inside her bra.

Within a year they were married, and within two they had a daughter called Isabella.

From the beginning she was restive like her horse. And he could only retreat. He had no defence against her particular form of self-assertion. If he had never met her, he would have been able to see himself as a complete person; but now, like Quilter, MacGeoch and Garlick, he could only see himself as a man who had once been defeated. He could never pretend to ignore her view of him, so pithily, so woundingly expressed. No matter what he achieved, no matter where he went, he would be aware of an alternative vision of his life. There is no fantasy more defiling than social fantasy; but in extenuation it had to be said that she smeared him not with her own excrement but with that of her horse. "My favourite animal is the horse," she said. "My second favourite is man." That was in the early days when he thought her witty and she made him laugh, in the days before he realised that she really compared him with her horse and was not surprised when she found him wanting.

For her thirtieth birthday he took her to see *Man and Superman* and winced when one of the characters said: "There are two tragedies in life. One is not to get your heart's desire. The other is to get it."

He looked at her superior profile in the theatrical half-light and he knew in his heart the dreadful thing he had to do.

Folkestone surprised him into a mood of forgiveness. He spent a bracing hour on the Leas looking across the Channel to France, after which he found a quiet tea shop where he drank a pot of tea and ate two buttered scones. He caught the 6:00 P.M. train, which must have left Dover Priory at 5:35, and quite by accident found himself in the same compartment as on the first day. He was absolutely certain. He recognised it from the graffiti on the ceiling. Men and women passed up and down the corridor, but no one joined him until they stopped at Tonbridge and Mrs. Gardener entered with a smile of surprised recognition on her lightly freckled face.

"On this train I'm pleased to meet a man I know, if only from across the road." She smiled half-mockingly in case he should attach too much importance to what she said.

She brought with her a touch of spring, not of autumn, yet it was of autumn she spoke as she sat down.

"What a glorious day it's been. It could only have come in October, it was so perfect in the woods."

"The trees are in their autumn beauty." He tried to impress. "The woodland paths are dry."

She was wearing a cream-coloured suit with a sorrel waist-coat and a frilled blouse, pure as the hearts of June roses. He swallowed at the sight of her stem-like neck, and she laughed indulgently but critically at his quotation.

"How can you see the woods as they are, if you clothe them in discredited lyricism? The trees are polychromatic in autumn because their leaves don't all wither at the same rate—because, as you would say, the pestilence-striken multitudes take an unconscionable time dying. Even on the same tree the leaves can be yellow, and black, and pale, and hectic red, and a dendrologist would quickly tell you why. I'm convinced that if poets and novelists had even the slightest smattering of science, their works would be shorter and a deal better."

"What you're saying at such length," he smiled, "is that ignorance of science is oats to Pegasus."

"I once read a long and banal poem about the Niagara Falls, and I laughed as I realised that what the misguided poet was celebrating was a spillage of H_2O—two atoms of hydrogen coupled with one of oxygen followed by yet another such combination endlessly."

She was teasing him and he did not wish to present her with more ammunition, so he told her in matter-of-fact prose about his walk on the Leas and the number of ships he counted in an hour. In recompense she told him that she was travelling by train because her husband's car had broken down and he had taken hers to the office that morning. It was all for the best. If she hadn't taken the train, she would have missed a cracking idea for her next painting. Mention of painting came like a godsend. He himself had once dabbled in the art, and he wasted no time in letting her know. Though the return journey had not turned out as planned, he enjoyed the sight and sound of her so much that he was sorry when they arrived in Wistwood. She may have been conscious of his sorrow because, as they parted, she invited him for coffee and a private view of her paintings the following morning.

He was so delighted that he barely noticed Jippo, the Colonel's golden retriever, as she jumped up to greet him in the hallway. He could see that she wasn't her usual collected self, and he soon realised why. She had found herself alone in the house with Garlick, of whom she had a passionate dislike. Garlick was not put out, however. He hung about solicitously in the kitchen, making small talk, while Keating cooked.

"So it's your first time in the suburbs?" He spoke quietly like a doctor in the presence of a patient who is seriously ill. "They are a fine and private place, the suburbs, a retreat for gardening, car washing and tea drinking. They are not a place in which serious events can occur. Here you will never meet a man whose life has been changed by an idea. Such changes as occur result entirely from salary rises."

"I haven't seen much of suburban man since my arrival, but what I have seen has led me to believe that he takes himself seriously."

"He is serious in the sense of humourless. He laughs loudest at his own jokes, especially if he's told them more than once. Yet, strangely, if you accused him of humourlessness, he'd feel offended. He mistakes the rictus of laughter for the spirit of comedy, but humour is a way of looking at life, not something you put on like a fancy waistcoat in the evening after a day at the office affecting solemnity to please your boss."

"I take it that you don't like the suburbs," Keating said.

"I find them seductive, but I refuse to be seduced. When I look at all this pinchbeck Tudorbethan, I long to escape from fakery into an unashamedly twentieth-century house. The only thing that keeps me sane here is the sight of passing goods trains carrying coal and aggregate on Sunday mornings. It helps to assure me that somewhere in this country stone is still crushed and coal mined, that we're not entirely given over to the service industries."

"Do you come from a Welsh mining area?"

"No, no, I come from a village on the marshes. My father was a doctor and my mother was a schoolmistress before she met him. Don't tell the Colonel, but I'm saving for a house of my own, a nice, plain little bungalow on the other side of Sevenoaks. I had a lovely house and garden once, but my wife claimed half of it when we got divorced. Are you married?"

"I'm divorced Irish-style, living apart and not paying alimony."

"What do you think of 'Foxgloves?'"

"It suits me while I'm looking for a job. I haven't had much luck so far, but the Colonel has promised to do his best for me."

"Don't depend on him." Garlick looked at the attentive Jippo and lowered his voice. "He promised to do the same for me once."

"And did he?"

"Did he fight in the Western Desert? He's fond of saying that the London suburbs are the heartland of English fantasy, but he himself is the greatest fantasist of all. He's convinced that 'Foxgloves' is a country house and that he's the owner. He even renamed it without telling the real owner."

"Who is the real owner?"

"The Brigadier, who is on furlough in South Africa. But shall I tell you something else about the Colonel? He's naive. He thinks the true test of class is whether your parents had leather-covered chairs. Sooner or later he will say that the suite in the lounge needs cleaning and he will ask you how you propose to do it."

"What should I tell him?" Keating laughed, but Garlick was being serious.

"Say, 'Leather is skin, and I'll treat it like skin—I'll wash it with soap and water.' You'll thank me for telling you, when the time comes."

"I'll thank you now."

"What do you really think of Quilter and MacGeoch?" Garlick moved closer, hugging his elbows. He smelt more sweetly than either the Colonel or the Major. He exuded the odour of resin so strongly that to come near him was to be transported to the depths of a pine forest in the height of summer. The Colonel made no secret of his dislike of resin. He was fond of telling Garlick that a man who baths once a day, or a woman who baths twice, has no need of deodorants. Keating did some thinking and found the diplomatic answer.

"Quilter and MacGeoch are Gog and Magog." He laughed at his reply. It was imaginative and ambiguous, and it was bound to please Garlick.

"How right you are. They are the sole founders and members of a Mutual Admiration Society, and, let me tell you, they're fully-paid-up members of the Swine's Club as well. Pay no heed to what they say. They're both journalists; the language they use is counterfeit currency."

"But you're a journalist yourself!"

"A technical journalist. I edit a medical magazine for under-paid nurses."

"There's nothing underpaid about Quilter."

"Quilter is a mystery. He's something on *The Telegraph*,

what precisely no one knows. For a journalist he keeps suspiciously regular hours, and he seldom mentions any paper except *The Times,* which he describes as 'written by the flatulent for the flatulent and for the relief of neither.' Yet he reads it every day from beginning to end, especially the 'dirty bits.' By 'dirty' he means badly written, of course. 'Did you see the piece about the Common Market on the middle page yesterday?' he will ask MacGeoch over breakfast. 'Now that's what I call a dirty read. It took three chapters of *The Princess Casamassima* and half a bottle of Bollinger to wash the taste from my mouth.'"

Garlick spoke from the depths of his boots with a dry clicking of the tongue in a surprisingly accurate imitation of the Colonel.

"His obsession with *The Times* is sour grapes," he continued. "As a young man, he was interviewed and rejected by Sir William Haley and he has never forgotten it. Carrying round *The Princess Casamassima* as an antidote to the fustian of The Thunderer is a typical piece of affectation, of a piece with his patronising use of Cockney rhyming slang when he's trying to be funny."

"Does MacGeoch also work on *The Telegraph?*"

"Now, he's another rum one. Though he works for *The Mirror,* our oldest tabloid, he takes care to leave words like 'bonanza' and 'clampdown' at the office. Like all Highlanders, he's a snob. He was brought up to look down on Lowlanders, and to him the English, with the exception of the Colonel, are only more lowly Lowlanders."

Keating, chopping chives for Ravigote sauce, tried not to let the vulgarity of Garlick's mind dissipate the afflatus required to make a sauce that must disguise the lack of flavour in a battery-reared chicken. There was nothing wrong with attacking Quilter, he thought, but it should be done with a rapier, not a bludgeon. Garlick's psychology was so crude that it was impossible to listen without being a party to an act of defilement and mutilation. He recovered his sense of serenity by putting an extra pinch of cayenne in the mixture.

"You're a stylish cook," Garlick said, "but don't let it go to your head. I've seen four so-called cooks come here and go in less than a year. The Colonel may like his food but he likes a joke even more. He once asked one of your predecessors to grill him a sirloin steak *in situ*. 'Certainly, sir,' said the idiot."

"And did he?" Keating teased.

"Of course not. You can't grill a steak without first cutting it from the steer."

"So what happened?"

"The Colonel sacked him for promising more than he could deliver. So look out. Don't become overfond of your reflection in those pots and pans."

"A true cook will always find another kitchen."

"You're more dedicated than the others," Garlick told him. "But I still don't understand why you're captain."

"What's so strange about that?"

"The others were only quartermaster-sergeant."

"I'm not content with being captain. I want to be major."

"We've got a thing or two in common, you and I." Garlick and the pine forest came closer, and Keating heard a puff and a fricative from MacGeoch in the hallway.

"Think about it," Garlick whispered and was gone.

Keating went to his room after dinner to think first about Mrs. Gardener's neck and freckles and then about her cut-glass ankle. At eleven he turned off the light, but after an hour he still had not decided which he should kiss first, given a choice. In the dark behind his eyes her neck rose from her collar like the stem of a mountain lough lily, he saw the reflection of a white rose with a fragrant heart and no thorn, and he felt the spring of soft turf underfoot after a night of rain. He turned on his side, then on his belly, wondering if masturbation was the only soporific. He hadn't had a go since he got married, he was out of practice, his imagination was not very vivid, and failure would only aggravate his insomnia. He went to the Ooja-cum-Pivvy, opened *The Book of Common Prayer,* and read "All thy garments smell of myrrh, aloes, and cassia," but that, he found, was not the literature of detumescence. Next he tried the *Mabinogion,* then Robbie Burns, and at last he found peace in chapter two of *Alice.*

The following morning he was up at seven, sitting by the window, watching early commuters and wondering if they caught even an echo of lonely herds lowing for them from remote ancestral shires. At seven-thirty Mr. Gardener appeared in a fur hat and sheepskin coat, a shapeless man who had stumbled unwittingly and undeservedly on a pearl of great price. Keating had seen what he wanted to see, not a bull but a bullock, so he went downstairs to prepare the smoked haddock and poached eggs that Quilter ordered for his birthday.

Mrs. Gardener, besmocked, bespectacled and bepaletted, opened the door and told him that she had quite forgotten her invitation. She looked reassuringly human, far from the icily perfect apparition on the train. She led him upstairs to a room full of pictures, warning him with mock-seriousness that in her house art took precedence over coffee. The pictures gave him a shock, not because there were so many of them but because she had used the same colours again and again. He looked at her severe steel-rimmed spectacles and realised that her pictures too were steely.

"Why did you take up painting?" he asked.

"I gained a doctorate for my work on the polymerisation of pigments. Like Margaret Thatcher, I'm a chemist."

"But she doesn't paint."

"When I came down from Oxford to get married, I was at a loss. I had acquired the habit of working with pigments, but I found that there is a limit to the number of times you can paint your house in a year. So instead I decided to put paint on canvas. That was the beginning, you can see where it's led me. Now I paint not to kill time but self-consciousness."

He looked at the paintings one by one, but he could only think of the floorboard that bore the brunt of her heel.

"What do you make of them?" she asked after a while. It was a question he did not answer directly.

"Why do they all look alike?" he countered.

"Because I've found myself, I've found a style."

"There's more to it than that. This one shows a bicycle being ridden by a theodolite and that one shows a croupier spinning a bicycle wheel, while three theodolites count their chips, and the one in the corner shows what I take to be two surveyors measuring angles with a pair of handlebars."

"What's odd about that?"

"In a sense they are the same picture."

"As I said, I have found myself. Once you've done that, you can only say the same thing in different ways. It's the price of self-knowledge. One day I'll show you my other paintings, the ones I did before I was condemned to one point of view, before pigment became subservient to experience."

"They have something else in common besides symbols. They are all bathed in the same light. The dark steely hues struggle against the pale background, as if the stimulating were losing the battle against the bland."

"They are part of a series to be called 'Wistwood Symphony.' Have you noticed, incidentally, that all the horses in the woods are grey?"

"No, I saw two lovely chestnuts yesterday."

"In that case you're a stranger. To suburban man all horses are grey. You have no business here." She laughed. "If you stay, you'll come to no good. In the land of the blind, believe me, the one-eyed man is a deviant."

She took off her smock and spectacles and made coffee in

the kitchen, which was as untidy as his cookhouse was clean. He was pleased to see that such daunting perfection came out of a house of such sweet disorder, not the bandbox he had expected. They sat in the dining-room with an oval table and a plate of biscuits between them. As he took the first sip of her coffee, an inexplicable faintness made him grateful for his sturdy chair. He felt certain that she could not have made this dark-brown brew in a coffeepot, that it had flowed naturally from some secret orifice of her body, an orifice unknown even to the anatomist Henry Gray. He took a tentative sip and asked her to pass the sugar.

"Is it all right?" she enquired.

"It's strong and pungent as I like it."

"I don't know your name."

"I'm Charles Keating."

"And I'm Ann Ede."

"I thought you were Mrs. Gardener."

"Who told you that?"

"Quilter, MacGeoch or Garlick, I can't remember."

"That's a good one. They call me Mrs. Gardener because I like gardening. You were naive not to realise." She laughed.

"Is Ede an English name?"

"Oh, yes, and it's older than most."

"It would suit you better if it were more musical. The best names are not those that are old, but those that are anapaestic."

"I'm afraid I can't help you. My maiden name is Seymour, a mere disyllable." She laughed. "You're Irish, are you not, but are you Catholic?"

"Yes, though not a good one."

"I'm a good one. Do you go to church?" She spoke without a hint of a jest.

"No."

"When did you make your last confession?"

"Seven years ago," he lied, because he couldn't bring himself to say ten.

"Disgraceful. I can see I shall have to take you in hand. The suburbs are full of paynims. We need all the support we can get."

"Surely there are no Muslims here in Wistwood?"

"I use 'paynim' to mean all non-Christians, including the modern heathen who like to seek respectability in agnosticism. My own husband is a paynim, though we got married in church."

He felt queasy after the coffee and uneasy because of the incisiveness of her conversation.

"What does your husband do?" He sought an innocuous topic. "I saw him leave early this morning."

"Though he'd be the last to admit it, he's a bagman."

"A bagman?"

"He travels for a paint manufacturer, but if you ask him what he does he will tell you that he's a Director of Operations. He reminded me last night that his function is 'to give positive direction to the firm's manufacturing and distributing facilities, to generate new ideas, to communicate with people, to take the initiative, and to get things done.' He's very successful. He's got six badges on the grille of his car."

"I would like to meet him," he lied again.

"You wouldn't take to him. Like most successful men, he's utterly humourless."

He felt tired of a sudden, as if he'd passed an uneasy night. He longed to retreat to the cookhouse, or better still the Arsenal, and think about her from a safe distance, but her clarity of expression, facial and verbal, held him spellbound. What she communicated was not so much unworldliness as incomparable objectivity. When she spoke of her husband and called him the Bagman, she was not being strident or vindictive; she was merely a bacteriologist discussing a culture which she had grown on herself as medium. The disinterest, you might say, was the more remarkable for being personal. He struggled to introduce a lighter note. Sex, he judged, was out of the question, so he turned to the next most absorbing subject in Wistwood.

"Do you know anything of foxes?" he enquired.

"Only that they're red, and if not red, silver."

"Have you ever seen one?"

"No."

"You don't have one in your garden?"

"No, and I don't propose to paint one either."

"Quilter says that everyone on this side has a residing fox, that only the socially deprived are without one."

"I think he may be pulling your leg."

He got up to go, and she followed him into the hallway.

"What do you seek here?" she asked.

"Only a job. I'm an out-of-work journalist."

"I didn't mean that, but never mind. Or rather mind how you go. This is Indian country, but if you keep your eyes skinned, you'll soon be able to distinguish between the suburban Shawnee and the suburban Sioux, between the suburban Apache and the suburban Cheyenne."

"Who's pulling my leg now?"

"To use the Bagman's favourite phrase, I kid you not. Go up to Wistwood station any morning at eight and you'll see more moccasins on platforms one and three than Custer saw at Little Big Horn."

"You mock me. I must tell you I already know that brogues, not moccasins, are *de rigueur*."

"Brogues in the East, but moccasins—I mean balding suede—in the West. You should try to get it right. It's as important as not slurping your soup, and as basic, if I may say so."

"Au revoir."

He retreated to "Foxgloves" and poured himself a bumper, not a finger, of whisky from the bottle he kept in his wardrobe for emergencies and sudden chills. She was a woman of overpowering personality, spiky as a briar, as his father used to say, and at the same time spiky in the English sense. How the Bagman ever got them off her, only God and possibly St. Michael could tell, and it was typical of his luck that he should fall for her, because she was in every way an incomparably superior Esther. Her knees, her ankles and her neck had bewitched him on the train, but today he was only aware of the cutting edge of her mind setting up sandbags and asexual buffers. She reminded him of the time Esther's sister, who was a nun in Nigeria, came back to Cork for a month. He and she went for walks every day, and all the time she excited him with intellectual whirligigs as she leant on him like a sister, blithely unaware of either the priceless pearl or the foul oyster that seeds it.

He drank another bumper and felt the fire of the Scotch warm the coffee that was not coffee in his stomach. He felt better. He should count not only his bad but his good. She was a Roman Catholic and he had the advantage of knowing the breed. They knew what they were about. They didn't sin lightly, which only meant that when they sinned it was not venially but mortally. He would hang around, because her mind was so ingenious that she could find as much theological justification for sinning as not sinning, if she so desired. And another thing, she saw the Bagman as a paynim. He had been mistaken in thinking that she saw him as a bacteriologist sees a bacillus—under a microscope. Truer to say that she observed him from a great distance, as if she had merely read about him a long time ago in a newspaper even less sensational than *The Times*. He had another advantage over the Bagman. He knew about painting, and he knew that she was doing things instinctively which her acidulous intelligence could not comprehend. It was just possible that she might appreciate a critical comment or two, provided they were delivered as questions rather than statements.

He would prepare for a long siege, however. He would disarm her suspicions by posing as a brother, so that in the fullness of time his thrust would give her a double thrill—the thrill of incest without repugnance and the thrill of adultery within the family. In the meantime he would seek an intermediate port in which to shelter. After all, he was in the suburbs, in the world of paynims and therefore in the world of houri.

4

HIS search for suburban crumpet began the following morning. He walked round the supermarkets and between supermarkets, eyeing trousered women pushing prams and noisy trolleys. He eyed them up and down and down and up, but not one of them eyed him back. He told himself that they were too fat and therefore too self-satisfied, sated not on sex but soft chocolate. He wished for a willowy woman with long legs and a pale, medieval face enfolded in a dark-blue wimple, but if such a woman was not to be found, an uncomplicated woman with a spiritual face and no opinions would make an acceptable surrogate. He went to the baker's and the green grocer's and saw only hard mouths and insensitive fingers surreptitiously squeezing loaves and tomatoes. The faces reminded him of Esther. She was thin when he married her, but within five years she had become a roly-poly, the clarity of her jawline lost not in the folds of a wimple but in folds of fatty tissue.

Suburban kisses, he told himself, did not fall on one's head like Newton's apple. But if they should fall, he would, like Newton, be receptive. He wondered if Newton ate the apple before or after formulating his theory of gravity, or if in his greed for knowledge he omitted to eat it altogether. He went back to "Foxgloves" and wrote in his diary:

> Kisses, like straws, upon the surface flow;
> He who would search for crumpet must dive below.

In the afternoon he crossed the road to talk to Ann Ede, pleasantly and purposelessly as a brother should. Afterwards he went to the woods with his book and read under a silver birch over and over again:

> I have a bothy in the wood—
> None knows it but the Lord, my God;
> One wall an ash, the other hazel,
> And a great fern makes the door.

After a time he closed the book and waited for a fox to come into view, but he could tell from the delighted twittering of the birds that neither fox nor vixen was in sight. The silver birches, however, made up for their absence. They were tall and slender like the woman he sought that morning, but she would not have their black "benchmarks," nor the horizontal rings where the bark had peeled like thin paper. Ann Ede said that the wood of the birch was whippy, just right for ascetic flagellation, but Quilter said that it was practically useless, good for nothing except chipboard.

Which, if either, was right? If everyone expressed the same opinion, the simple truth might be easier to discover. As things stood, he had to sift every word, weasel and otherwise, and try to postpone judgement until all the evidence was heard. He was not the best man to hear it. He knew instinctively when the wind changed and when the tide was on the turn, and he knew about assonance in Irish syllabic poetry. He knew also about the country fox, but he now realised that he knew nothing about his suburban cousin.

Nevertheless, the days passed pleasingly, as if he were in the country, each bringing its own tune and dance. The mornings were often damp, with mist like a thick wall at the end of the road, and the yellowing trees dripped, though it had not rained in the night. At eleven the mist would lift, the sun would come out to dry the lawns and pavements, and it would be warmer out than in. Pink and golden sunsets illuminated the evenings like ethereal conflagrations behind the darkness of the trees, and moonless skies and lively breezes made the nights soothing and cool. He varied his daily round to enhance his well-being. He spent one day creosoting the timbering, he spent another mowing the lawns, and yet another stewing apples from the garden until the whole house reeked like a cider press.

The Colonel's library was another pleasure. It was well stocked and the Colonel knew it. He once said to Garlick, "There are more books in my library than are dreamt of in your principality," but he omitted to say that most of them were on the same subject—the First World War. He seemed to have collected every history, biography, novel and poem about those four fruitful and fruitless years, which he was too young to remember but which captured his imagination in a way the Second World War did not.

Some days came close to perfection, especially those on which Keating crossed the road for coffee and a metaphorical conversation about paintings and paynims with Ann Ede. One day she took him round the house, pointing out with unsuburban pride the rooms she had never redecorated. "This is my boudoir, where I sulk," she said, "and this is my carrel, where I study while the Bagman is in the pub." Her bedroom was plain and austere, with white walls, a white table and chair, and a white coverlet on the bed which reminded him of the bed in his boarding school cubicle twenty years ago. The only thing that wasn't white were the curtains. They were lilac and so flimsy that they rose and fell like streamers on light breezes. Again, he floated on a sense of spring and the freshness of a medieval day, and he turned to her and asked her what she would most like to be.

"An abbess," she replied without smiling.

"You must have an unworldly streak."

"Not at all. An abbess, particularly in the Middle Ages, was a woman of substance and social consequence. She was addressed as 'My Lady' and she had a retinue of monks and priests to 'pander' to her every spiritual whim."

He did not pursue the subject because he felt it might expose the black carnality in his heart. Instead he invited her to "Foxgloves" for coffee the following morning. He would have to be more alert, he told himself. He had seen her ankle. He must now discover her Achilles heel. But she looked at him with eyes that seemed to have solved the conundrum of how to be wise as serpents and harmless as doves.

That night in bed the image of the abbess in white tormented him, and when he finally slept it was to dream of bells ringing on a windy night by the sea. They were both in an abbey, and while she was attending to something in the calefactory he lay naked on her bed, warming her sheets with his straining body. On the stroke of midnight she stole into the darkened room and stretched beside him, hip to tingling hip and right ankle to left, while their hands joined over the pit of her groin. She smelt of starched linen newly ironed, and her hand felt cold and puny in his uncompromising grip. A bell began ringing in the distance, then another and another, all swelling and fading, their peals borne forwards and backwards on the fitful wind.

At first the bells tormented him with their unpredictability, now near, now far away, and then it seemed to him that they were calling him to a life of visionary brightness where bells rang singly and every bell had its time and purpose—the signum in the early morning, the squilla at breakfast, the campanella to summon monks from their cloisters, the tinniolum at bedtime, and the corrigiuncula to call the ascetic to his flagellations. The flimsy curtains swaddled both himself and the abbess and bore them through the open window into the bell-burgeoning night, high into the heavens, so high that he woke up breathless but refreshed, thinking not of monastic but of pagan Ireland, when heroes hunted the deer and slept on hillside rushes without caring where the sun rose or set on them. It was a world of single sounds—the troating of bucks, the baying of hounds, the cry of curlew over ebbing tides—but on a fateful day in A.D. 432, St. Patrick's mass bell rang in the duality inherent in all impossible yearnings. Henceforth, all was seen with two eyes, not one, and the curse was that both eyes squinted and never saw simultaneously. He focused on the bare mock-Tudor fireplace and told himself that he was being fanciful, that all he really needed was a good ride.

The days passed into late October, but in his fascination with the place of trees all things tempted him from the common pursuit of true crumpet—Quilter in his covert coat taking Jippo for a walk, affecting a deerstalker and a rustic stick; Jippo standing passant in the hallway and the Colonel stooping to shake his right forepaw; MacGeoch going out the back before shaving in the morning, venting with his nose up like an otter and checking his udometer before tapping the barometer by the stairs; and Garlick cutting his bacon rind so meanly that it became a thread while he waited stoat-like to pounce on Quilter if he should leave even one *t* uncrossed.

Garlick was a man of moderate habits, but Quilter and MacGeoch drank heavily two or three evenings a week. On these evenings they came rolling home from "The Fox and Billet" after closing time and pressed Garlick into playing a few tunes on the piano, which invariably included "Lili Marlene" and

"Knees Up, Mother Brown." Then, having sung their heads off, they would sit down to discuss politics, which at this hour of the evening meant the colour of Margaret Thatcher's knickers. Of these, they claimed to have found multiple foreshadowings in the works of Edmund Burke, Walter Bagehot and Benjamin Disraeli. In spite of their intimacy with the works of the trio, and the intimacy of the trio with the vexed question, they could never agree on an answer. But it seemed to Keating that Quilter had the best of the argument, and he contended that she favoured what he described as "long blue winceyettes reinforced with a double canvas gusset."

Sunday morning was a time of ease. All four of them got up late and read the papers over a leisurely breakfast, after which the Colonel would play baroque concertos on what he called his gramophone, but which Garlick called a music centre. Sometimes, in a bantering mood, he would play "O Lord, the Maker of All Things," "Passetyme with Good Companye" and other Tudor songs, and remind Garlick that he was the music man and that it was time he composed for Wistwood man a mock-Tudor madrigal.

At five minutes to twelve, Garlick would leave for "The Fox and Billet" and Armada Square so as to be assured of the lion's share of the cheddar. "The Fox and Billet" was renowned from Lewisham to Sevenoaks for the toasted cheese, anchovies, olives, prawns and pickled onions that the landlord put on the counter on Sunday mornings to intensify the thirst of his too-temperate patrons. His generosity attracted hordes of trippers from Bickley, Chislewick and Orpington, hard-faced, tight-fisted men who worked in the city during the week and knew the value of a buckshee breakfast. Garlick forgave them their interest in the prawns and anchovies, but he argued that the toasted cheese was for the locals. He was not greedy, but he believed it his duty as a Wistwoodlander to eat as much toasted cheese as he could before "the Huns, the Ostrogoths and the Visigoths" descended on the spread. With this admirable purpose in mind, he would first attack the toasted cheese in the saloon bar, and, having made short work of that, he would matriculate to the cocktail bar to demolish whatever was still in need of demolition.

Quilter and MacGeoch, as befitted officers of their rank, remained aloof. They never went to "The Fox and Billet" before 12:30, and by then all that was left on the counter was empty dishes. Keating shunned "The Fox and Billet" because he saw pubs as places where curiosity outstripped discretion, and where men got to know one another too quickly. But he would fondly watch the Colonel and the Major walk the length of Raleigh Way to Armada Square, the Colonel in his thornproof tweeds and the Major in the kilt he called "my Buchanan." The Colonel walked with shoulders back, head up, and hands clasped behind him, while the bowlegged Major walked with his arms hanging like a penguin's flippers as he rolled and nudged the Colonel with his shoulder at every step. In spite of the disparity of their stature, their gaits were oddly complementary. If you ever saw them walking together, you could not imagine them walking alone.

On November first, the Colonel came down to breakfast in higher spirits than usual.

"A good day for a fox drive, eh, Major?" He turned to MacGeoch.

"Visibility couldn't be better," MacGeoch spluttered.

"Do you know what happens today, Keating?" the Colonel asked.

"No, sir."

"Fox-hunting begins in England. Within the hour the countryside will be ringing with view halloos."

"It's a pity we can't organise a hunt in Wistwood." Garlick

tried his own brand of the sarcastic, which he referred to as the sarcaustic.

"We can do better, we can eat goose." The Colonel was not amused. "Captain, will you see to it that we have roast goose and the usual sage and onion stuffing for supper."

"As you wish, sir."

"Why goose?" Garlick was being awkward.

"Because the fox likes goose, you fathead."

"It's the equivalent of sympathetic magic," MacGeoch explained. "It's sympathetic degustation."

After they had dealt with the kedgeree, the Colonel drew Keating aside in the kitchen.

"We'll have to do something about Garlick," he confided. "He was late on parade this morning. If the bugger didn't have to earn a living and make his contribution to the household exchequer, I'd have him confined to barracks. Perhaps a round of sanitary fatigues at the weekend might bring him to his senses."

"He must have slept through reveille, sir. I'd be lenient just this once if I were you."

"You know my policy, Keating. Strict discipline in battle and in bivvy. But I'll give what you've said a thought. Another thing: have you noticed anything strange about his conversation?"

"No, sir!"

"No veiled references to toasted cheese?"

"Oh, that. I thought it was a joke."

"Some joke! What does toasted cheese mean to you?"

"Very little, except in a sandwich."

" 'Well, many's the long night I've dreamed of cheese— toasted mostly—and woke up again, and here I were.' Whom does that bring to mind?"

"Ben Gunn?"

"Garlick is obsessed with *Treasure Island*. When he gets up in the morning, he asks himself, 'Which Stevenson character shall I impersonate today? On Sundays, as you may have heard, he goes to 'The Fox and Billet' to impersonate Ben Gunn. No wonder Lachlan MacGeoch says he defiles the memory of a great Scotsman."

"Come to think of it, he did show me a copy of the book."

"He's got over a hundred copies. He collects illustrated editions. His favourite, as he will tell you, is the 1911 Scribner with pictures by N.C. Wyeth. So have a care. If he asks for pigeon pie, tell him you know his game. It was pigeon pie the Squire gave Jim Hawkins on the night he brought him the Captain's papers. If I were you, Keating, I'd have another dekko at the book on the q.t. To be forewarned is to be forearmed."

"I'll see if I can get a copy in the library this morning."

"And perhaps you could take my brogues to the snob shop on the way."

"The snob shop?"

"You will find it on the other side. The name is Walton. He's our regimental boot repairer. And, Captain, don't forget the goose."

The library was almost empty, ideal for study, but both copies of *Treasure Island* were out. Keating decided that instead he would do some research on the fox, but again he was disappointed. Quilter had told him that Wistwood Library had the best collection of books on vulpinology in the country, but that there was a waiting list of at least ten for every one of them. He thought it possible that Quilter could have been exaggerating.

"I'm looking for a book on the fox," he said to the assistant, a burly, round-shouldered youth with long hair, long fingernails and a platinum earring.

"Ah, the Fox. I doubt if we've got a book devoted entirely

to the Fox, but we've got several on North American Indians in general."

"I thought you specialised in the fox."

"Not as well known as the Shawnee and the Sioux. Even the Blackfoot are more popular in Wistwood than the Fox."

"What I want is a book that will help me recognise a dog fox from a vixen."

"Ah, foxes. You want a book on foxes? Very difficult."

"Are they all out?"

"Is it for a child?"

"No."

"We've got several books in the junior library, stories about B'rer Fox, the fox and the grapes, the fox who lost his tail. . . . "

"I was thinking of something a shade more scientific."

"We have next to nothing for adults, I'm afraid."

"Are they all out?" Keating enquired again.

"Most readers borrow fiction or biography, and foxes don't fit into either category."

"Don't you find an interest in the fox, then?"

"I can see you've written a monograph on the fox." The assistant smiled. "Authors are so difficult to please, and they will insist on writing impossible books. All librarians, on the other hand, take after Melvil Dewey. They love to catalogue and classify. To a good librarian a good book is a book that is easily classifiable."

"Are books on the fox in great demand here?" Keating almost shouted with impatience.

"If there was a demand for books on the fox, we'd have books on foxes. Now a biography of a fox—or a day in the life of a fox—would go down well. We don't cater for vulpinologists, you see. We don't cater for specialists of any coat or colour. To be honest we cater mainly for housewives."

So much for Quilter's famous collection, thought Keating,

going back to the stacks. Was this whole business of the fox a gigantic leg-pull? And what about the goose? Was he really meant to buy one, and if he did, would they all laugh at him? There was so much fiction in the suburbs that it was impossible to establish fact.

Here every man is his own novelist, he thought. Here fiction is the staff of life, fiction about oneself and fiction about other people.

He looked over his shoulder and almost lost his balance. A small woman in a grey nylon dress and impossibly high heels was reaching for a book, and as she reached higher, her dress clung to her underwear like wet material, and her protuberant buttocks took shape like two smooth turnips before his unbelieving eyes. It must have been a saucy book, because, as she read, she kept flexing her gluteal muscles so vigorously that her dress got caught in her cleft.

Distinctly cheeky! He decided to move closer. Beyond question, my lord, there's a *prima facie* case for further investigation.

He followed her out of the library, telling himself that she was well enough dressed to be an Eastsider. As if to please him, she turned left and crossed the footbridge over the railway, the outline of her backside appearing and disappearing like fox fire as she walked. But that was not all. To complicate his fantasy further, her left buttock rose an inch as she put her right foot forward and fell again as she put her left foot forward, while her right buttock behaved similarly in relation to her left foot. This was a phenomenon he had never observed in Ireland, and he wondered if it was an adaptation peculiar to the Anglo-Saxons and, if so, what feature of the English cultural environment induced it.

Before he had time to speculate further, she went into the delicatessen on the right, where she bought a small jar of gentleman's relish, and then, as if to confuse him utterly, she walked back over the footbridge to the West. He still followed at a distance, trying to puzzle out why in looking for a tall woman he had found a short one, but before he could discover the answer she turned into Warner Road and disappeared into a house called "Delta," next door to one called "The Worples."

"Delta," compared with the neighbouring houses, looked shabby. The paint on the upstairs windows was peeling and the walls could have done with a lick of emulsion. There was no prefab garage and no multicoloured crazy paving, only a narrow footpath of cracked concrete leading between sprawling rhododendrons to the door.

He walked back to the shops and found himself looking at plastic grass in a butcher's window, which suddenly reminded him of Quilter's goose. Putting all ischial undulations for the moment from his mind, he decided that the Colonel must surely be teasing him, so he bought five pounds of pork for the Hunt Supper. As soon as he got back to "Foxgloves," he put the pork in the fridge until the afternoon, took down the F-volume of MacGeoch's encyclopedia, and made a quick reconnaissance of the articles on Fish, Flowers and Fruit. After which he put the volume in MacGeoch's second-best briefcase, straightened his tie before the hall mirror, and set off for Wistwood West with a pleasurable hint of sexual excitement in his chest and groin. Then, as he reached Drake Parade, he remembered that all salesmen are optimists, so he nipped into the chemist's and bought twelve French letters specially made for "sensitivity with safety."

Wistwood West was different from Wistwood East. The houses were smaller and plainer, and understandably perhaps there were more gnomes and plaster boots in front gardens. However, Quilter was less than accurate when he spoke sneeringly of Wendy-houses. To Keating, they looked as if they could accommodate a husband and wife with two children in modest comfort. Garlick told him that they were built in the 1930s for the better class of artisan, but that they found themselves demoted, at least culturally, in the post-war social revolution. They were now the homes of hard-pressed junior accountants, assistant managers and programme analysts with an all-consuming ambition to make the short but significant transition to the other side. Keating doubted all that. To him they were solid, self-righteous houses. A few were even serious-minded, as if an awareness of their better appointed cousins in the East had conferred on them the self-knowledge that can only come from self-criticism. The self-righteousness, he decided, must have derived from their contempt for the excess of architectural curlicues that local estate agents found so congenial in their meretricious cousins.

As he approached "Delta," he wondered what on earth he would say to her. Should he begin with a word of praise for her front garden, as all good salesmen do? But her garden was a wilderness, and a word, however subtle, might only embarrass her. A reference to the unusual name of the house might break the ice. Perhaps she was a Greek scholar who would appreciate the conversation of a man to whom "Delta" was not Greek. Would it be a meeting of true minds without impediments, or a case of Greek meets Greek bearing a Greek gift? He clutched MacGeoch's briefcase and raised the knocker.

"Good morning, madam. I deal in works of reference. I happened to be passing, and not unnaturally I wondered if the owner of a house with such a scholarly name might provide a home for a weighty tome or two. In short, I was curious to know if you and your husband were Greek scholars. I'm afraid I'm not a Greek scholar myself, but I've met scholars. So I should be most grateful if you could spare me fifteen minutes."

He held up the second-best briefcase like a Chancellor of the Exchequer holding up a battered dispatch box. The tiny woman on the doorstep looked up at him in wonder and laughed so heartily that the fragrance of her breath nearly knocked him over.

"So you're a salesman." She smiled. "I thought at first you were a Regius professor."

"A salesman, yes, but never a bagman. I sell books, not sausages—what we describe in our profession as works of reference. May I come in?"

She opened the door wider and closed it promptly behind him, garotting him with a stricture of stagnant air that brought back to him the crypt, the jumble sale and his second-hand hacking jacket. She led him into the sombre front room and in a failure of imagination he returned to "Delta."

"It's not a name I would associate with Tudor England." He stroked his chin.

"When we first came here, it was called 'The Dells,' which, cheek by jowl with 'The Worples,' proved too much for my late husband."

"I know. He called it 'Delta' so that he need only change two of the five characters."

"Not quite. It's named after the Delta connection."

"The title of a book?"

"No, a term used by electrical engineers. My late husband was one of the best."

As she spoke, he watched the muscles of her face and neck. She must have been fifty, if not more, but her skin was still fresh. Her hair, swept up to increase her height, was dark and glossy, her eyes danced with intelligence, and her enormous breasts jutted straight out, as if supported by a hidden cantilever. A sudden dizziness broke his grip on himself. He found himself lying on top of her with her breasts like conical hot-water bottles under his chest, and then he realised that she was merely waiting for him to say something. He reached for

72

MacGeoch's briefcase and produced the F-volume with a magical flourish that amused her.

"First of all let me tell you a few things about our encyclopedia. It comes in twenty-four cloth-bound volumes, each of them weighing an average of six pounds. The total weight, as I'm sure you've already calculated, is one hundred forty-four pounds, or, to put it in more meaningful terms, ten stone and four pounds."

"What does it cost?"

"The cost comes later, because it is secondary to knowledge, which is an end in itself. Obviously, I'd need a pair of packhorses to lug all that erudition around, so I content myself with the F-volume because it contains what we encyclopedists call the seminal articles—those on Fish, Flowers and Fruit. This trinity of subjects form the footing of the encyclopedic edifice, and what I'd like to do now is sit beside you for half an hour and go through them one by one to acquaint you with what modern scholars call the 'nexus of epistemological inter-relationships.'"

He got up to go to her, but she stopped him in his tracks with a jolly little laugh that seemed to have its footing in an unassailable sense of superiority.

"I don't like saying, 'Not today, thank you,' but I'm afraid that's simply what I'll have to say. I was getting ready to go to a funeral when you knocked. Perhaps you could call again tomorrow and I'll give you coffee to make up for this morning."

"That's perfectly all right."

"Can you come at eleven?"

She led the way into the hallway and the perfume of her breath made the words in his mouth crack crazily, but not like her concrete footpath.

"It's my second funeral in a fortnight." She turned to him.

"The first was Miriam Trek's. Such a lovely woman. I just don't understand why anyone should want to murder her."

"These are troubled times," he told her soothingly.

"Do you think funerals come in threes?"

"I'm afraid I'm not superstitious. It's one of my blind spots."

He sought to change the subject. He looked round and made a move towards the door.

"What's that, a good luck charm?" He pointed to a shrivelled skein on the wall.

"No, it's a piece of withered seaweed. My late husband didn't hold with barometers. He kept a handful of seaweed in the hallway and always felt it before going to work in the morning. If it was moist to the touch he'd take his umbrella, and if it was dry he'd sing, 'We do love to be beside the sea-side' on the way to the station. He was a lovely man."

Utterly dotty, he thought as he lurched between the rhododendrons towards the gate. But I've discovered the way to her heart, not through the senses but the memory of her dead husband.

He spent an energetic afternoon in the cookhouse, but the Colonel was not as appreciative as he had hoped.

"It smells of anything but goose," he shouted as he came in. "And at the same time there's a hint of goose."

"It's mock goose," Keating told him with hastily mustered gravity. "I tried to get a real goose, but not one was to be found either on this side or the other."

"What's mock goose?" the Colonel sounded doubtful.

"Pork stuffed with sage and onion like a real goose."

"Keating, you're a corker! I knew you wouldn't let me down. And what are you giving us for starters?"

"Mock turtle soup followed by pâté crêpes—*pâté de foie gras*, to be precise."

"Excellent. What can I say, if not *il miglior fabbro*. A little emendation perhaps. We'll have the crêpes first and then the soup."

The Hunt Supper was an unqualified success. The mock-goose, like mock-Tudor architecture, in the absence of the real thing, served its purpose. And it was enhanced by three bottles of red burgundy preceded by a bottle of dry sherry.

"I had a brain wave last night," the Colonel said over the port. "I realised for the first time how little we know about the Wistwood Fox. We hear the clatter of a dustbin lid in the night and no more. Much research needs to be done, and the best way to do it is by radio-tagging. We shall put a collar with a small radio transmitter round his neck, and then his every move will be known to us."

"But who will collar it?" Garlick probed.

"Think of the myths we could explore and possibly explode." The Colonel disregarded him.

"We are surely here to create myths, not explode them," Garlick reminded him.

"Think of the questions it will answer. Does it never cross the railway? And if there are West-foxes, as some believe, will East-foxes mate with them?"

"These are serious questions," MacGeoch agreed. "It is all too indicative of the state of current research that not one of them is answered in the recent *History of Wistwood*."

"This is not an occasion for censure." The Colonel smiled. "It is an occasion for celebration. And to mark it with due ceremony I suggest that we all gather round the piano for a robust rendering of 'The Fox Went out on a Chilly Night.' Do you know it, Garlick?"

"Of course I know it."

"Do you, Keating?"

"Indeed I do."

"There are times when I have my doubts about you gentlemen," the Colonel said. "But I must grant that though you may not have gone to the right university at least you've gone to the right nursery schools."

Garlick sat down at the piano and the others gathered round and sang with a lightness of character that surprised them into the laughter of contradiction:

> The fox went out on a chilly night,
> And he prayed to the moon to give him light,
> For he'd many miles to go that night,
> Before he reached the town-o, town-o, town-o,
> For he'd many miles to go that night,
> Before he reached the town-o.
> He ran till he came to the farmer's pen,
> Where the ducks and geese were kept shut in.
> "A couple of you will grease my chin
> Before I leave this town-o, town-o, town-o.
> A couple of you will grease my chin
> Before I leave this town-o."

When they had sung the last verse, the Colonel asked Keating to serve an extra tot of "porto," and Keating went to bed early with the excitement of tomorrow's salesmanship in his blood.

5

HE was glad that the wind in the chimney woke him because it filled the night with intimations of comfort. Here he was in an Englishman's castle with firm foundations and solid walls and three of the most incurious men in England. The wind sucked at the swan-neck of the guttering, expressing the surprise he felt at the thought of how he now lived. He had begun to feel secure, but not so secure that he could afford to drop his vigilance. The Colonel, with his journalist's command of the language, had expressed it well enough: here they fleeted the time carelessly as they did in the golden world. He had expected enemies, but he now knew that the only enemy he'd encounter here was the enemy within. With smug self-confidence, he turned over and slept till the alarm woke him.

After breakfast he told Quilter that he still had not heard from the sports editor of *The Sunday Mirror*.

"I've seen him around," said Quilter. "I should forget him if I were you. He's what our night editor calls an SS—a shit and a snollygoster."

"Perhaps you could keep a weather eye open," Keating reminded.

"It would help if I had something from you to show."

"Cuttings? I'm afraid I left them behind in Newcastle. What I was thinking is that I might write a couple of paras which you could shove under the right nose."

"What about?"

"Politics perhaps?"

"Everyone thinks he knows about politics, but the results of every general election in my lifetime tells a different tale."

"I suppose you're right."

"What do you really know about?"

"Old Irish nature poetry."

"An acquired taste, I imagine. Why not write about something everyone else knows about, but which you see differently because you're new to it. Write eight hundred words on the epidemiology of the garden gnome."

"Full of pitfalls. I don't even know what a garden gnome is made of."

"What about the taxonomy of lich-gates in mock-Tudor suburbs?"

"No, I'll write a piece on the man himself, the man who dreams of lich-gates and garden gnomes. Suburban man."

"Capital. If you let me have it this evening, I'll slip it under the editor's nose first thing in the morning. But let me say this: write something fresh with an original angle. How about suburban man as a link in the evolution of man from ape?"

"Sounds highly unlikely."

"You've heard of *Homo habilis,* have you not?"

"No."

"An early ancestor of ours with sufficient skill to use crude tools."

"I'm afraid I don't see the connection."

"Suburban man shares his preoccupation with elementary technology. There's nothing he likes better than gadgets with an acceptable noise level—electric drills, power saws, you know the kind of thing. He spends his weekends at his workbench, using his hands, to recover the masculinity he's lost, using his noddle, during the week. Think about it, Keating. There's a feature there for *Punch*."

He sat at the dining-room table waiting for words to explode into thought. The sun coming through the mountain ash cast a labyrinth of light and shadow on the blank page. He sharpened two pencils and checked the ink level in the cartridge of his pen, but though words came, they did not explode and neither did they follow one another in the order prescribed by the best subeditors. He went to the French windows and stood with his back to the warmth of the fire. The garden was a summation of a life he did not comprehend. Dry leaves—dirty green, yellow and brown, but not hectic red— whirled and danced like bodies without souls. A rusty wheelbarrow and a broken push mower squinted like Darby and Joan in the failing sun, and on the lilac tree, a few remaining leaves floated like crispy mobiles between open doors. They were airy, translucent, about to drift away, as if they had finally taken leave of the summer substance that had been holding them earthbound. He knew in his heart that Quilter's *Homo habilis* was a load of horse manure. He still had an hour to kill before it was time to investigate the Delta connection, so he decided to kill it in the woods.

Garlick told him that Wistwood without the wood would be a place of sand, but then Garlick was not one of life's concelebrants. Keating knew the woods as a place of doubts and mysteries, the antithesis of the straight-running roads around them, roads that enclosed houses of facile certainties, in which two and two always made four, and in which, at least according to Garlick, self-regard had driven out self-knowledge. He sat under an oak tree trying not to count the acorns bouncing off his head, thinking that unfortunately he saw everything at second hand, through the fantastic eyes of Quilter, Garlick and MacGeoch, and wondering if in half an hour he would be seeing them through the equally fantastic eyes of the Deltaic Widow.

A pretty girl on horseback bore down on him with what seemed like an unpardonable waste of muscle. The horse was so large compared with the light-boned rider that he could not help sensing a disproportion between the energy expended and the weight transported. The horse thought otherwise, however. With a rococo flourish of his undocked tail, he defecated with an ease which might be the envy of many a costive commuter, but, though he defecated, he never once put a hoof wrong, never once modulated the rhythm of his trot. The girl, however, was not so splendidly unselfconscious. Perhaps associating a loss of power with a loss of heat, she administered a sharp touch of crop on stifle and thus escaped the mint-keen fragrance which she bequeathed to Keating and all in her wake. He picked himself up as if he'd been ridden down and, crying "Christ Almighty!" flailed madly with his arms at the dung-whetted air.

He emerged from the woods into disinfected air breathed by accountants with miniature pocket calculators. Crossing the footbridge by the delicatessen, he noticed a dead dog on the line, only to realise with disbelief a second later that it was not a dead dog but a dead fox. Quilter told him that to embarrass Westmen the Eastmen filled their conversation with phrases like "there are no atheists in fox-holes," and that in the library on Saturday mornings they complained loudly that the books were so foxed that they could not read them. The fox below him was facing west. Strange that he did not have the cunning to use the footbridge. But his carcase proved one thing: although now dead, he once existed.

The widow had the kettle on the boil when he knocked. Her thin upper lip puckered as she pronounced a plosive in the doorway, and he wondered if the teeth in her lower jaw were acquired or home grown. They seemed a fraction of an inch farther back from the inside of her nether lip than he would have wished, but he had to admit that the relationship of lip to teeth would make an excellent embouchure for a trumpet or trombone. As she turned her back, he noted again the high-rise heels and the primly straight seam of her dusky nylons. Her coffee was strong and the single biscuit that accompanied it so hard that he doubted if anyone could have cracked it with a denture. He was pleased to see that she herself had one from the same tin.

"Do you believe in dreams?" he asked.

"In my life, when dreams don't foreshadow, they sum up."

"The first time I called, you told me about your friend Miriam Trek, and then I went home and dreamt that I saw her in Battersea Park sitting on a seat with one leg curled up beneath her." He was lying of course, but his lie contained more than a grain of truth.

"Did she ever sit like that?" he asked.

"How?"

"Did she sit so that you could see only one leg, not two?"

"I don't think so. She suffered from varicose veins, you see."

"In my dream I sat beside her and kissed her left ear. Then I asked her who she was and she said she was a seafaring woman with one leg."

"It doesn't sound like Miriam."

"Did she ever mention *Treasure Island?*"

"No, but she bought *Coral Island* for her son when he was ten. I remember, because he told her that he didn't have to read it, that he could guess the ending."

"What did she look like?"

"She had fair hair and fair skin with freckles across the bridge of her nose."

"That's the woman I saw in my dream."

"Was she tall?"

"She was tall and slim with long fingers that threatened to break off as she sat knitting."

"The woman you saw wasn't Miriam. Miriam was just my size and her fingers were short and pudgy."

"What does it mean then, my dream?"

"Well, it doesn't sum up, so it must foreshadow," she laughed.

He took the F-volume from the briefcase and opened it at the article on Flowers, but she told him that what she would like most would be to keep the volume for a day and a night and sample it for herself. Then, when she had read the articles on Fish, Flowers and Fruit, he could come back and explain to her their bearing on the nexus of epistemological interrelationships. As she said this, she laughed so merrily that he considered it possible that she might be teasing him.

"I'll be delighted to have something to do." She smiled. "I sometimes borrow two or three books from the library but I never seem to get through them, simply because I don't have to. Knowing that you'll be coming back will give me an incentive. It was different when Henry was alive. I used to read four books a week then, because he read them too and we'd discuss them in bed before going to sleep. Books weren't his passion, though. His two greatest things were requiems and the Cinque Ports. He was daft about the Cinque Ports, just the original five, and of them, Hastings was his favourite. Every summer we used to go to Hastings for our holidays, and he always brought back a memento. He found that ashtray in a junk shop in All Saints Street, I remember."

He picked up the ashtray and read aloud: *"You have to kiss a lot of toads before you kiss the Handsome Prince."* She gave a little laugh and he smiled as innocently as he could to conceal his sense of tiptoeing over a well-tended grave.

"Henry found that very funny, and so do I. Have you ever been to Hastings?"

"No."

"Then you must go. Henry used to say that he'd prefer to be Lord Warden of the Cinque Ports than Prime Minister."

"You said that he liked requiems as well." He was conscious that the conversation was not following the course he had so carefully planned.

"He had recordings of over twenty requiems, but Berlioz's was his favourite."

"He must have had an artistic streak." He tried to sound interested.

"In many ways he was a prosaic man—he once gave me a spring balance for Christmas. But he was the kind of man you couldn't but get on with. He said one Christmas morning that Berlioz wrote a requiem that would wake the dead, and when I laughed, he felt embarrassed and I loved him for it."

"I've never heard Berlioz's but I've heard Mozart's."

"Are you in a hurry?"

"Not really. My next appointment isn't until after lunch."

"I'll play you the Berlioz if you like. Not the whole thing, just the *Dies Irae,* the part that Henry loved."

They sat on opposite sides of the room and heard the intermittent thunder of overweening brass, while he wondered where on earth or in heaven all this would lead to.

"He always listened to music before turning in. One night I told him I was going up, and he looked at his watch and said, 'Already? I thought I might have time for another requiem.'"

"Why was he so fond of requiems?"

"It wasn't that he was morbid. He just felt that they embodied some kind of truth that escaped other kinds of music. One day I came back from the shops and found him lying on his back on the floor, his hands folded over his breast and his face set like a death mask while the *Dies Irae* from the Berlioz was playing."

"Presumably, he wanted to hear it as it will never be heard."

"That's precisely what I thought."

"Did he play an instrument?"

"No, but he wanted to write music. The year before he died he took up D.I.Y. and he took it so seriously that he decided to compose a requiem for his own funeral. Curiously, it was to be a requiem of rigorous moderation, the antithesis of the *Grande Messe des Morts*. It was to be written for four male voices, and in the interest of unity and economy the four were also to act as pallbearers."

"Did he in fact compose it?"

"He could neither read nor write music, so he began taking evening classes. He was a man of extraordinary will power. If he hadn't been called away, I'm sure he'd have seen it through."

Her voice rose in a stifled cry of distress, her thin lips puckered, and her hands flew to her face. He went and sat beside her, but all he could find to offer her was a crumpled paper handkerchief.

"Don't distress yourself," he said feebly, wishing he had a linen handkerchief and that he could put his arm round her without accusing himself of unforgivable fraudulence. It was a rare opportunity to offer something more tangible than sympathy, but the image of the well-tended grave ensured that any fibrillations he felt were confined to the region of the heart, a source of embarrassed self-accusation rather than the rackety vitality he had planned on the way.

"I know how you feel." He placed a cautious hand on her elbow.

"Please excuse me." She dabbed her eyes with a triangular handkerchief which had little perforations like those in the uppers of the Colonel's brogues.

"I must be off now, but I'll come back when you've looked through the F-volume."

"Come tomorrow at the same time, if you like." She was

smiling again, like an uncertain sun on a day of unpredictable showers.

"Don't forget to look up the article on the fox." He laughed as he said good-bye.

"Why the fox?" she responded. "I thought you said Fish, Flowers and Fruit."

"You're right. We mustn't introduce unnecessary complications."

As soon as he got back to "Foxgloves," he went through the Colonel's records and found four requiems—Mozart's, Berlioz's, Fauré's, and one of Cherubini's. He put the Berlioz on the record player and lay flat on his back on the dining-room table with his eyes closed and his hands stretched stiffly by his sides. As the mighty music rolled round the catafalque, he tried to obliterate conscious thought, to will himself into becoming an empty urn that still retained the possibility of an echo. Before him hung a heavy black drape that muffled the thunder of the *Dies Irae*. Then out of the dark came blue lightning that split the drape down the middle and revealed the opening of graves and the scurrying of the newly risen dead, awesome and awestricken, making rustling noises like dry sedge in a high wind. He thought he understood Henry's fascination with death. It was simply a fascination with his wife. But in himself Keating found something else, a desire for ultimate experience, for a baring of the breast before all that is overwhelming both here and hereafter.

He spent the afternoon before Quilter's typewriter in the hope that it would bring him more inspiration than the sharpened pencils of the morning. As the sun went down behind the garden trees, he watched its golden light strike individual blades of grass on the lawn, illuminating them, it seemed, not from above but from their roots below. Three gardens away, a snake of smoke coiled itself round the branches of a copper beech, an Indian cobra pretending to do the Indian rope trick.

Inspired, he went back to the typewriter and knocked off a thousand words about Red Indians, which he subbed down to eight hundred and then retyped for the Colonel.

To his surprise the Colonel was critical. He cackled irreverently as he read it through the first time, then he reread the offending paragraphs aloud, denoting the end of each sentence with a snort:

The Sioux lived on the plains, whereas the Iroquois made their home in the woodlands of the north. The Iroquois grew corn and beans, and, interestingly, suburban man spends much time at weekends growing vegetables in his garden. The Sioux, like the other tribes of the plains, lived in tepees that looked as much alike as the mock-Tudor houses of suburbia. Other curious parallels abound. In wearing suede shoes with rubber soles rather than conventional leather, suburban man is obviously again taking a leaf out of the book of the woodland Indians with their soft-soled moccasins. Similarly, the briefcase, in which he carries his (news?)papers and cucumber sandwiches resembles the parfleche which the Red Indian made from buffalo hide and in which he carried dried meat on long journeys. And, finally, the Indian potlatch or tribal feast has survived in the suburban party, though with certain interesting modifications. Whereas the Indian chief overwhelms his guests with presents, the suburban host expects to receive presents—without the slightest sense of shame, he invites his guests on condition that they "bring a bottle."

"My dear Keating, this will never do. To begin with, it simply isn't true. Suburban men, at least suburban gentlemen, wear brogues not suede. And the language is as flat as a pancake. Try to be folksy, try to catch the rhythms of Billingsgate and Smithfield, and never, never start an article with 'Though . . .' Concessive clauses smack more of Balliol than Billingsgate, and in Fleet Street the smack of Balliol is the smack of death."

"You forget 'Though yet of Hamlet our dear brother's death the memory be green. . . .'" Keating tried to be superior.

"I have not forgotten it, Captain. Great journalist that he was, he did not begin the play with it. He begins with the more colloquial 'Who's there?' I shan't show this to the editor, because I think you can do better. So try again. And this time say something at once provocative and true. A good journalist is a man with a ready-made opinion on everything from epeirogenesis to episiotomy, so don't be shy. Don't just write with the bloodless intellect. Remember you've also got a heart, a liver, a cock and a brace of balls. And think again about *Homo habilis*. I'm certain it could be the germ of something good."

Keating went to bed despondent. Though he was grateful for the easeful life of "Foxgloves," he did not wish to remain the Colonel's head cook and bottle-washer forever. He wanted a proper job, and journalism was the only job he knew. Even at his best he was never flash with words, but at his best he could achieve a modest competence, which, to judge by the newspapers, was all that most Fleet Street journalists could depend on. Perhaps the Colonel was right. He was certainly old enough to know the ropes. The sensible thing surely was to swallow his pride and try again.

He slept on his resolution until something woke him. He could see the window at the foot of the bed and a slit of grey that wasn't light, only a shade less dark than the room itself. He turned to sleep and found himself swimming against a headsea, while at the back of his mind he knew that someone had opened and closed the street door. The loose tread halfway up the stairs creaked. Wide awake, he pricked his ears, but there was no further sound, no step on the landing, no click from a bedroom door. He was on the verge of sleep again when someone flushed the loo. He got up and stood in the dark behind the door. Again there was silence on the landing.

He switched on the light and went across to the Ooja-cum-Pivvy. The window was open, the cistern was hissing, and in the bowl was an unflushed faecalith of equine proportions, the Turd of the Unknown Journalist. He went back to bed thinking that the perception of madness is nowhere keener than in the small hours, while the mind is still between waking and sleeping, before it has switched on the fail-safe mechanism with which it normally confronts the chancy small change of the day.

He woke in a lather at seven. The Widow had dragged him to Miriam Trek's funeral, and after the cremation she invited him for a meal at the crematorium cafeteria, which was divided like the chuch into two aisles. On the right were the self-important Eastsiders who could afford to pay for their tournedos chasseur, and on the left were the Westsiders who, because they were Westsiders, were given a free lunch, broiled braxy from the furnace, the stench of which burst above them in a sulphurous head of steam. The Widow dragged him towards the Westsiders. He shrieked in horror and fled into the sane sunlight between the cypresses, but he knew that the reality of life was inside, not here.

He lay on his back with the bedclothes over his head and a weight like a bag of cement on his chest. He felt befouled by experience, his own and other people's, negative experience that muddied the waters of spiritual serenity, and he wished for a bothy in a wood, spring water sparkling, birdsong, and the love of God. He wanted to stay in bed, but if he didn't get up, the Colonel would send him to the M.O., who would undoubtedly prescribe a Number 9. And if he refused to take the Number 9, he would be confined to barracks for the day. So he went to the bathroom and wondered at the *tabula rasa* that emerged from under the shaving lather with the help of six or seven razor strokes. Hurrah for pogonotomy and King Camp Gillette. He felt whole again in mind and body, and he asked himself if, in a curious way, guilt, not cleanliness, was next to godliness.

When the Colonel had gone to work, he sat down to the typewriter to see what he could make of *Homo habilis,* but all that came were flat-footed phrases stumbling erratically like drunken cripples across the page. It was a blowy morning. From the table he watched the wind weaving the branches of the silver birches, lifting a skirt on one clothesline and making a windsock of a doubly hung sheet on another. Seeing these visible manifestations of the invisible made him think again of the strangeness of Henry's relationship with his wife. He sat looking at them for an hour, until it was time to go to "Delta."

Her eyes were red as if she hadn't stopped weeping since he last saw her. As soon as she closed the door, she burst into tears in the hallway.

"It's Jewel. She's been run over, poor thing, and she had barely recovered from her bronchitis."

He led her into the front room and sat beside her on the brown corduroy sofa. This time he had taken the precaution of buying a linen handkerchief in Drake Parade on the way, and she put it to her eyes, while he thought that all cats were not practical. When he spoke, however, it was to tell her not to fret. His left arm was round her waist, her tiny left hand was in his right, and his lips were brushing her lightly scented cheek when he wasn't kissing her behind the ear. After he had pretended to feast at some length on the lobe itself, he risked a kiss on her closed eyelids and lastly on her lips, which tasted of beef consommé, though it was still an hour off lunchtime. They kissed for twenty-two minutes by his watch, while he counted cars passing in the road, and then he found his hand chugging up the steep incline of her leg into a no-man's-land beyond the nylon, which was smooth and soft like a peach, and warmer too. He detected in himself a growing reluctance to proceed, as if he were about to prod a wasp's nest with his forefinger just for devilment and at the same time dreading a sting.

Yesterday he went up into the loft to hide the Colonel's knife, which he thought might not be safe in the bathroom ventilator, and, peering about him in the half-light under the tiles, he froze at the sight of a wasps' nest hanging from a rafter above his head. As a boy in the country, he had seen wasps' nests in trees, and he had thrown stones at them from a safe distance for the amusement of his friends, but this nest was different. It was unnatural. It did not belong in the house. It reminded him of the Turd of the Unknown Journalist. He touched a seam of the papery ball and three or four wasps circled menacingly round his head. He flailed the air with his arms, he almost fell through the trap-door behind him. . . .

He changed position and all reluctance dissolved. She was now beneath him, the boisterous cusps of her breasts making rash promises to his chest, and his risen tickler stranded in the valley between her knees. His left eye, close against her neck, observed through a microscope with critical reductiveness. It was a dry neck, the loose skin somewhat coarse like wartime paper or paper that's been recycled at least twice. He remembered being trapped halfway down a sea cliff when he was twelve, hunkering precariously on a ledge while the men above prepared the ropes, and seeing a tiny flower between two rocks, about two inches from his eye. He knew that he must not look down, that he must concentrate on the delicate flower and the yellow worm that came wriggling up through the loose earth at its root.

Her breasts were fizgigs exploding through the light cotton of his shirt. He hoisted himself carefully with neither block nor tackle until the tickler was in a position to assert riparian rights. Her hand plunged like a sounding-lead. Playfully, she nipped the tickler at the root and with an appreciative giggle piloted him through the shallows of the estuary into the safety of the oily waters above the tideway. For a while he lay motionless and breathless, wondering if she had nipped him deliberately so that his pleasure would be the greater for succeeding pain.

The oily waters spat and boiled with currents, crosscurrents and wriggling elvers. He ignored the sucking and the buffeting and tried to recall the stem-like delicacy of Ann Ede's neck, but like the Holy Grail it could be seen only by men of perfect purity. Still he must not complain. He had found what he sought, and only a snob would reject it for coming from the wrong side of the railway. He was neither a perfectionist nor a saint. If he could not ride and tie, he would ride and be thankful.

"What's your name?" she asked in the stillness that followed a struggle so determined on both sides that it seemed as if only one of them could survive. He was pleased to find that they both not only survived but won as well.

"Charles Keating."

"I'm Sarah Stooke. I think we owe our introduction to poor Jewel."

"I'm sorry about Jewel, but I'm glad we met."

"Dearest Jewel. And Miriam was so fond of her. To lose them both within a month of each other was more than I could bear alone."

"Was Miriam Trek a good knitter?"

"Why do you ask?"

"I heard two men on the train the other day talking about a woman who knitted pullovers," he lied. "I just wondered if she were the woman who was murdered on the way from Dover Priory."

"Miriam used to knit now and again, but I wouldn't say her knitting was special."

That evening, as he watched the news with Quilter, Garlick

and MacGeoch, he felt that he could have predicted, if he had taken thought, that another Wistwood woman would be strangled. She was a middle-aged widow, living alone in the West, and her body was found in her garden shed with a page from *Foxe's Martyrs* stuffed down her bra.

"She was obviously a Catholic," Garlick told them.

"Why Catholic?" Quilter sounded contemptuous.

"*Foxe's Martyrs* describes in lurid detail the sufferings of Protestants at the stake under Mary Tudor. Could the murderer have chosen a mock-Tudor suburb in which to avenge the deaths of Cranmer, Ridley and Latimer?"

"Codswallop, Garlick. The murderer is not a religious maniac, but an incorrigible punster. He has torn a page from Foxe's book for the same reason that he put a fox-fur round the neck of his first victim."

"I agree entirely," said MacGeoch. "The fox is his hallmark."

"If not his touchstone," said the Colonel.

"I think you should report that to the police," Garlick said.

"The police may be slow, but they get there in the end. They need no help from either you or me."

Keating looked at Quilter, Garlick and MacGeoch, but the light from the small screen shone impartially on their inscrutable faces. One of them had gone out last night after the others had gone to bed, and sometime in the night a woman had been murdered. One of them had gone to the loo and dropped an unflushable faecalith. Question: Was the man who went out and the man who failed to flush his deposit one and the same?

6

WITHIN hours of the discovery of the second murder, Wistwood was overwhelmed by police—police on foot, police on motorbikes and police in obtrusive panda cars. They mingled with shoppers in Drake Parade, they took registration numbers in Armada Square, and they knocked on doors in the narrower avenues of Wistwood West. Keating did his shopping as quickly as he could and stayed indoors for the rest of the time, except for brief walks with Jippo in the woods. He rang Sarah Stooke to remind her that she still had his F-volume, but when she invited him for a drink the following evening, he said he was going away for a day or two, that he would call on her one morning next week. Being seen in Wistwood West after dark and stopped by a bobby for questioning was the last thing a journalist with neither job nor cuttings could wish for.

He sat beside the telescope in the Arsenal, gazing disconsolately across the road at Ann Ede's empty garden. She had gone to the country "for a day or two" without thinking it proper to tell him the hour and minute of her return. She had a cottage somewhere in Suffolk to which she retreated to meditate, paint and garden whenever the materialism of the Bagman and other such paynims got on her most Christian of wicks. It was "a cottage with dormer windows and cream weatherboarding" that had been left to her by a maiden aunt, and it was so far away from the nearest pub that the Bagman went there once and never again. It pained him to think that in spite of the dormer windows and weatherboarding, he could not picture it, because she had not told him how it stood in relation to the garden, so he thought the best thing to do was to go downstairs and read the biography of Geert Grote which she gave him before she left.

He had invited her for coffee the day before she was due to go, and she came through the door with breathless urgency, waving the biography as a lesser woman might wave a bottle of champers.

"You haven't heard of Geert Grote?" She put on her act of condescending amazement. "He was a fourteenth-century Dutch preacher, a forerunner of Thomas a Kempis. Don't tell me you haven't heard of him either."

"The name seems to ring a bell."

"For you Irish Catholics religion is not a thing of the intellect; it's to be lapped up like mother's milk—unself-consciously. Even the most tedious of paynims has heard of a Kempis."

Their conversations were all like that. She obviously enjoyed his company, otherwise she'd hardly invite him for coffee, but talking to her was an act of fraudulence and concealment, because he could never give his whole-hearted assent to even one of her assumptions, and the game would be up if he once made his predicament clear. At least it was impious as opposed to pious fraudulence, deception practised to bring carnal, not religious, fulfilment to the person deceived. However, he felt that he was deceiving himself more than her. While he couldn't think of her without lusting after her, he knew that what prompted the thought in the first place was hunger of a kind that no amount of sex would satisfy.

As soon as she came back, he invited her again. He sat by the window, watching her door, wondering if he could conceal from her that he'd read only the first and last chapters of her book. Luckily, as she came through the door, it was flowers, not Geert Grote, that was uppermost in her mind.

"There's a distinct lack of flowers in this house." She sniffed significantly in the hallway. "Even one plant would help to draw the tang of pipe smoke from the air."

"It's a mannish sort of house. Not a trace of a woman's hand."

"It's heavy and stuffy, like one of those ghastly gentlemen's clubs in Pall Mall."

He laid the cups on the dining-room table, because he didn't like the lounge in the morning, but as soon as she saw the sunlight streaming through the French windows, she suggested that they sit in the garden. The sky, after a week of morning fog, was blue and clear. The sun was warm for November, and the unswept leaves on the lawn had lost their sogginess and were again crisp and rustling. Only a few tired leaves remained on the apple trees, and curiously they were all on the top branches, all red, while the weeping willow in Giles Oxbone's garden had faded to dirty yellow.

She pulled up her dress slightly and sat on the other side of the table with her back to the house. The garden chairs were low and the table was rather high, so he was aware of looking at her face "above board" and the next moment stealing a glance at her legs below, which were so long that she had to sit obliquely for comfort.

When he looked at her, he was transported from November to May. He saw a secluded mountain stream, cool bright water falling musically among ferns, and he was filled with a sense of freshness and cleanliness, of a sea wind cooling a verdant shore. He recalled the smell in her bedroom, a sea smell, which transformed itself into the taste of fresh oysters on his tongue. If only she would put him to the test . . . he would drink her water and tell her that she had not made a drop too many. But that would not be her idea of a test. She would not see the act as the self-abasement of romantic love but as proof positive of his fallen nature. She would value her body not as the end of one man's quest but as the temple of the Holy Ghost with herself as the unworthy caretaker.

"On a morning like this I feel as if I might escape." She raised two open hands to the sky.

"You sound unhappy. Are you?"

"No."

"Are you happily married?"

"My husband thinks so, and that, I suppose, is what matters. He believes that I'm a typical suburban housewife, that I give the morning to shopping, the forenoon to coffee-drinking and the afternoon to gardening and cooking. He needs to feel that in his absence I am capable only of the trivial."

"But he must know you paint."

"He's pathetically jealous. He calls it "picturising," not painting. But he still doesn't know my secret. Four years ago I discovered he was being unfaithful, and I never said a word. From time to time I get mysterious phone calls from breathless women, trying to check up on him, I suppose. His dishonesty is painful to me, but it is a consolation to know that the other women are being treated equally shoddily."

"Have you met any of them?"

"How should I meet them? He doesn't discriminate, he recruits from the typing pool. But don't think I'm sour. The modern typing pool performs the function of the Victorian brothel; it leaves serious-minded wives free to pursue their hobbies in peace."

"I don't understand why you stay with him."

"Because in a way I value his company. When he's off on business, I miss him. When he's here—when he's not boozing in 'The Fox and Billet,' that is—we rarely have anything to say to each other. But his presence is soothing, nevertheless, like the presence of someone else's dog. I suppose you might say that in spite of all, he's still my best friend."

She pushed up her hair with both hands and laughed without a trace of ill-feeling. Keating laughed too, but his laughter was tinged with wonder at the saintliness of a woman who could talk so lightly about a subject that gave her pain.

"The pity is that I can't help thinking about his infidelity, which is a shameful waste of a life. Just now I thought I might escape from petty preoccupations into something generous and fine."

"But you do escape to your cottage."

"I meant into a more innocent form of spirituality, the spirituality of the Middle Ages. I should like to recapture the life of a former age, if only to experience the contradictions of my own nature more fully."

"Impossible. Even historians can't do that. Think of the difficulty of recalling the emotions of childhood when you're only eighteen."

"Yet you can have insights from time to time. In the fourteenth century, in 1395 I think it was, Lady Alice West of Hampshire left eight pounds, ten shillings in her will to have forty-four hundred masses said for her soul within a fortnight of her death. I find such simple, uncomplicated faith affecting. She obviously believed that the quicker the masses were said the sooner she'd get out of purgatory. How many middle-class Catholics would believe that today? If you gave a fiver to a priest tomorrow to say a requiem for the repose of some tormented soul the following day, he'd say, 'What's the hurry?' Even priests don't believe in either the efficacy or urgency of prayer. At mass I often think of Lady Alice West of Hampshire and wish I had half her faith."

Keating was at a loss for words. She uncrossed her legs, revealing the fullness of her thigh through the light material of her dress and the shadow of the valley of life between the shimmering nylon of her knees. The garden became a sanctuary enveloped in the smell of myrrh, aloes and cassia. He thought of benediction on Sunday evenings in Cork and the weight of woodbine in the air between country hedges. He thought of chantries, priories, crucifers and thurifers, and charcoal and incense burning. Finally, he thought of Geert Grote, and as he thought of him, her left leg vanished before his eyes. It was most disconcerting. One minute it was there and the next all that remained was the leg of the chair in which she was sitting. He closed his eyes and opened them again and asked himself if the hallucination could have a rational explanation.

"Have you ever thought of committing adultery yourself?" He decided to change the subject.

She looked at him for a full minute before breaking into a smile, which was the smile of a schoolmistress who's been asked an awkward question.

"Whom did you have in mind?" As she spoke, her left leg rematerialised, obscuring the leg of the chair, and he breathed more easily, pleased that he was awake again in the twentieth century, not bewitched by the world of Lady Alice West of Hampshire.

"I was thinking in the abstract." His voice crackled.

"I've never considered it, even in the abstract. He would have to be impossibly perceptive, impossibly handsome, and in a state of grace to justify the sin."

"Do I qualify?"

"You're not perceptive. You've got no eye for inscape,

you're too concerned with the surface and contour of things.
And you're not handsome."

"I thought I was."

"In Ireland maybe, but not here. Furthermore, from what
you say, you're not in a state of grace."

"Why is it desirable to be in a state of grace before committing adultery? Surely you must believe that adultery is a falling
from grace."

"I couldn't commit unpremeditated adultery. The act must
have my full consent. To mean anything, either here or in
heaven, the sin must not be venial, but mortal."

He caught a flicker of contempt in her eyes. He had never
seen her tongue, and he wondered if, like a serpent's, it
flickered too. She was leading him in a theological dance, and
he lacked the nerve to follow her. He would not reveal his
ignorance. He would do what all sensible men do in the company of superior women; he would seek refuge in the phatic.

"Many women commit adultery out of boredom." He felt
pleased with the ordinariness of his observation.

"Since I took up picturising, I never get bored, but I often
get distracted. The day is full of irritations that grip the mind
like crab claws and keep you from listening to yourself. Do
you have an inner voice that speaks?"

"If you mean, do I have a little red man in a green waistcoat
and check trousers who talks to me, I'm afraid I must disappoint you."

"Then you're missing something, if only the uncertainty.
You can listen all day without hearing anything, just as you
can fish all night without catching anything. But when you do
catch something, even a dab, it's an affirmation of your existence. It starts a singing inside you that you can hear for days.
It's as if for a brief moment you'd taken full possession of

yourself. Most of the time nothing happens, and then I feel I'm just a mirror in which other people are reflected."

"That can't be true. If it were, your happiness would depend entirely on the people round you."

"For most people life would be richer if they were surrounded by more enriching people. The Bagman, bless him, is such an extrovert that he fears he will vanish in a puff of smoke when the pub empties at closing time."

"I think this listening of yours is a listening for the numinous. I've never found it inside my head, but I've found it sporting with Amaryllis in the shade, and Amaryllis told me she found it too."

"Do you ever think of anything but sex?"

"It's the only thing I can think of without trying to."

"I found my faith as an undergraduate at Oxford when all about me were losing theirs." She decided to ignore him. "I dreamt that there was no God, no one about in the Quad, and I woke up with tears running down my cheeks and a pain like the burning of sulphuric acid in my throat. I had woken up in tears before and brushed them away, but this time they kept flowing like saltwater into the corners of my mouth. I saw the earth full of seedy cities and worthless little men, and women who gave birth to more little men, all under a sun that was mercifully losing its heat."

"*Fiat Deus.* So you created God."

"That's cheap. What I experienced was a revelation, not a revelation of the Divine Presence but of the Divine Absence, which, to me at eighteen, was just as potent. Perhaps it's the only kind of revelation possible in an age that's spawned nothing but negation."

At the word "negation," she crossed her legs tightly, and he did the same, seeking to feel what she felt, seeking to unwrap the vexatious mystery of her womanhood, but the insistent bulk of the scrip and tickler between his legs communicated nothing but a ludicrous sense of discomfort. If he were a pure spirit, he could presumably sit with her inside her dress and know what it was to be Ann, not Kate or Nan, but just then she uncrossed her legs and a subtle breeze exposed her porcelain thigh, driving all thought of angelology from his mind.

"We've been talking about me since we sat down, and I can't imagine why," she said. "What do you seek here, apart from occasions of sin?"

"I told you before."

"You said a job, but that doesn't answer my question."

"I'm looking for the kind of peace I once found in the country and find in the country no longer." It was not true but it would provide a useful red herring while he tried to make out whether her thigh was Spode of Meissen.

"What do you think of the suburbs?"

"They are far from the country, farther in some ways than Piccadilly Circus, but they provide trees and grass and flowers and the opportunity to observe birds and small animals in near-natural surroundings."

"You over-simplify. A half-acre of garden will amuse a bank clerk until it is time to retire to the country. But a garden is nature in a procrustean bed, nature without the dripping tooth and claw. The ravin doesn't occur in the suburbs but in the city during the working week. And then at weekends the suburban garden becomes a place in which ravin is remembered. The flowers and the vegetables are lifeless as garden gnomes. If they fail to grow in a bad summer, it doesn't matter. The gardener will not go hungry."

Her hand went emphatically to her groin, making him wish the hand were his. Her dress fell back over her knee, but now it didn't matter. He'd seen enough; the porcelain was unquestionably Meissen.

"You said you seek peace, but you'll only find it in true relationships. Here there are no true relationships. We relate to one another on levels that have little bearing on the course of our lives. We have settled for a travesty of life, because the travesty makes less demands than true living. You said you want peace, but you can't have peace without truth. Here you'll be lucky if you see truth's reflection."

"Surely you can find as much truth in a semidetached as in a country cottage, if you have a mind to. No matter where we live, the second last enemy to be destroyed is illusion."

"I am talking about something else—about the quality of knowing and feeling. A man who spends his life in cities knows nothing truly, because the things that matter do not matter to him truly. He's been dispossessed of his real heritage, and in his impoverishment he seeks to capture the plenitude of nature on the postage stamp that is his back garden. He may tell you about the Catastrophe Theory and the Optimisation Theory, about Critical Path Analysis and Site Catchment Analysis, about the Skinner Box and Pandora's Box, but he will never speak of them with the passion of a poacher discussing trout tickling."

Keating breathed a sigh of relief when she got up and asked if she could use the loo.

"Of course you may. But first let me make sure that it's fit for a lady. You know what gentlemen of the press are like. One of them is very forgetful."

"It doesn't matter."

"Oh, yes, it does. I'd hate you to think it was me."

He ran up the stairs, checked that the bowl was empty, replaced the girlie magazine on the music stand with *Alice in Wonderland,* and briefly explained to her the significance of "Ooja-cum-Pivvy" before she entered. Impatiently, she closed the door in his face, as if retiring to an ashram from a wicked world, and he went slowly down the stairs, clomping deliberately in case she should think he was spying on her through the keyhole. In the hallway he read the barometer and studied the train timetable that was posted on the door of the Orderly Room, but neither the barometer nor the timetable held his attention. All he could think of was the Ooja-cum-Pivvy, and if it were invested with the odour of oysters and the sea.

"The things she does best she does unwittingly," he told himself. "But would her sea smell be noticeable by the sea?" Then he felt a sadness near his heart as he remembered that if she committed adultery it would be premeditated.

"There's someone talking in one of the upstairs rooms," she said when she came down.

"There can't be. The others are at work. I'm the only one here."

"I heard it distinctly, a testy voice saying, 'Split infinitives, split infinitives.'"

"Maybe someone forgot to switch off the radio."

"This is the room," she said when they reached the landing.

They both listened. The door was locked and from behind it came nothing but silence.

"Never mind." He took her hand and gave her a light kiss on the side of the neck.

"Why did you do that?"

"It was unpremeditated—a venial, not a mortal, sin."

"I don't want you to excite yourself." She drew away.

"Excite myself?"

"I have no desire to lead you into sin."

"I promise to be good."

"To be pure? Have you ever entertained impure thoughts about me?"

"Yes."

"When?"

"In bed before sleeping. I think of the largest freckle on your nose and the evening light making honey of your hair."

"I would call such thoughts extraordinarily pure."

"They may be pure but they keep me from sleeping."

"Do they excite you?"

"Yes."

"In a gross sense?"

"I'm afraid so."

"Then you must put impure thoughts from your mind. You must never touch yourself as you think of me. Promise me that."

"It's easily promised. I was never any good at it. But I think that if I could touch you in the flesh now and again, I should be better armed in the nightly struggle with Satan."

"To be an occasion of sin for you is the last thing I want. Perhaps if I allowed you to hold my hand occasionally, you would see me as I am, a sinner with a soul to save like yourself, rather than the embodiment of your outré sexual fantasies. There, you can take it, if you promise not to kiss it."

"It has the quality of near-transparency. The blue veins under the pale skin remind me of the blue and white of Wedgwood pottery."

"When I was eighteen, you couldn't see those veins at all."

"You're still only a girl, but when I look at your face I think that no man loves a woman who does not love in her the years at which the locust has bitten, who does not see in her face the mystery of a face in final repose."

"Do you see clay when you look at me?"

"I see fine dust gleaming in the sun and I hear the *Recordare* from Mozart's Requiem with its boundless compassion for the living and its unrivalled glimpse of a life we have still to know."

He congratulated himself. He could see that he was getting to know what she liked.

"In spite of your prurient mind, you could be a man of the most refined spiritual nature. I can't understand how you can neglect the sacraments as you do."

"I'm waiting for a revelation, and I think it will come to me through you."

"How I should love to save another soul. A person who saves two souls is more gifted than Goethe. Do you sometimes thirst for visible grace?"

"Visible as manna was visible to the Israelites?"

"If only I could have a conversation like this with my husband. I was sweeping up leaves on the patio the other day, and when they were all in a heap I found a little mound of fine dust beneath them. I stood looking down at it, and as I was about to brush it into my dustpan a gust of wind came and blew it away. I never felt so close to God, but when I told the Bagman he laughed and said that Death, not the Deity, is the true centre of Christianity."

They were coming down the stairs when Quilter opened the door. He looked at Ann and then at Keating, and Keating knew that he had jumped to the wrong conclusion.

"Good morning to you." He spoke to Ann.

"One of the best we've had since September." She took care not to show the slightest awareness of his thoughts.

"I forgot a document I shall need for a meeting this afternoon. I had to come all the way back from town."

When Ann Ede had gone, the Colonel directed at Keating the fire of his hooded eye.

"What did Mrs. Gardener come to borrow? A garden hoe?"

"She didn't come to borrow anything. I just invited her in for coffee."

"I'd like a word with you in the Orderly Room, Captain."

The Colonel placed a square piece of carpet before the table and told Keating to stand on it. Then he sat in the armchair on the other side of the table.

"You astound me, Captain, after all my admonitions. I said quite clearly, no bints in bivvy, didn't I?"

"Mrs. Ede is not a bint. She's a respectable married woman."

"I don't care if she were married ten times over. I told you this house is an oasis, and I told you what happened to your predecessor when he brought in a floozie against my wishes. He was court-martialed and cashiered, and he now lives in rankless disgrace on the other side. I saw him the other evening slinking out of the station and taking the wrong turning at the ticket barrier, pretending that he still lived in the East."

"I don't see what's wrong with floozies, as you call them."

"We're all divorced men here, men who have suffered at the hands of women. We have known them with the rags on and the rags off, and we've listened with longanimity to them chewing the rag which is neither on nor off. In a word, Keating, if you want to get your Saturday night finger out, don't do it here—unless, that is, you're paying for it."

"It's an extreme point of view, Colonel."

"I'm the most compassionate of C.O.s. My ambition as a young man was to be an abbot in a contemplative order, so if you have a sexual problem, come to me. You will not find me lacking in understanding. One last thing—the M.O. is coming to dinner this evening, so I should like to see you on your best behaviour. Have you got a dinner jacket yet?"

"No."

"Then you'd better buy, borrow or steal one. It's always black tie for the M.O. I hope you haven't got yourself a dose of the clap, because the M.O. unfailingly conducts a short-arm inspection."

7

THE Colonel's reference to a short-arm inspection puzzled Keating. He had heard of shorthand, shorthorn and short hairs, but not short-arm. As soon as the Colonel left, he looked it up in his dictionary, only to have his puzzlement compounded. A short-arm blow, he discovered, was one delivered with the arm not fully extended, so perhaps a short-arm inspection was an inspection of the arm while bent at the elbow. But why should the M.O. inspect the arm if he was on the lookout for V.D. symptoms, as the Colonel suggested? It was a real tickler, not a problem to be solved by using the dictionary, so he rang *The Daily Telegraph* Information Service. The girl who answered told him good-humouredly that if he cared to ask her a more serious question, she would do her best to answer it, that it was really a matter for the Ministry of Defence or perhaps the Department of Health. As he put the phone down, he laughed out loud. It had dawned on him that his short-arm might conceivably be his penis.

The whole thing was most bizarre. He knew from casual hints that the Colonel had a high opinion of the M.O., but who was he? The Colonel's doctor? If so, he would surely come as a guest, not to examine the four of them for traces of the demon gonococcus. He smiled as he pictured the Colonel, MacGeoch, Garlick and himself lined up naked for examination. That was one of the impossible things about "Foxgloves," the difficulty of knowing where "reality" ended and fantasy began. It was typical of the Colonel to call him into the Orderly Room to carpet him, but it was impossible to tell if he was being serious or just indulging in a bit of gentle leg-pulling. He mentioned a dinner jacket. Was that also a joke? Two weeks ago he thought the goose was a joke, but now he knew better. He decided to play safe. He would ask Ann Ede if he could borrow the Bagman's monkey suit in case the others should decide to dress for dinner.

"My husband doesn't have anything as common as a 'monkey suit,' but he does have something he calls 'my D.J.,' which he wears to the Royal Institute of Bagmen's annual dinner. Feel free to borrow it if you're stuck, but I'll expect it back sponged and pressed, because bagmen believe that apparel, not manners, proclaims the man. Where are you dining? At the Chinese take-away?"

"We're dining at home. Quilter has arranged a dinner party for some army quack who hopes to combine diagnosis with degustation."

"You're all quite mad, but that's no business of mine. I suppose Quilter thought I had nipped across for a spot of morning fornication."

"It did look as if he leapt to the wrong conclusion. As a journalist, he is paid to think the best of himself and the worst of everyone else."

"Did you tell him I went upstairs just to visit his confounded Ooja-cum-Pivvy?"

"I told him nothing."

"Good. I should hate to think that he knew I once sat on the same toilet seat as he. I know all about men and their filthy fantasies. They derive more pleasure from the heat of their imaginings than they do from the antic act itself."

The jacket fitted perfectly but the trousers were half an inch too short in the leg. Nevertheless, they would do. He knew that he was in the doghouse, and he was determined not to end up in the glass-house. It was in his interest to remain at "Foxgloves" until he landed a job. Furthermore, at "Foxgloves" he was within hailing distance of Ann Ede. All told, it was not the time to get the Colonel's back up.

MacGeoch and Garlick came home early, jabbering like two excited monkeys.

"You know the M.O. is coming to dinner?" Garlick asked.

The Colonel told me this morning." Keating was busy putting the finishing touch to a pigeon ragout which he hoped would prompt Garlick into asking for pigeon pie.

"He always keeps it secret till the last minute."

"You'd better get out of civvies and into uniform," MacGeoch said. "They'll be here any minute."

"I'm going up to wash my hair, I always wash it for the M.O." Garlick chuckled.

"Did you leave the radio on this morning?" Keating asked him. "I thought I heard voices coming from your room."

"You may have heard a voice. That'll be Flint. Surely the Colonel must have told you about my parrot."

"Mad as a hatter," said MacGeoch when he'd gone. "He spent all last winter teaching the stupid bird to say 'Split infinitives.'"

Keating went to his room to change and subject his tickler to a preliminary examination. He had been right to take the Colonel seriously. Dinner jackets were obviously *de rigueur* for short-arm inspections. At eight Quilter arrived with the M.O. who, to Keating's surprise and delight, turned out to be a stunning young woman in what looked like a khaki jump suit.

"This is Jilly Dingles, who, as M.O., makes sure we all remain in the pink of health," he introduced her to Keating.

She smiled sweetly and turned to MacGeoch, who gave her a playful tickle on the cheek with his moustache. She was about twenty-six, tall, slender, and boyish in spite of the fullness of her breasts. She was wearing copper-coloured makeup that went well with her khaki jump suit and reminded him of outdoor girls advertising sports cars in the Sunday colour supplements. She had strong cheekbones, dark-brown eyes with a streak of green beneath them, and a nose that turned up slightly at the tip—an imperfection that only increased her sex appeal. Her hair was her most distinctive feature. Long and brown with straw-coloured strands, it was combed upwards from her neck and passed through a bronze ring so that it fell like an undocked horse's tail rather than a ponytail from above her left ear. He had never seen such a breathtakingly erotic creature, and he felt a sting of jealousy when the Colonel put his arm round her waist and poked his nose lubriciously up under the horse's tail. It were an act of animal spontaneity that made Keating resolve not to get in the way of his Commanding Officer.

While they drank their sherry and waited for the ragout, which was twenty minutes behind schedule, they gathered round the piano and sang First World War songs with ribald gusto. Jilly Dingles asked Garlick to play "Tipperary," which she sang in a slightly husky voice, as if there were a large tadpole but not quite a frog in her throat:

> It's the wrong way to tickle Mary,
> It's the wrong way you know;
> It's the wrong way to tickle Mary,
> There's another way, you know.

As he listened, Keating could sense her warm breath floating gently from between her lips, caressing his cheek though he was standing four feet away. He felt an urgent growth of muscle in the left leg of the Bagman's trousers, which caused him to wonder about the strength of the fabric and about the spectacle he'd present if he had a sudden "accident." He moved to the other side of the piano for cover, as Jilly changed to "They Were Only Playing Leap-Frog."

When she finished, they all clapped exuberantly and the Colonel gave her horse's tail another wanton sniff.

"I haven't had such fun, Jilly, since the evening you had a stinking cold and Major MacGeoch made you inhale Friar's Balsam," he told her.

"I don't remember." She laughed.

"Why, you stuck your nose into the jug of boiling water and said, 'Friar's Balsam smells of Balsam's Ass.'"

Conversation over dinner centred on sexual perversions of the most outré order, a subject on which the M.O. was impressively well informed. The Colonel seemed to know the names of the "diseases," but, as befitted a medical officer, Miss Dingles could cite fascinating case histories from personal experience and describe the etiology and symptomatology of conditions that aroused more than the interest of her eager patients. To give her her due, she tried several times to talk about the weather, but the Colonel always perpetrated a double entendre of such enormity that she had no option but to return to medicine. Keating enjoyed the dinner more than any he'd ever cooked, and this he attributed to the wit and beauty of Miss Dingles, whom the Colonel toasted as "not only a spanking Medical Officer but the best Mistress of Misrule who's ever entered an officers' mess."

As Keating poured the coffee, Garlick lit his one cigar of the day, a cheap and particularly nasty one to which, nevertheless, he'd been looking forward since morning.

"Why did you give up cigarettes?" Miss Dingles asked him, as the acrid aroma enveloped them all.

"A friend who smoked lost a lung."

"Thus cancer doth make cowards of us all." The Colonel winked at the M.O.

"A cigar is an occasion if you smoke only one a day," Garlick told them. "It is almost a forbidden delight, the pleasure it gives, as you inhale, so immediate compared with the slow puff of a pipe."

"I wish you wouldn't wax so lyrical in front of Miss Dingles," the Colonel reproved him. "A cigar is like anal intercourse, whereas the pipe is straight sex in the missionary position."

"You speak in riddles, Colonel." Miss Dingles barely touched his wrist.

"What I mean is that a cigar is fun once in a while, but the pipe is a pleasure to which you always return."

"What can I say, Colonel?' Garlick smiled acidly. "I can only bow to your superior pipemanship."

A bubble of male irritation hung over the table. Miss Dingles, sensing that it might burst, turned to the Colonel and with her forefinger traced a little path between the hairs on the back of his hand.

'We've had an evening of frivolity.' She smiled at them all. Let's be serious for five minutes. I couldn't help noticing all the police as I came out of the station. Have they called here?

"Why should they come here?" MacGeoch asked. "The murder was committed on the other side. Nothing to do with us."

"Of course it has to do with us," said Garlick. "The country is going to the dogs and all we can think about in this neck of the wood is foxes. We have turned the fox to social account, and I'll bet that now we'll see murder itself transmuted into an acceptable status symbol."

"What nonsense!" MacGeoch shouted. "There isn't one person on this side of the bridge who wouldn't give a month's salary to see the criminal brought to justice."

"Careful now." Garlick wagged a finger. "When yobbos from you-know-where first began coming to Wistwood on the ninety-four bus to enjoy an evening's breaking and entering, everyone was equally horrified. Everyone was saying, 'What are we coming to? Is no suburb sacrosanct? If this continues, we'll all have to move out beyond Tonbridge.' But when it became apparent that the yobbos confined their attentions to this side, having one's house burgled became a mark of social distinction."

"I've yet to meet an Eastsider who asked to have his telly and record player stolen." MacGeoch smiled derisively.

"It's more subtle than that, Captain. How many times have you heard Eastmen who have just been burgled broadcasting their 'misfortune' among the hapless Westmen, with the implication that in the West there's nothing worth burgling."

"I've never heard such a load of old codswallop." MacGeoch looked at the M.O., who smiled not at him but at the Colonel.

"We can only wait and see," said Garlick. "Will the murderer discriminate like the burglars, or will he choose his victims from both sides of the railway?"

"You expect him to strike again?" Miss Dingles asked.

"I'm certain of it."

"Tell us more." The Colonel stared at the Lance-corporal.

"If the police knew their business, they'd be looking for a man who thinks he's a fox." Garlick blew a putrid smoke ring towards MacGeoch. "They'd be making enquiries about men who have recently undergone physical change. A man with a changed voice perhaps or changed features."

"I haven't heard such rot since I was last in the Lowlands."

MacGeoch rolled the "r" of "rot" so ferociously that the ash from Garlick's cigar fell into his coffee.

"It's called lycanthropy," Garlick lectured. "The patient imagines he's a wolf or some other animal. In this case he's obviously under the illusion that he's a fox."

"And where does that lead us?" the Colonel enquired.

"He's obviously a Westman, because Westmen are more preoccupied with foxes than we are. It is easy to visualise a man who becomes so touchy about the lack of a fox in his garden that he deludes himself into thinking that his own name is Reynard or Charles James."

"It's a fanciful theory, but I don't believe it," said Miss Dingles.

"We still haven't heard your theory." The Colonel turned to Keating, who had already decided to keep his theory to himself. If the murderer was present, it would be foolish at this stage to give him cause for alarm.

"It's easy to leap to the wrong conclusion," Keating said. "It's possible that the two murders may be totally unconnected. I know that the first was associated with a fox-fur and the second with *Foxe's Martyrs,* but the second murderer could have pinched the signature of the first in order to confuse the police. Moreover, the first murder took place on a train somewhere between Ashford and Tonbridge and the second in Wistwood—miles away."

"What do you think?" the Colonel asked the M.O.

"I think they're sexist murders, and I'm glad I'm not living in Wistwood. The police should be looking for a woman-hater—unlike Captain Keating, I think they should be looking for one man."

"I agree with the M.O." The Colonel smiled at her. "The murders have several things in common. Both the victims were women and both were in the habit of moving outside their territory. Both were Westwomen with friends on this side whom they frequently visited. And the first woman was travelling first class, not quite the territory you associate with Westsiders."

"From all that you could easily construct a profile of the murderer," Miss Dingles encouraged him.

"Yes," said the Colonel. "He's a misogynist and a snob, perhaps a South African with a strong sense of apartheid."

"Perhaps he expects all Westsiders to carry a passbook." MacGeoch agreed with his Commanding Officer.

"So you refuse to be serious," said Miss Dingles. "Let's see how flippant you'll be now that it's time for the short-arm inspection."

"At last," said the Colonel. "But first the seeding."

"I shall need a spray of pampas grass or maybe two," the M.O. confided.

"Pampas grass? Whatever for?" Keating asked.

"Like the rest of us, you'll have to wait and see," said the Colonel.

"I spied a clump of it in a front garden in Essex Ride," the M.O. told them.

"Captain, would you mind going out and commandeering a plume or two," said the Colonel. "I'll see to it that the ceremony doesn't start till you get back."

"That's a promise." The M.O. smiled at him sweetly. "And take a secateurs, I like a clean cut."

He stole up Essex Ride, looking to right and left, but luckily there was no one about. It was all quite crazy, but he had to keep in with the Colonel and he rather liked the lively Miss Dingles. Quickly, and with one eye on the house, he cut two sprays and hurried back to the fun.

"Well done, Captain." The Colonel smiled.

"They're just the thing." Miss Dingles caressed the silvery white plumes. Then she drew a foot rule from a pocket in the leg of her jump suit and brought it down with a smack on the palm of her hand.

"Off with them, gentlemen," she commanded. "On the jildi. Toot sweet—and the tooter the sweeter."

Keating watched the others getting out of their trousers.

"What's wrong, Keating?" the Colonel shouted. "Have you never had your short-arm inspected before?"

Keating did not reply. After a moment's hesitation, he took off his jacket and shirt, and finally his trousers and underclothes. The four of them stood at ease in the buff with their backs to the fire, while the M.O. inspected them fore and aft and gave the Colonel a playful smack on the bottom with the flat of her rule.

"Where's the Game Book?" she demanded with mock-severity.

"You'll find it under the sheet music in the piano stool," the Colonel told her.

"The seeding will take the following form"—she stood in front of them with the Game Book open on the table—"I'll measure each short-arm in its flaccid state and enter the length in centimetres in my little book."

"Inches are imperial and therefore more military," said the Colonel. "Furthermore, I'm certain that in this context an inch means more than a centimetre to both you and us."

"Inches it is then." The M.O. smiled as she checked her rule. "After measurement will come tactile and visual stimulation. And after the stimulation I'll measure each short-arm again in its standing position and work out a coefficient of elongation."

Here she drew a pocket calculator from her handbag and placed it on top of the Game Book on the table.

"Pardon my asking," said the Colonel, "but will that give a true reflection of strike capability?"

"I haven't finished. I shall measure the time of stimulation in

116

each case, and adjust the coefficient of elongation accordingly. Need I add that the longer the stimulation time, the higher the score."

She reopened her handbag and took out a stopwatch, which she placed beside the pocket calculator. Keating felt that he must be dreaming, but at a side glance the Colonel's scrip and pecker looked real enough. The scrip was as full as the crop of a stubble goose, so full that the pecker did not dangle but lolled horizontally on top of it.

"I shall begin with you, Lance-corporal, and end with you, Colonel. That way the last shall be first and the first last, as you might expect from a Mistress of Misrule."

She measured their short-arms with a speed that deceived the eye but not the short-arms themselves. A muscle began to throb in Keating's left buttock, he ground his molars, and shivered at the icy touch of the metal rule. In a second she had gone to the next short-arm. He heaved a sigh of relief and cursed the muscle in his buttock for ticking like a watch. After entering the figures in the Game Book, she took off all her clothes except her knickers, which were lilac, loose-fitting, and trimmed with goffered lace. Keating glanced at the other short-arms, but none betrayed even a hint of recognition, though they had seen all this before.

"Now comes the crunch, but not, I hope, the climax." She laughed. "I'll ask you to cup my right breast in your left hand and knead my bottom with your right while I tickle you gently between the legs with one of these plumes. Remember that nothing will touch your short-arm except the grass. But the stimulation will be visual as well as tactile."

"You say we are to knead your bottom." The Colonel's throat was cracklingly dry. "Do we knead the covering fabric or the skin itself?"

"You may do either or both, as befits men under a government that supports free enterprise. Lance-corporal, you're first."

She kissed the tip of the plume and drew it gently like a cello bow across Garlick's privates. Garlick felt her right breast with his left hand and the silk of her knickers with the palm of his right. The effect on his pecker was terrifying to see. It rose slowly and mechanically like a bascule-bridge, and as soon as it was open to shipping, the M.O. checked her stopwatch and took a second reading on her metal rule. It seemed callous to Keating to leave poor Garlick in such a state of hypertension, but now, he realised, was not the time to worry about the Lance-corporal, because he himself was standing next to him.

Before he could quite adjust to the idea, the M.O. lightly tickled the hairs of his scrip with her wand and things began happening to him at two removes from where he stood. It was like discovering Newfoundland and realising that you'd already explored it in a dream. But there were differences as well. Her breast was heavier than he'd expected, like a loaf of bread without leavening, and the nipple was stronger than any nipple he'd ever touched. He put his other hand down inside her knickers, only to find that the perfection of the bottom was balanced by the imperfection of the cleft. The bottom itself was cold and smooth like polished marble and the cleft was what a mineralogist might call plagioclastic—it did not run vertically but obliquely, yet curiously the area of one buttock did not exceed that of the other.

He splayed his fingers and began polishing the polished marble with his palm. He dwelt in marble halls so spacious and airy that you could not walk across them in a day, and strangely the marble goddesses on marble plinths bled when you touched them there. The halls vanished like summer mist, the M.O. was checking her stopwatch and taking a second reading on a rule that now seemed colder than before. He was hardly aware of how the Colonel and the Major fared. By the time he regained common consciousness, the M.O. was seated at the table doing some complicated sums on her pocket calculator.

"Whatever the outcome, it was a rip-roaring success," the Colonel declared. "One of your more ingenious ideas, my dear Dingles. We shall certainly try it again."

The M.O. got to her feet and read from the Game Book:

Major MacGeoch	154
Captain Keating	157
Lance-corporal Garlick	183
Colonel Quilter	184

"I congratulate you, Colonel." She gave his hand a friendly squeeze.

"It was a close-run thing," Garlick complained. "Shouldn't we have a recount?"

"No, Lance-corporal," said Miss Dingles. "In these matters the decision of the M.O. is final."

The Colonel went upstairs with the M.O. while Keating, Garlick and MacGeoch put on their trousers below.

"She's full of imagination, she always comes up with something new," said Garlick.

"And it's always a good wheeze," said MacGeoch, who seemed cheerful enough in spite of being seeded fourth.

At last the Colonel came down and Garlick took his place with unseemly alacrity, or so it seemed to Keating.

"What do you think of our M.O.?" the Colonel asked him.

"She's original." Keating tried to be objective.

"There are two types of women, homemakers and homebreakers," said the Colonel. "Miss Dingles is a homemaker without a home. In a perfect world she'd make a loving wife for a randy aristocrat with a proper contempt for bourgeois values."

"I wouldn't have thought it," Keating said.

"When you go upstairs, you'll see what I mean. She has a warmth about her that would dissolve flint grit. Every so often she comes down from London to bleed us in the interest of mental hygiene, and all she will accept in return is a case of dry sherry. As officers and gentlemen, we have a duty to return her warmth with gallantry and humanity. She will enfold you, my dear Keating, in the place where it most matters, and she will draw the toxins from your system, not by vein puncture, venesection or cupping, but in a manner to which all true officers and gentlemen respond most heartily. Now you know why there is no need to bring floozies here. It would quite simply be gilding the lily. Don't you agree, Major?"

"I most certainly do," said MacGeoch.

She came out of the Ooja-cum-Pivvy as he came up the stairs. He put an arm round her waist and led her into his bedroom, wondering what medicines she carried in her doctor's bag.

"How would you like it—sunny side up or once over lightly?" she challenged him.

"I'm afraid I don't know. I'm suffering from what I think is delayed shock."

He didn't know why he said it. He just felt that he didn't want to follow Garlick.

"No need to go the whole hog if you're off form." She sat beside him on the bed. "That box of tricks you see there has something for everyone. As women become more liberated and ferocious, more and more men are coming to me for a common or garden cuddle. They used to pay me for sex, now they pay me for love."

"I don't even want a cuddle. I just want to be quiet for a while."

"Well, I'd better leave you to your thoughts."

"No, stay, I don't want the others to know."

"What shall we do?"

"Perhaps we could talk." He took her hand, which was light and shapely, a beautiful hand which seldom got up to any good. "The Colonel said you were reading for a degree with the Open University."

"An extracurricular hobby, not my bread and butter."

"What are you reading?"

"Anthropology. The Colonel calls it the study of Man, and I don't like talking about it to men."

"Where do you live?"

"I have a flat in Shepherd Market. I run an afternoon play school for backward boys. You might consider coming along sometime." She smiled.

"And why do you come all this way on a Friday evening?"

"It's a labour of love. I talk to other punters but I communicate with the Colonel. He's an extraordinary man."

"So you come down to see the Colonel?"

"I come down because I'm an artist, because I like the quality of imagination you all bring to the evening. If these are the suburbs, they're more stylish than Mayfair."

"I'm glad you like us."

"I like coming down here so much that I can't believe it's the scene of a murder. I was actually afraid to come on my own this evening, so I got the Colonel to collect me. I was surprised to hear that the four of you had such different things to say about it all. Garlick, I thought, was the most original, though not the truest."

"It's a strange business. I can't imagine the kind of man who would look up *Foxe's Martyrs* before murdering someone."

"You say a man. Could it be a woman?"

"I'm sure it's a man, a suburban man. He probably reads *The Financial Times* and takes the Cannon Street train from platform three every morning."

"A middle-class murderer who doesn't distinguish between a killing on the stock exchange and a killing in the suburbs?"

"He may be quite ordinary, a little man with a briefcase and umbrella. Why, he could even be one of us here at Foxgloves.'"

"It seems pretty farfetched to me."

"Supposing it were true, which one of us would you expect it to be?"

"You all look equally unlikely. But since you brought up the subject, I must tell you that it could be you."

She smiled and lit a cigarette, and they lay on the bed exchanging pleasantries but not kisses until she told him that it was time to call MacGeoch.

It was well after midnight when the Mistress of Misrule declared that their revels were now ended. The Colonel drove her back to Mayfair and Keating and the others went to bed. He lay for a long time in a state of nervous excitement, struggling with the thought that two hours ago he was stretched beside the most attractive woman he'd ever seen without as much as turning on his side to kiss her.

He fell asleep with a sense of regret uppermost in his mind and dreamt that the Bagman had never been born, that he himself was married to Ann. He was deliriously happy and so was she. It was summer, and the sunshine danced between the branches of the apple trees, clear and green as if it had absorbed the chlorophyll from the leaves. Ann came out into the garden and announced that she was leaving him.

"But we're so happy," he said.

"That's the problem, we're too happy to save our souls. Ours will be a polite parting with neither hurt nor ill-feeling. I'm not running off with another man, I'm going to cook for the Carmelites in Aylesford Priory."

"But how shall I live without you?"

"I've thought of everything, you'll be well cared for." She

patted his hand. "I've spoken to Mrs. Stooke, who is willing to marry you. I'll organise the wedding to stop the neighbours talking, and I'll be bridesmaid too."

He could not believe that it was happening, and he could not express his grief. It was as if he were only ten and his mother had come home from hospital in a coffin. But he got into the taxi with Mrs. Stooke and the wedding guests waved good-bye. Ann came forward and kissed him again, and the grief in his chest and in his breathing burst like ichor from a festering wound. He turned to Mrs. Stooke, and she smelt of old crypts, damp stonework and worm-eaten pews. He woke up with the ichor on his cheeks. It was morning and the milkman's float was in the road below. He stood by the window, trying to take in the glorious ordinariness of the slow-moving vehicle, overjoyed that life was really simple, that what he'd been through was a dream.

8

A WEEK passed and he still did not ring Mrs. Stooke. Instead he gave his time to Ann Ede without gaining an inch of ground. Every morning he told himself that he would collect MacGeoch's F-volume before lunchtime, but evening always came and he still had not gone. In the first week of December she rang to say that she had read the seminal articles on Fish, Flowers and Fruit, but that she would like to see the S-volume before finally making up her mind. When he promised to bring it round the following morning, she said that she always felt dyspeptic after getting up, that if he came for lunch he might find her more willing to invest.

She poured him a glass of white wine and gave him a large plate of whitebait followed by biscuits and brie, which he ate without asking if she had forgotten to take the roast out of the oven.

"You may be surprised at the absence of an entrée." She seemed to have read his thoughts. "It's not an oversight. It's just that I eat only one meal a day. I have the hors d'oeuvre and the cheese at lunchtime and the main course and dessert in the evening."

After they had finished the wine, she showed him Henry's

pipes and pipe rack, and the unfinished tobacco in his humidor, which was dry as snuff but not as aromatic. Then she sat on his knee, no heavier than a seagull's feather, and kissed him with everted lips till he was breathless. As he waited for second wind, he pecked at her ear and opened his legs a little to make elbow-room for his burgeoning short-arm. He kissed her again, but this time he inhaled deeply before starting, so that she had to surface for air before he did.

"What are you thinking of?" She tickled his neck.

"I'm thinking of a soufflé."

"Why?"

"Because that's what you feel like on my knee, light as a feather, as if you might float away."

"I'm glad the way to your heart is through your stomach."

"What were you thinking of?" he asked.

"The double bed upstairs. It hasn't borne the brunt of a man for over a year."

They went upstairs, and she made him lie on his back with no pillow under his head. Then she put her ear to his abdomen, like a Red Indian listening to the ground for the thunder of approaching horses. She probed his belly with her fingers till it hurt, and she listened again as if for the croak of water in ancient souterrains. When she had completed her investigations, she lowered herself gently onto his waiting dowel. The dowel became a dovetail and the mortise gripped it with a hundred vices. Quite without warning the dovetail collapsed and the mortise lost her savour. Mrs. Stooke plunged and panted, fighting against time and an ebbing tide. Robbed by death, she administered the kiss of life, while Keating watched from a great distance across the wilderness of his abdomen, like a patient observing the frenzied efforts of a surgeon operating without an anaesthetic.

The operation was a resounding success. The patient rose in angry bafflement from a death he loved more than life, and within the space of two minutes he was wreaking a vengeance on the surgeon that amply made up for his former faineance.

"Why did you put your ear to my tum?" Keating asked when the serenity of satiety had been restored to the bedroom.

"Henry once gave me a book on splanchnomancy, the art of telling the future from inspection of the intestines. I suppose I was trying to guess what you had in store for me."

"What you had in store for me was better than a soufflé. It was two soufflés in one."

"Have you ever kissed a woman you-know-where?" She put her lips to his ear and whispered.

"I couldn't do that. I only kiss by the book."

"But not by the *Kama Sutra?*"

"I'm a simple Irishman with simple tastes."

"Henry was a simple man too, but he loved nothing better than a muff-dive."

"Men differ."

"And men and women differ more. What do you think is the greatest difference between men and women?"

"When women boil water, they boil just enough. Men always boil too much."

"You're so like Henry. He always said that when women *make* water, they make just enough, not a drop too many, not a drop too few."

"Now what did he mean by that?" Keating was puzzled.

"I didn't suppose you'd understand. In his last few years he developed a belated interest in uriposia."

"What on earth is that?"

"The drinking of urine for pleasure."

He laughed at the madness of it, but he stopped when he thought of Ann Ede. Albion was not perfidious but perverted.

"Why are you laughing?"

"I couldn't help wondering if he drank it warm or chilled—with a cube of ice perhaps."

"I'm serious. We were happily married. It was mine he drank and no one else's."

"I still find it difficult to credit. I suppose you must blame my sheltered Irish upbringing."

"Have I ever told you how he died?" she asked.

"No."

"He died in his pleasure, lying on top of me here on this bed."

Keating shivered.

"He had a massive coronary," she continued. "He shouted like a man in grief. Then he went limp, but his penis still kept throbbing inside me. I'm sure he would have been pleased to know that it was the last part of him to die. I'm afraid I panicked. I tried to get out from under him but I couldn't. Then I managed to roll over, and we both ended up on the floor. Curiously, the last thing he said to me before we made love was, 'The auditors are coming in tomorrow.' He didn't know they were already coming up the stairs."

Keating stepped into his trousers, anxious to be alone at "Foxgloves." The walk home did him good. The raw wind purified his flesh and dislodged the tatters of unwanted experience that obscured the light inside him. As he saw it, Mrs. Stooke was serious about only one thing—death. She did things deliberately, as if for the last time. She saw her life as a long autumn, a shedding of leaves, one by one, till only the naked branches would remain.

"Every day of your life," she told him, "you lose as much of yourself as you gain. We are things of shreds and patches, and vague memories of outgrown garments. No wonder we surround ourselves with objects—furniture, paintings, ornaments, books—anything that might reassure us that we can know and be known."

He went into the garden, not to bemoan loss but to put a hundred miles between himself and Mrs. Stooke, and try to forget what he knew to be painfully true—that he had found a clearer reflection of himself in the widow than in Ann Ede. He had seen himself swimming in the pupils of her eyes and had shrunk from what he saw. It was as if Esther had arranged it all to prove beyond doubt that every word she'd ever spoken to him was true.

The garden was strewn with wet leaves, and a coiled hose-pipe hung from a sawn-off branch of the mountain ash. He pulled up the runner-bean canes that stood like skeletal wigwams deserted by tribesmen gone long ago to happier hunting grounds. He lightly pruned one of the pear trees, while Farmer Giles on the other side of the fence sprayed his apple trees with tar-oil wash. In the fork of a branch two spider's webs hung side by side, fine droplets like miniature pearls on the threads. The two looked so similar and yet so different. Did each spider spin the same web over and over again throughout its life? Did they all share a theme on which each wove endless variations? The physical world was an inexhaustible goldfield for anyone who wished to mine it. He longed for the objectivity of the scientist immersed in the orderly acquisition of scholarship, and for an escape from the suffocating untidiness of personal relationships. He recalled Quilter's advice on his first day at "Foxgloves":

"Keep your distance and you'll keep your head. If you must tread, tread carefully. The fox preys farthest from his hole. So don't befriend suburban housewives. If you wish for a juicy steak, you don't befriend the bullock from which you will cut it."

Homely wisdom. The advice of a disillusioned romantic or a sour misogynist? Certainly not that of a disinterested philosopher. He went into the warm kitchen and made coffee. His body glowed after the cold, but the sting of ice in his ears lasted till he had written a letter of application for a job with *The Guardian*.

That night he put a hot-water bottle in his bed for the first time and fell asleep with it resting between his feet. When he woke, he knew that it was several hours later, because the hot-water bottle was barely warm. He lay on his back wondering if he had woken because of the cold, or because of a noise or movement in the house. If someone had gone out, for example, the door latch might have clicked. And if he lay awake, he might catch whoever it was coming back. He knew it was irrational to suspect men who gave no cause for suspicion, but he could not put suspicion from his mind.

All three, he thought, were capable of crime—Quilter out of intellectual perversity; MacGeoch to add a couple of cubits to his stature; and Garlick to assuage his sense of injured merit. Of the three he would back MacGeoch, if only because he liked him least. He thought he heard a noise like the click of a briefcase closing, but he could not be certain if it came from downstairs or from one of the other bedrooms. He crossed the landing to the Ooja-cum-Pivvy, but the Nocturnal Crapper had not yet struck. He went downstairs in the dark, stopping halfway as he saw a chink of light beneath the door of the officers' mess, aware of a sense of menace that made him look up at the landing above his head. Deciding to be brave or at least imprudent, he switched on the hall light and opened the dining-room door.

"You've found me out," said MacGeoch. "Long though the fox runs, he's caught at last."

He was sitting at the table with a plate of chips and a half-empty bottle of Scotch before him. He couldn't have been to bed because he was still wearing the suit he wore at dinner.

"I'm having a beano. Would you like to join me?" He speared a chip with his fork and took a kiss-like sip of neat whisky from his glass.

"I thought I heard a noise and I thought it might be a burglar."

"I heard the same noise, someone coming in." MacGeoch looked at him. "I thought it might have been you."

"Why me?"

"I don't know. We all went up at the same time. I suppose I just imagined you couldn't sleep and had taken Jippo for a walk. Care for a drink?"

"I'm afraid it's too early for me." Keating tried to laugh. "Did you make the chips yourself?"

"They're oven chips. I keep a bag of them in the freezer in case of insomnia and night starvation."

"I didn't know you drank Scotch." Keating sat opposite him.

"I know the Colonel thinks the grain inferior to the grape, but I always keep a bottle of Barleycorn in my room. It's a great comfort on cold nights, and it's at its most consoling with chips. Whisky-and-chips is best described as *suaviter in modo, fortiter in re.* The chips, you see, have a gentling effect on the Scotch without in any way reducing its firmness of purpose. Those who eat fish with chips are boors and snifflers who should be promptly pickled in the vinegar they're so fond of. But don't mention my beano to the Colonel. He has set ideas about the proper conduct of officers between retreat and reveille."

MacGeoch burped at considerable length and Keating realised that, though he did not look it, he was probably drunk.

"It's coming right," MacGeoch addressed the last chip on his plate. "Nothing like a burp to relieve the osmotic pressure on the grey cells. Come on, Keating, get yourself a glass and pretend it's an Irish funeral."

Keating got a tumbler from the sideboard and poured himself a finger of Scotch.

"Short measure, Captain. You poured as if death was not in the pot but in the bottle."

"Talking of death," said Keating, "I had a dream before I

woke up that left me in a sweat. I thought the murderer came into my room and pulled the cord out of my pyjamas while I slept. I could hear him padding about downstairs before he went out, but no matter how hard I tried I couldn't wake up. Then I heard on the news in the morning that a woman from the other side had been garrotted with a pyjama cord."

"Did you have a cord in your pyjamas?"

"No, just elastic."

"Then don't worry, it can't happen."

"I know it can't happen, but it still disturbed me."

"Stop bellyaching, Keating. You've fallen on your feet here. Think how drab your life would be if you were living on the other side. Here you're among the élite. You are the élite."

"I'm not aware of it."

"The Colonel wouldn't have any old Scotsman or any old Irishman at 'Foxgloves.' Garlick's the odd man out. He just isn't officer material."

"Is it an accident that the Colonel chose an Irishman, a Scotsman and a Welshman to share with?"

"No, it was deliberate. He wants this house to be the nation in miniature."

"God help the nation if it is," said Keating.

"Why?"

"It's a house of distorting mirrors. Everything here is new but everything is untrue."

"That's what the Colonel likes. He says every man must struggle with his antithesis, and that the Celt is the antithesis of the Anglo-Saxon. He loves distorting mirrors. If he wanted to, he could easily find received reflections among other Englishmen at his club. But he doesn't set too great store by what literal-minded people call the truth. He wants amusement, imagination and the joy of the arsy-versy. The Colonel, you see, is condemned to live in the imagination, because England is no longer wide enough to accommodate the sweep of

---

his dreams. He's a man without a vocation. By temperament he's a leader of men, but as a journalist what can he do but denigrate? He's got more talent for leadership than any other man I've ever known."

"More than the Brigadier?"

"You've never met the Brigadier."

"Garlick told me about him. He said that 'Foxgloves' without the Brigadier is a house that has lost its reason."

"And without the Colonel it would be a house of only bricks and mortar like all the other houses in the road. The Brigadier is too objective. The light he sheds on things reduces them to the sum of their parts, no more. We weren't sorry when he went on furlough. It gave the Colonel an opportunity of raising this house from the dead by making it a meeting place of nations. In that he is a true Anglo-Saxon. Without your Anglo-Saxon, the history of these islands would be a ragbag of sub-plots without direction. No man is more Scottish than me, but I have to admit that whereas the Anglo-Saxons provide the theme, the Celts only provide the variations."

"Are these murders the theme, or are they the variations? Do they come from the centre or do they come from the fringe?"

"What do you mean?" MacGeoch, though drunk, looked up sharply.

"There are times when I feel I have a special insight into this murderer's mind. I felt uncomfortably close to him in my dream."

"It's the police who should have special insight into his mind, but this is one case they won't solve. The police are plebeian, out of their depth in a place like Wistwood. When they think of a murderer, they think of a man with dirty fingernails."

"Who will catch him, then?" Keating probed.

MacGeoch licked the whisky off his moustache, sweeping it with his tongue like dew off aftergrass.

"Another Wistwoodlander, an Eastman more than likely. Only a man who has ridden to hounds will run the Wistwood Fox to earth."

MacGeoch wasn't talking to Keating but to his almost empty bottle, and his words came like precious drops from the condenser of some far-off Highland still.

"I haven't ridden to hounds."

"The Wistwood Fox, I wouldn't mind betting, has not one earth but several." MacGeoch disregarded his comment.

"What does that mean?"

"He's not just a hedgehog with one trick."

"He's not suburban then."

"Oh, yes, he is. Suburban man may look like a hedgehog to the uninitiated, but if you want the police to have a chance, go and tell them in the morning that the proper study of suburban man is the fox."

"I'm going back to bed. We're barmy, sitting up talking at this hour." Keating decided that MacGeoch was too drunk to make sense to anyone who wasn't drunk too.

He went to bed wondering if he should believe the Scotsman. "I heard the same noise, someone coming in," was how he had put it. "And I thought it might have been you." Did he really hear a noise or had he just come in himself? And if he hadn't been out, why did he not think it might have been Quilter or Garlick who had taken the dog for a walk?

Keating listened to the news at seven, but there was no mention of another murder. He listened again several times during the morning, but it was not until lunchtime that the dreadful business came to light. Though he was expecting trouble, he was not expecting what he heard. During the night, the newsreader said, an attempt was made on the life of Mrs. Sarah Stooke, a widow who lived alone in Wistwood West. The murderer entered her bedroom and, after attempting to strangle her, left her for dead in the bath. Several hours later, she came round to find herself clutching a wisp of dried grass. She was now in hospital under sedation and her condition was as good as could be expected.

Keating felt the weakness of panic in his bones. His fingerprints were bound to be round the house, possibly in the bedroom itself. It would be foolish to try to conceal his relationship with her. He would have to visit her in hospital, for example, but he was sufficiently cunning to go to the police and ask them where she was. He would tell them casually that he was her friend, and if his fingerprints were later found, their presence could be easily explained.

He waited patiently for the others to come home, because there was one among them who would surely give something away.

"Why the withered grass?" he asked them.

"Perhaps it was reddish," Garlick suggested.

"The police and the papers are equally puzzled. This time there's no obvious connection with the fox," MacGeoch said.

"It's as plain as day," the Colonel replied. "The withered grass must be foxtail."

"If it is, it's the same old pattern," MacGeoch said.

"We don't know yet. We mustn't jump to conclusions," Garlick admonished.

"I think we do know," said the Colonel. A new common denominator has come to light. The women had a square the size of a postage stamp cut from their skirts a few inches above the knee.'

"How do you know?" Garlick asked.

"Don't you read the evening paper?" The Colonel was stern. "The police apparently kept it quiet until today."

"I know the woman," Keating said. "I struck up a conversation with her in the library a few weeks back."

"I know her too," said the Colonel. "Or rather I knew her husband, poor man, before she drove him to an early grave."

9

"Get out of bed!
Get out of bed!
You lazy blighters;
I feel sorry for you, I do."

THE Colonel clapped his hands and Keating woke to the realisation that he had slept through the alarm. He went to the window, knowing from the brightness, before he drew the curtains, that it must have snowed during the night. Below him was a world of gleaming clarity, and above was pure sunshine and blue sky. The sun was shining on the black-and-white fronts of the houses, on white roofs, white walls and white gardens, achieving without effort the static perfection that Ann Ede sought in vain in her paintings. The snow made white legging round the telephone wire that crossed the road in front of the house. A bulky thrush with feathers fluffed out against the cold lit on the wire and a handful of snow drifted down like fine dust into the trackless garden. Well-wrapped figures with briefcases filed past the gate. Some wore hats, some caps and some balaclava helmets. And all wore thick-soled boots or wellingtons with their trouser bottoms tucked into long woollen socks. They looked like the remnants of a broken battalion answering with simple heroism the call to the breach once more.

"The spirit of Dunkirk is abroad this morning," Garlick remarked at the breakfast table.

"Dunkirk my foot," shouted the Colonel. "It's the spirit of the Western Front that matters. ' "He's a cheery old card," grunted Harry to Jack as they slogged up to Arras with rifle and pack . . . But he did for them both with his plan of attack.' Get it, Keating?"

"Yes, sir."

"This morning suburban man looks as if he's off with Scott to the Antarctic," the Colonel told him. "Here we conspire to exaggerate the severity of winter weather. We shall talk of little else today and tomorrow. We'll all set off for the station an hour late and when we arrive even later at the office we'll boast that we had to wait over an hour for a train. That, Lance-corporal, has little to do with Dunkirk and nothing to do with Passchendaele."

The Colonel got up from the table and looked back before closing the door.

"I am just going outside and may be some time." His voice cracked with mock-heroism, but neither MacGeoch nor Garlick responded.

When they had gone, Keating washed up and listened to a cello sonata by Marcello on Radio 3. The two conifers at the bottom of the garden had put forth balls of white fluff like arctic fruit, while the dead roses on the trellis by the window peeped like little red petticoats from beneath the white of the snow, making visual poetry against the black laths. Red, white and black. A wounded raven bleeding to death in the snow. Pleased that he had forgotten to dead-head them, he put on his overcoat and tweed cap and went out.

Giles Oxbone, puffed and red-faced, was clearing the snow from his driveway.

"Punting about, that's all they're good for." He dropped his shovel and picked up the yard brush. "When they're not punting about, they're buggering about, and when they're not buggering about, they're taking registration numbers."

"Who?" Keating asked.

"The police, who else? They still haven't caught the murderer. Did you hear the news this morning?"

"No, I was late getting up."

"The withered grass, they say, was foxtail."

"It's all so unreal, and it's happening only a stone's throw away," Keating said.

"Fox-fur, *Foxe's Martyrs,* now foxtail. Where will it end?"

"He's obviously a madman."

"You say you can't believe it. Well, I can. The rot set in with Sir Robert Peel. This country hasn't been the same since the repeal of the Corn Laws."

"It's an unusual theory, but you could be right."

"I know I'm right. A typical example of the effrontery of the mercantile middle class. The landowners should have stood their ground. The mercantile middle class have taken over. They're all round us. Why, mine is the only tractor in the parish."

"It's just the thing for the roads today." Keating tried to bring Farmer Giles back to earth. "The cleats will grip where a car wheel won't."

"I'm taking it to Bromley before lunch. If you'd like a lift, you're more than welcome."

Keating thanked him for his offer and told him that he would prefer to take the centrally heated train.

There were three police cars outside "Delta," and a young policeman was walking up and down in the road. Keating told him that he was a friend of Mrs. Stooke, and after five minutes' conversation he managed to find out that she was in Orpington Hospital.

"How nice of you to come," she said, taking his box of liqueur chocolates.

She looked paler, drier and thinner, as he imagined she might look after a night of debauchery. Her eyes were lifeless and her fingers twitched as if she were trying to grasp an object he could not see.

"I'm drugged to the eyeballs." She half-smiled. "It all seems far away."

"Don't worry, you'll be better in a day or two."

"I'm so pleased to see you. I don't like women visitors, they put me at a disadvantage."

"Would you like to talk about it? If you did, it might help, you know."

"I talked about it to the police. I told them everything I remember, which isn't much. It all happened so quickly, you see. It seems like a miracle that I woke up again."

"What time of night did it happen?"

"I have no idea. It was dark. I woke up dreaming. There was a man behind me in the bed with his arms round me, holding me tight. I thought at first it was a nightmare and then I thought it was you. I tried to get up but I couldn't. His arm was pressing against my throat and he was whispering quietly in my ear. 'I'll let you off if you can spell the word "consensus,"' he said. 'Is it "concencus," "concensus," or "consencus?"' 'It's none of them,' I said. 'It's "consensus."' 'You're wrong,' he said. 'Women who can't spell are an even greater threat than women who can.' That's all I remember. When I came round, I was lying in the bath in my nightie with a square hole cut out of the front of it. I waited for a long time in case he was still in the house. Then I crawled downstairs and rang the police."

"What kind of voice did he have?"

"He just whispered with a hiss."

"Did he have an accent?"

"I don't know."

"Was he working class?"

"I think he was well educated."

"Did he have a distinctive smell? Did he smell of after-shave?"

"It's difficult to say, but I think he smelt of drink."

"Scotch?"

"Possibly. I thought at the time that it was a heavy drink like rum. But it could have been Scotch and spicy food. Why are you asking all these questions?"

"I want you to remember everything so that you'll be able to give a more detailed account to the police. It's the only way they'll catch this bastard."

"I told them about 'consensus.' I knew I had the right spelling—I solve the *Times* crossword every day. So the murderer is a man who can't spell 'consensus.'"

"There's a lot of them around."

"The police looked it up. I was right."

"At least it's a clue."

"Don't tell anyone. They told me to keep it quiet. They're going to give a spelling test to every man in Wistwood."

When he got back to "Foxgloves," he looked up the dictionary to make sure. He was excited at the prospect of a test for which he knew the answer and in which Quilter, Garlick and MacGeoch would not have the same advantage.

They were late home because of the snow and in no mood to discuss anything but the travail of travelling and the number of cancelled trains. Over dinner the Colonel asked MacGeoch to describe his ordeal, and MacGeoch said that he got to work after twelve, that he froze for two hours outside London Bridge in an unheated train. Garlick made a farting noise with his lips and remarked drily that MacGeoch's ordeal by snow must surely be the equivalent of a Blighty One. The Colonel snorted and took a copy of Scott's journal from the bookshelf.

"Listen carefully, Lance-corporal." He opened the book at the last page and read:

> *Thursday 29 March 1912:* Since the 21st we have had a continuous gale from wsw and sw. We had fuel to make two cups of tea apiece and bare food for 2 days on the 20th. Every day we have been ready to start for our depôt 11 miles away, but outside the door of the tent it remains a scene of whirling drift. I do not think we can hope for any better things now. We shall stick it out to the end, but we are getting weaker, of course, and the end cannot be far.
>
> It seems a pity, but I do not think I can write more.

"We have a lot to be thankful for," said MacGeoch.

"I want you all to think of Captain Robert Falcon Scott as you go to bed tonight," said the Colonel. "I can assure you that the sheets will seem warmer if you do."

"Tell us about your ordeal, Colonel," Garlick teased.

"I take no account of the weather, but I listened carefully to one Westman telling another on the train that he sighted a pheasant in his garden this morning as he shaved."

"Impossible," said the Major.

"I tell nothing but the truth," said the Colonel.

"I don't see that it matters," said Garlick.

"It matters a great deal," said the Colonel. "It could be the start of an attempt by Westmen to find a symbol of rurality that could supersede the fox. I can foresee the day when every Westman will have a pheasantry in his garden."

"You're right," said MacGeoch. "The pheasant will quickly oust the fox."

"Surely the fox will eat the pheasant," Keating said.

"You haven't thought the problem through," the Colonel

told him. "The pheasants will attract foxes to Wistwood West and within a year the characteristic distinction between East and West will have vanished. Property values will fall in the East, and rise correspondingly in the West."

"We must nip the pheasant in the bud—or at least clip his wings," said MacGeoch.

"How?"

"We must find a way of preventing Westmen from rearing pheasants in their gardens."

"That's what's wrong with this country," said the Colonel. "Too much tunnel thinking when what we need is a touch of the lateral. Ask yourself what is the greatest difference between the gardens of the East and the West."

"The gardens of the West are foxless," said MacGeoch.

"Wrong," shouted the Colonel. "What do you say, Keating?"

"The gardens in the East are bigger."

"Correct, Captain. That is what we must exploit—the size of our gardens. We must find a symbol that will reinforce the fox. His primacy in Wistwood must never be challenged."

"What are you suggesting, Colonel?" MacGeoch seemed excited.

"We shall beguile him with geese. They are bigger than pheasants and more traditional to a fox."

"It's an expensive way of making up to Charles James," said Garlick. "Geese are twice as expensive as turkeys."

"My strategy is two-pronged," said the Colonel. "The goose will keep the fox in the East and at the same time will itself become a secondary symbol. The symbol will no longer be the fox, but fox and geese—in short, a kind of bimetallism. Do you agree, Keating?"

"I'm afraid it's all rather too complicated for me."

"Then I shall explain it as simply as I can. You need at least a quarter acre of garden if you are to rear geese. In fact a quarter acre will only accommodate twelve in comfort. Ergo, they can only be reared on this side."

"I'm beginning to see the light."

"As I said, the geese will keep the fox in Wistwood East but the fox won't be able to get at them. It's all a question of fortifications, as we military men should be the first to know. Furthermore, the goose will transform the cultural life of Wistwood East. We'll eat goose eggs for breakfast, we'll have roast goose on Sundays and bank holidays, and we'll found goose clubs from which Westmen will inevitably be black-balled. If the symbol takes, as I hope it will, we could have a goose fair in October, complete with gooseherds. We could even make Tudor Way into a drove road, closed to vehicular traffic for the duration of the fair."

"It's positively ingenious," MacGeoch marvelled. "The goose could become a more potent symbol than the fox."

"Exactly," said the Colonel.

"What a load of old cobblers," said Garlick. "A goose, like Celia, unfortunately shits. It's dirty, smelly and very noisy."

"What do you think, Keating? You come from farming stock. You must know."

"They're easy to keep. Between March and October they'll live entirely on grass."

"Capital," said the Colonel. "We'll no longer have to mow our lawns. And we'll no longer have to worry about whether we've got a fly-mo or a push-mower. We'll have a greater status symbol—the Toulouse goose."

"That's something you'll have to decide," Keating said. "There are several kinds of geese—Embden, Toulouse, Brecon Buff and Chinese."

"We'll have the heaviest," said the Colonel. "Nothing but the best for Wistwood East."

"The Embden is the heaviest," said Keating.

"Then the Embden it shall be."

"You speak with all the knowledge of a goosegirl, Keating," Garlick scoffed.

"Don't be a shit, Lance-corporal," said the Colonel. "Keating comes from farming stock, he speaks from the heart."

"I feel strongly about geese," Keating replied. "I lived in mortal dread of my grandmother's gander when I was a boy."

"Do you think the goose will make a good status symbol?" the Colonel asked him.

"It's entirely appropriate in that it's a species that has survived unchanged. In spite of the twentieth-century passion for cross-breeding, the modern goose is pretty much the same as the goose our Victorian forefathers ate at Christmas."

"A true blue. I knew I was right," boomed the Colonel.

"We could start a new political party," said MacGeoch. "We could promise a fox in every garden and a goose in every pot."

"You're all mad." Garlick rose from the table.

"Why are we mad?" The Colonel became combative.

"You're deluded enough already, and geese will delude you more. It's well known that if you look at them long enough, they turn into swans."

Garlick banged the door behind him and the Colonel turned to Keating.

"Does the goose have any other disadvantages? If it has, I wish to hear the worst."

"Only this. It's difficult to encourage both the fox and the goose simultaneously. The fox is an ancient enemy of the goose. As the proverb says, 'It's a silly goose that comes to the fox's sermon.' In short, I think that this particular form of bimetallism won't work. The fox will drive out the goose."

"You're much mistaken, Captain. We'll raise our geese in fox-proof houses, which will nevertheless keep the fox on the qui vive. You've heard of a tantalus in which bottles of wine are kept locked while still remaining visible. Our goose-houses will serve the same purpose. They will stimulate the fox's appetite for *confit d'oie* and at the same time deny him satisfaction."

"Your case for the goose is watertight, Colonel," said MacGeoch. "The only question is: Will the idea take? Suburban man, as we know, is conservative. Will he eat goose if he can get roast beef?"

"Then we must appeal to his patriotism and love of all things Tudor. Queen Elizabeth the First decreed that goose should be eaten on the twenty-ninth of September to commemorate the defeat of the Armada. I know there are certain lily-livered historians who question the historicity of her decree, but we shall mollify even them by giving them the option of celebrating Nelson's birthday on the same day. And those historians who claim that Nelson was born on another day shall be deported to Toulouse where they will be force-fed on geese farms till their livers are enlarged in direct proportion to their scholarly pretensions."

"Bravo, Colonel," MacGeoch shouted. "When England was at her mightiest, everyone ate goose, not turkey, for Christmas. If we now put a goose in every pot, the rest will follow. We'll leave the accursed Common Market, if only because they'll no longer have us, if only because a goose is not a commercial bird to be fattened in a battery and standardised and decimalised like a turkey."

"Now what have you got to say, Keating?"

"I still think the fox is antipathetic to the goose."

"Perhaps in Ireland, but not in England. Here talk of foxes is never far from talk of geese. Here the fox and goose are as complementary as roast beef and Yorkshire pudding."

"When do we start, Colonel?" MacGeoch could not contain his enthusiasm.

"We'll start when the grass grows in March, first with a modest number, perhaps half a dozen goslings. They will feed in the garden, and by Bartholomew's Day—that's August twenty-fourth—they'll be ready for the table."

"Who will look after them?" Keating asked.

"In the absence of a quarter-master-sergeant, you will, Captain."

"And how shall we spread the goose news?" MacGeoch wondered.

"We'll found a goose club and hold discussion groups in the Memorial Hall. Perhaps we'll even get the landlord of 'The Fox and Billet' to resuscitate the royal game of goose."

The bell chimed in the hall, and when Keating opened the door, he found two police officers standing like expectant penguins in the snow. He ushered them into the lounge where they were joined by Quilter, Garlick and MacGeoch. They said they were interviewing everyone in Wistwood, because every scrap of evidence, every opinion and every theory, no matter how unlikely, might have a bearing on what, they assured the Colonel, was an extremely tricky case. They talked for ten minutes, asking routine questions and taking notes, and then they gave the four of them a sheet of paper each and asked them to write down the correct spelling of ten commonly misspelled words.

"Why spellings?" the Colonel asked.

"We have reason to believe that while the murderer is obsessed with correct spelling, he is not such a hot speller himself," the fatter of the officers told them.

"But this is preposterous," the Colonel laughed. "We're all journalists here. Spelling, you might say, is our business."

"I can assure you it's just a matter of routine, sir. We're not accusing anyone. We're merely doing our job."

The other officer read out the words, all of them words that were frequently misspelled even in the Colonel's own newspaper: dessicated, accomodation, concensus, abbatoir, indispensible, reconassance, liquifaction, supercede, courtmarshall, and grafitti.

"I'm surprised you didn't ask us to spell 'floccinaucinihilipilification.'" The Colonel laughed as they handed back their sheets. The fat policeman put them in his briefcase without as much as a glance of curiosity.

"I suppose you'll be sending them to All Souls to have them corrected by one of the fellows," Garlick said.

"I know it's silly, gentlemen, but the misspelling is our only clue."

"Well, I hope you catch the bugger," said the Colonel. "Not content with giving us a bad name, he's now suggesting we can't even spell."

"He's not your run-of-the-mill murderer, sir. He's a joker, if you ask me, but it's possible that one of his jokes will trip him up in the end."

The following morning Garlick announced that he was taking the day off. At ten he went to the newsagent's and came back an hour later with a cigar and a bundle of newspapers.

"Listen to this," he said to Keating. "*The Mirror* has nicknamed the murderer 'The Wistwood Fox.' Do I detect the influence of MacGeoch?"

"I heard him use the phrase a few days ago."

"But *The Times* is not to be outdone. It has a learned article, by a fellow of All Souls no doubt, likening the murders to the London garrottings of 1862. Totally out of touch with reality. No wonder it makes the biggest loss in Fleet Street."

Garlick was reading on a high stool in the kitchen, while Keating chopped an onion. Keating thought that it might be a good opportunity to sound him out about the murders, but he wasn't sure how to start without showing his hand.

"We'll always be outsiders in this house, you and me." Garlick folded *The Times*.

"I can't say I share the Colonel's every interest, but I can't say I feel left out of it either." Keating trod carefully.

"But you are, and so am I. We never sailed with Flint, that's our trouble. We're in on only half the fun. We're living in a club of which we're not members."

"Who is Flint?"

"The man the Colonel calls the Brigadier. He worked for years in Fleet Street. It was under him that Quilter and Mac-Geoch cut their subeditorial teeth."

"They look up to him?"

"They're pleased to have him out of the way, but they owe him too much to forget him. You could tell by the cut of his jib, if you saw him, that he wouldn't know how to play second fiddle. If we had him here for even a day, we'd solve the mystery, I can tell you."

"Which mystery?" Keating sensed danger.

"You know."

"The biggest mystery for me is what the Brigadier is doing in South Africa." Keating sidestepped.

"He's writing a book on gold."

"Why gold?" Keating felt that he was being conducted blindfold through a pine forest where sunlight never penetrated.

"The metal is typical of the man. You couldn't imagine Flint writing a book on platinum."

Keating could not be sure if Garlick was teasing him. It was the first time he had heard a word of praise on his lips and it sounded out of character.

"Is he a metallurgist?"

"No, a stylist. His proper métier is literary aurification. It is said that those who sailed with him, even the men before the mast, would walk the plank rather than split you-know-what."

"The mainbrace?"

"No, the infinitive. You splice the mainbrace, but you split the infinitive." Garlick winked at Keating, and Keating felt so uneasy that he almost sliced his thumb.

"My greatest regret is that I never sailed with him," Garlick confided.

"Why?"

"If I'd sailed with Flint, I might be editing *The Times* by now, and—who knows?—in line for a knighthood. Not one of his men have done badly."

"Is the Colonel serious about the fox and geese?" Keating tried to get Garlick to talk about something he might understand.

"Quilter pretends to be an eccentric, but behind the mask he's as conventional as the suburbanites he affects to despise. Let me tell you a story to prove it. One of your predecessors in the cookhouse kept a pet fox called 'Alopecia.' He kept him in a makeshift kennel out the back, but he used to bring him into the kitchen once a week for an egg-and-lemon shampoo."

"The Colonel must have loved him for it."

"Not a bit of it. He sacked him because he couldn't stand the stink. He may talk of nothing except the fox, but poor Reynard is too smelly to share the house whose market value he is said to enhance by his presence."

"Is the Colonel pulling our leg? Does he go on about the fox in the hope that we'll take him seriously?"

"That's how it all began, but now he's gone so far that he's deluded himself into swallowing every word he says on the subject. What Quilter longs for more than a public school background is a hero-worshipper, and he thinks he's found one in MacGeoch. He accepts MacGeoch because he doesn't pose a social threat. He accepts you because you flatter his taste buds. But he's wary of me because, unlike himself, I've been to public school. The only men Quilter likes are men he can despise. He's a fake, let me tell you. He had a bad war. That's why he detests Churchill, and why he'll never talk about the last war, only the first, which he's too young to remember. Another thing, he prefers Robert Graves to Siegfried Sassoon. Sassoon had a bad war too. Now you see how twisted is our Commanding Officer."

"You make him sound very complicated."

"He is. He never mentioned, for example, that he was once close to the woman who was almost strangled."

"He did say he knew her."

"But he didn't say how well. He said nothing about having an affair with her while her husband was still alive. There's more to these murders than meets the eye."

"What do you mean?"

"Henry Stooke was a thorough-going crackpot. He took it into his head that the fox was a carrier of *toxocara canis* and that fox faeces were alive with the parasite. He began writing to the local paper about the dangers to children who might handle fox faeces in back gardens. Then he announced that he was going to found a Foxocara Society to campaign for the extinction of the suburban fox, and when he got no support he wrote another letter saying that foxes were prone to rabies and that a rabid fox from Wistwood East pursued him across the footbridge and bit him on the left ankle. It was obvious to all that he was a crank—to all except Quilter, who called a meeting of Eastmen in the Memorial Hall to found a Foxymoron Society for the appreciation of you-know-who. Needless to say, no one turned up except MacGeoch. Quilter was furious. He said that Eastmen lacked the courage of their convictions, that they had made the fox their mascot and now wouldn't lift a finger to protect him against the class-hatred of the lower-middle class from the West. He couldn't see that suburban man saw not a hap'orth of difference between himself and Stooke."

"I can see that they were both equally immoderate, and therefore equally suspect."

"The funny thing was that when Quilter failed to launch his Foxymoron Society, he wrote to Stooke and they became close friends. They were birds of a feather. Though they took opposing views of the fox, they both acknowledged his supreme importance."

"And where did Mrs. Stooke come in?"

"She became Quilter's vixen."

"Were you living here at the time?"

"No, no. And neither was MacGeoch. Both he and Quilter were still living with their wives. But I was told the story in 'The Fox and Billet.' There are one or two regulars who remember it well."

"But surely all this has nothing to do with the murders."

"All I will claim is that Quilter is saying less than he could."

"It's all past and buried. He's probably forgotten it."

"She jilted him after she got him to leave his wife. A man who can't forgive Churchill for having a good war, will hardly forgive a woman who's made an ass of him."

"It's all beyond me." Keating could not bring himself to show open disloyalty to his Commanding Officer, especially in front of Garlick.

"As Squire Trelawney said about Captain Smollett when his back was turned, 'I declare I think his conduct unmanly, unsailorly, and downright un-English.'"

"Well," said Keating, "we shall see."

10

OVER the week the snow lost its purity. Dog and fox tracks marred the blank whiteness of the lawns, and traffic churned the roads to grey slush, turning them into nineteenth-century lanes rutted by iron-shod cart wheels. As he shaved one morning, he thought it was snowing again because he could barely see the trees at the bottom of the garden. When he went out, however, he realised that what he took for snow was an icy fog that hung like gritty particles in the air and clutched at his crotch, throat and chest. By lunchtime the temperature began to rise, and at nightfall it seemed as if the heavens had suddenly opened. Water was falling at the back and front of the house, spilling from the guttering as the snow on the roof melted, spilling not like rain in a storm but out of the depth of a far-off silence. Then the phone rang and he heard Mrs. Stooke's voice telling him across a great ocean that she'd come home.

In the morning he brought her flowers and she clung to him tearfully and said that he must never desert her. She dreaded living alone, though the police said they'd give her every protection. She knew they meant well, but not even the Commissioner of the Metropolitan Police himself could now put her mind at ease.

"I was thinking that if you came to live here, I'd feel safe again."

"It's difficult," he said. "Even if I lived here, I wouldn't be here all the time."

"But you'd be here at night, which is the worst time."

"You mustn't let it get on top of you. There are lots of women in Wistwood who have to live alone."

"But they haven't been through what I've been through."

"I'll come to see you more often."

"Then get me a gun. I'd feel safe if I had a handgun."

"But where would I get a gun?"

"If you have the money, there's nothing you can't get in London."

"What would you do with it?"

"I'd put it under my pillow."

"I've got a knife," he said. "I'll give you that instead. You can put it under your pillow at night and in your handbag when you go out."

The following day he brought her Quilter's knife and watched her weigh it in the palm of her hand.

"You must have something in return," she said.

"It's nothing. If it makes you feel safer—"

"You smoke a pipe?"

"Now and again."

"Then I'll give you Henry's humidor. It's almost new. He bought it only a month before he died."

They made love in the bedroom upstairs with the curtains drawn against the light, and she lay beneath him, giving as good as she got, and said "Oh, Henry!" twice as he urged her into the final straight. In the hallway she gave him a carrier bag for the humidor, and he asked for the F-volume and the S-volume in case MacGeoch might notice the gap on his shelf.

As he hurried out the gate, he looked back at the forlorn windows and felt a tightening of the anal sphincter, as if a hostile ghost had goosed him from behind.

He went to see her every day, not because he wanted to, but because seeing her was what Ann Ede would describe as "one of the corporal works of mercy." Every time he saw her they made love, and after the lovemaking she gave him a glass of brandy and port and told him that if she hadn't loved him she wouldn't have called him Henry. Her brush with death seemed to have brought her even closer to her dead husband and to the music of the Requiem Mass, which used to move him even more than a visit to Hastings.

"Was he obsessed with death?" he asked her.

"Not at all. He saw death as a celebration of life —the final and greatest celebration. He was always making jokes about his own funeral, and how he'd love to hear the music. Before he started composing his own requiem, he used to say that he wanted the mourners to come back here to drink sherry and listen to the *Grande Masse des Morts.*"

"Why did he choose the Berlioz?"

"Because he couldn't come to terms with it. Sometimes he thought it vulgar and sometimes he thought it the greatest of all requiems. He once told me that he liked it because the terrors it contained were deliberately theatrical. He said it contained more comfort for the living than the so-called liturgical requiems with angels of consolation waiting in the wings."

"Did you play it at his funeral?"

"It was an awful day, Charles. It rained throughout the morning and again as we came back from the crematorium in the afternoon. I invited nineteen of his friends back here. Counting me, that made twenty, two for every section of the Berlioz. Everyone was on edge, but the sherry soon settled that. When they had drunk three or four schooners, I put on the requiem, but they were in no mood to be quiet. At the

Dies Irae Peter Quilter got up on a chair and began conducting so strenuously that he fell off during the summons from the brass to the Final Judgement. I persisted with the rest, but by the time we came to the Sanctus solo most of them had begun to chat. I was so glad when the record ended that I ran upstairs for a good cry. I couldn't help feeling that it summed up Henry. He wasn't of this world. He never realised that most of his friends felt more at home with Glenn Miller."

"I didn't know you knew Peter Quilter."

"He and Henry were friends. They were both musical and they both liked requiems. But he wasn't a true friend. Once when Henry was visiting the Cinque Ports, he came round here and tried to seduce me. How do you come to know him?"

"I live at 'Foxgloves.'"

"All the more reason why you should come to live with me."

He wondered if she was telling the truth, or if, as Garlick claimed, she'd had an affair with Quilter, but he told himself that her evidence was no more objective than Garlick's.

Two days later Quilter announced that he had the gout. It was not the first time. He'd had attacks before, but this time the pain in his toes was so sharp that he could not face the journey to work.

"You *will* have rich food and strong wines." Garlick laughed.

"I know I can't expect sympathy," the Colonel said. "For some unfathomable reason gout brings a smile to every face except the patient's."

"That's because people think that the patient belongs to the other half, that he gets no more than his deserts."

"Then I shall go to Lord Chesterfield for comfort. He said that gout is the distemper of a gentleman; whereas the rheumatism is the distemper of a hackney coachman.'"

Garlick said that the gout had outlived gentlemen, and Quilter, ignoring him, asked Keating to bring in his gout-stool from the garden shed. He went to the doctor after breakfast and gloomily handed Keating a diet chart when he returned.

"I shall be off work for at least a fortnight." He sighed. "No more pheasant en chartreuse and no more brandy and port in the evening, at least till I purge myself of all this sodium urate."

Keating took off Quilter's shoe and placed the gout-stool under the ailing foot. He wanted to take off the sock and read the foot as a gypsy might read a hand. If he did, would he hear a stealthy footfall behind an unsuspecting victim? Would he see the victim's face with the murderer's face behind it? He looked at Quilter's face, slightly mottled, more than puffy, the face of a man who did not wrestle with the pleasure principle.

"I've had an idea," Quilter said. "Since I can't eat what I like, I'll write about it. I'm thinking of starting a book to be called *Cooking for the Rising Man*—cooking for men who want to forget their origins."

"Men who want to forget about bubble and squeak and toad in the 'ole?"

"And who wish to know about sole Colbert."

"But surely they can find out about sole Colbert in any one of a hundred cook books already in print."

"My book will be different. It will teach people who can't afford good food to talk knowledgeably about it without having eaten it. I often listen to Westmen in 'The Fox and Billet' boasting about the expensive dinners they've eaten. It's all too obvious that they eat out only to talk about it, and sadly the prices are the only thing they can discuss with any degree of conviction. They don't possess the vocabulary to discuss *haute cuisine*. They remind me of those literary men you meet in Fleet Street pubs who discuss the titles of books rather than the books themselves. We, my dear Captain, shall give them the gift of tongues."

"We?"

"You are going to help me. It's an excellent opportunity for you to earn some money while you're looking for a job. You and I shall give them the vocabulary to appraise the borsch in a way a structuralist critic might dissect a poem."

"But I'm only a cook, not a critic," Keating pleaded.

"You'll provide the recipes and I'll provide the analysis. The beauty of it is that our readers will no longer have to eat out to impress their friends. They'll simply look up our book before the next cocktail party to find out what to say about any dish that takes their fancy. It will sell like hot cakes, I do assure you. In fact it's possible that the restaurateurs of the London suburbs may pay us hush money not to publish."

"It sounds too good to be true."

"I'll let you have thirty-three and a third percent of the royalties. I take the lion's share because I came up with the idea."

They spent the next few days listing the recipes they would put in the book, after which the Colonel pronounced it a surefire bestseller and promised Keating that that they'd start writing first thing in the new year. Keating didn't like having the Colonel in the house during the day, but he told himself that the gout might prove one thing: if there was another murder while the Colonel was laid up, he would not be among the suspects.

To escape from the C.O., he crossed the road one morning to see Ann Ede, who asked him to come to Rome with her for Christmas.

"What about your husband?"

"The Bagman. Oh, he's spending Christmas in 'The Fox and Billet.'"

"It's a strange thing to do, going away at this time of year."

"I can't bear Christmas in England."

"How can you be so unpatriotic? It was the English who invented Christmas, or at least reinvented it."

"As a Christian you should know better."

"Well, at least you invented the Christmas card."

"We have a lot to answer for. In the last century Dickens sentimentalised Christmas, and in this century the paynims came and smeared it with their excrement. Now it's a feast for manufacturers and consumers and all the parasites in between—the little man in the high street, the wholesaler who supplies him, the modish adman and the common rep. On the day, of course, it's the feast of the telly comedian. Above all it's a feast for distillers, brewers and publicans and the drunks they prey on, a feast for confectioners and overweight gluttons. The Christian afloat on this filthy modern tide can only try to keep from swallowing the stinking flotsam and long for the vernal purity of Easter."

"Will Rome be different?"

"I shall be staying with Italian friends, simple folk who don't judge a day by the amount they swallow. Will you come? It could be the remaking of you."

He would have loved to go with her, but he couldn't go without a passport.

"I don't think I can, not this time. I've promised to go to see some friends in Newcastle."

Without her, his Christmas was less than perfect. Mrs. Stooke kept pestering him to move in with her, and gout and abstemiousness made the Colonel combative. When Garlick asked if the M.O. would be calling during the festive season, he told him curtly that though she knew how to cure a roaring Jack, she had no power over the gout.

Ann Ede came home in the first week of January, but seeing her again failed to cheer him. He was in the dead-letter office; he could go neither forwards nor backwards. He was incapable of escaping from Mrs. Stooke, who rang him three or four times a day, and he was equally incapable of getting Ann Ede to take him seriously.

In the chill days of January he could not put Henry Stooke from his thoughts. He felt that he himself was ɛs dead as this strange eccentric he had never seen. He was dead to family and old friends. He was cook-general in a madhouse that was probably saner than any other house around. He had come into what Ann Ede called "a dry place without rivers of water," a place he viewed through an icy fog and could not yet identify. He was suspended between two shores, between perception and apperception, and nothing he said or did possessed the value of authenticity. He was immobilised by the toxins of his psyche, and when he listened for an inner voice, all he heard was: "He shall return no more to his house, neither shall his place know him any more."

This dry place without rivers of water, was it a place of preparation like purgatory, or was it a place where God sent people he wished to make mad? If He was a humorist, His fun might consist in making the madness of one madman seem like the quintessence of sanity to another. The mad and the dead do not doubt their perceptions; only the quick and the sane know uncertainty. But he knew that even here he was deluding himself. There was no God and there was no purgatory. There was only a dusty track and a black hole at the end of it.

In his loss of hope, like Henry Stooke, he turned to the music of the requiem mass, the *Missa pro defunctis*. What he wished for, however, was not the music of consolation, based on the lie that man's life mattered, but the truth about his melancholy end. He found to his surprise that even the so-called pagan requiems sweetened the pill. They simply failed to encompass the desolation at the heart of every unaccommodated man, man without his box of tricks—his house and car, his bank statements and friends, man without the arrogance of health and wealth. When he shared his thoughts with Ann Ede, she told him he was looking for fool's gold and, what is more, looking for it in the wrong place.

"Art is man-made," she said, "and therefore, unlike truth, imperfect. Don't seek truth in art because art delights, and delight is only delusion."

Every day he thought of the murderer, until he could not tell whether his hopelessness found expression in images of another man's violence, or whether it was the consciousness of a crime he could not expiate that blackened his thoughts. The murderer sat on his back, his legs locked about his neck, his fingers entwined in his hair. He knew that only cunning would unseat him, but every act was an act of faith and in this dry place he was faithless.

Every night he dreamt of Mrs. Stooke. In one dream he would be lying helpless on his back on the bed while she bent over him like a heartless surgeon. In another he would find himself lying naked on top of her, while she aged visibly under the brunt of his masculinity. Her skin would crinkle into grey papier mâché, her skeleton would crumble, and finally he would find himself lying on a mound of dust, which a gust of wind would suddenly blow away. Every night, as he covered his head with the bedclothes, he would try to think of Ann Ede, but she always managed to elude him, even in his dreams.

One afternoon, while she was giving him tea, he pretended to go to the loo and instead pinched a pair of her knickers from her bedroom. That night he put them under his pillow to see if he would dream about her, but he dreamt instead that Mrs. Stooke was dancing round the room, playing macabre tunes on the flute, demonstrating the perfection of her *embouchure*. In the morning he put the knickers in Henry's humidor to keep them fresh, and the following night he met with partial success, because at least the owner figured marginally in his dream. He dreamt that over afternoon tea she took them off, not because she felt hot in em, but so that he might wear them as a protection against fellatio by Mrs. Stooke. They were white as a curate's surplice and roomier than he expected, but no sooner had he put them on than they began to contract and crush his testicles. He cried out in pain to Mrs. Stooke, who ripped them open with Quilter's snickersnee and immediately examined the manufacturer's label.

"What does it say?" he asked, still clutching his bruised fardel.

"Just as I thought. Knickers by Nessus. I swear by Saint Michael myself."

He continued to visit Mrs. Stooke throughout January and February, but her burgeoning paranoia and predatory sexual appetites made communication with her impossible. He sensed that she needed more help than a mere layman could offer, but he could not bring himself to tell her so. Now nothing would please her but to lie on top of him, her mound biting into him, bone seeking bone, grinding like quern-stones in a fury. He would turn his head away in case she should kiss him on the lips, and after she found rest he would go to the bathroom to wash out his mouth with some of her hydrogen peroxide. One night after he came back she told him she had an earache. She warmed olive oil over the gas, tilted her head, and asked him to pour a spoonful into her ear, but all he wanted was to get away. His hand shook with impatience and the oil ran down her neck.

"You don't care about me." She jumped from her chair in a rage. "If you loved me, you wouldn't have missed my ear. My ear and my ache are nothing to you. All you can think of is my pussy."

"You flatter yourself, madam," he thought of saying. "Your

pussy is a matter of total indifference to me. I would as soon fill it with hot oil as hot semen."

He placed the teaspoon on the table and told her not to ring him again, that he would not be coming to see her anymore. He disliked being forced into cruelty, but he knew that he had only past weakness to thank for both his and her suffering.

On the way back to "Foxgloves," he stopped outside "The Fox and Billet," wishing he could enter and buy oblivion for less than a fiver. He had heard from Garlick of the magical atmosphere within, the plenitude of anecdote, the mock-Tudor fireplace, the heavy beams, and the prawns, bacon rind and toasted cheese mine host laid out on Sunday mornings. Reluctantly, he turned away. "The Fox and Billet" was an emergency ward for men whose lives now and again became intolerable. It was a palace of dreams, where guilty men came to shed their guilt, and hard-faced businessmen shed gravitas and responsibility for an hour. He visualised his local in Cork and his old schoolmaster wagging his finger at an ex-pupil:

"Keep thy foot out of brothels, thy hand out of plackets. But if you must rummage in plackets, remember only the first one matters. The rest is silence."

He smiled at the schoolmaster's folly, but he wished nevertheless that his aphorism were true.

With the coming of Lent, Ann Ede came into her own. Though she stopped short of going about in sackcloth and ashes, she wore a girdle borrowed from one of the White Friars at Aylesford, not to support her slightly protuberant tummy but in the hope that she might acquire some of the virtues of the Carmelites, whose piety she admired even more than their pottery. He visited her every morning, but now, as a token of self-denial, she made him sit on the other side of the table in case he should accidentally touch her hand. He fell almost too easily into the role she had conceived for him, persuading himself that present discomfort was an investment that could pay ample dividends once the rigours of Lent were over and she woke to the thrill of spring. He was not a lapsed Catholic for nothing. He well knew that Catholic women, even the most devout, are at their most vulnerable after a long fast or a long retreat.

Lent also seemed to have a salutary effect on the Colonel. His gout, which made table talk at "Foxgloves" acidulous during January and early February, improved so much after Ash Wednesday that he announced on St. David's Day that the M.O. would be coming to dinner that evening. MacGeoch and Garlick were delighted, and Keating trembled with pleasure at the thought of her icy footrule. A hint of warmth in his stomach spread to his legs and arms, and he knew that he expected her to bring him not just sexual excitement but resolution. She was an intelligent woman who knew more than anyone about the Colonel, the Major and the Lance-corporal, perhaps even the Captain too. He felt that her purpose was to make clear to him what he felt in his heart but still could not see. He would watch her every gesture and mark her every word. He told the Colonel how much he liked her and with his connivance sat beside her at the dinner table.

"It seems a long time," she said over the soup.

"It was all the Colonel's fault," Garlick told her. "For that old enemy the gout had taken him in toe."

"You should have called me in," she said. "I was once given the cure by an old woman from Monkwearmouth, but it sounded so outlandish that I've never once prescribed it."

"Tell us more," said MacGeoch.

"First you find three white stallions. Then you arrange for them to defecate simultaneously into a vat, and lastly you immerse the gouty leg in the boiling dung."

"Very ambiguous," Garlick commented. "Must the stallions excrete boiling dung or is it permissible to put a Bunsen burner under the vat and bring the contents to a temperature of one hundred degrees Celcius or two hundred twelve degrees Fahrenheit?"

"The latter, I imagine." The M.O. refused to smile.

"You may laugh at the gout, but at least it isn't a malady of milksops," the Colonel reproved them.

"Have you managed to shake it off?" She placed her hand on his.

"It was not the gout that held me back, it was something rather more serious. My shot was falling short. The striker-pin felt O.K. but the rifling had completely gone."

"What you needed was a rebore, my dear Colonel." She suddenly kissed him on the cheek.

"And that's just what I got." He squeezed her hand and laughed, and when the Colonel laughed, it was a signal for all to join him.

After dinner, when the port had been round the table twice, the Colonel said that it was time for the seeding.

"I should like to try something new tonight," the M.O. told them. "A kind of quiz with only one question. I shall need the cooperation of Major MacGeoch, who, I feel sure, will oblige by changing into his Buchanan."

MacGeoch and the M.O. went upstairs together, and after ten minutes or so he reappeared in his kilt, complete with sporran and skean-dhu and a silver pin in the front flap, which he said he inherited from his maternal great-grandfather. He loudly clicked the heels of his brogues, put one arm round the M.O.'s waist, and adjusted his glengarry with the other.

"The seeding will take the following form," she announced. "The first to guess what the Major is wearing under his kilt will be first unto the breach. The second closest guess will be second and so on, and I shall be the only judge. Major MacGeoch himself will also be taking part in the quiz, and for once

even the Scotsman won't know the answer to the most con-
troversial conundrum in the cultural history of these islands."

Keating looked at the Colonel and the Colonel smiled at the
M.O. MacGeoch, trying to look innocent, adjusted his sporran as if he wanted to relieve an itch under his kilt without
giving anything away. Garlick looked sharply from face to
face, and Keating sensed that he too expected the game to reveal something more serious than knowledge of the secret
which all Scotsmen are born with and which Englishmen
spend the best part of their lives trying to discover.

"Surely, MacGeoch will have a head start on the rest of us.
Surely he must have a fair idea from the weight and feel of it."
Garlick voiced suspicion.

"I can assure you he's as innocent of the correct answer as
the rest of you," she told him. "I shall start with the Colonel
and work down to you, Lance-corporal. Before you guess you
may ask one question, provided it is a question that can be
answered with a simple 'yes' or 'no.' Your turn, Colonel."

Colonel: Is it something unusual? M.O.: Yes. Colonel: Is it a
cricket box? M.O.: I am sorry, Colonel, it is not. Mac-
Geoch: Is it vegetable? M.O.: Yes. MacGeoch: Is it one of
those orange penis gourds with which certain African tribes
adorn their willies? M.O.: No, Major, it is not. Keating: Is
it made of cotton? M.O.: No. Keating: Is it an orgone box?
M.O.: It is not an orgone box. Garlick: Is it symbolic?
M.O.: I don't know the answer to that off the cuff, but I can
try to find out.

Here the M.O. put her hand up MacGeoch's kilt and rum-
maged about vigorously, as if she were going through a trin-
ket box. The Major's rubicundity increased by fifty percent.
He closed his eyes and raised his face heavenwards as if to pray
for the concealment of a growing caber.

M.O. (withdrawing her hand): Yes. Garlick: Then I know. It's Saint David's Day today, and it's a daffodil. M.O.: It is not a daffodil. Colonel: Is it an article of dress? M.O.: Yes. Colonel: Is it a masonic apron? M.O.: It is not a masonic apron. MacGeoch: Is it worn by men exclusively? M.O.: Yes. MacGeoch: Then it's a codpiece. M.O.: No, my dear Major. You are not wearing a codpiece.

Just then it occurred to Keating that the winner of the game need not necessarily be the murderer. He was convinced, however, that under the Scotsman's kilt was the clue that would lead him to the truth, and he couldn't help wondering why the Colonel said a masonic apron. Perhaps it was an apron of a different colour, and perhaps the Colonel was preparing the ground to give the correct answer next time. It was possible that the M.O. had told him the answer on the way down, and that he was trying not to make his advantage obvious. Keating decided it was time to pip his Commanding Officer.

Keating: Is it a special kind of apron? M.O.: Yes. Keating: Then, it's a bishop's. M.O.: Well done, Captain. It's a gremial. In other words, a bishop's apron. The Major has made history. He is, unquestionably, the first Scotsman to wear one under his kilt.

MacGeoch pulled the apron out from under the Buchanan, and Garlick laid it flat on the table like an exhibit in court.
"Where did you get it?" Keating enquired.
"From a very special punter." She smiled.
"Ecclesiastical?" the Colonel asked.
"As ecclesiastical as archiepiscopal." She laughed. "But now I must decide on the batting order. First, the Captain, then the Colonel, then the Major, and finally the Lance-corporal."

"I declare no contest," Garlick shouted.

"Why?" The Colonel turned on him.

"This apron is made of silk, and silk is animal. The M.O., quite distinctly, said vegetable."

"A slip of the tongue," she said.

"No time for shilly-shallying now," said the Colonel. "Let's get started before the Lance-corporal finds yet another pretext for nitpicking."

Keating took the apron from Garlick and held it up against the light, as if searching for the watermark on a banknote, but one glance told him that the message he sought wasn't there. He put the apron to his nose and sniffed like a bloodhound on a fresh trail.

"What have we here? A silk fetishist or an honorary member of the Caledonian Society?" The M.O. laughed.

"Well, Captain," said the Colonel, "is it a counterfeit gremial or is it genuine?"

"It's genuine all right."

"But what is it—brocade, crêpe or satin?"

"If I knew that, I might know too much," Keating replied.

"Let me tell you, then," said the M.O. "It's none of those. I've had it from the horse's mouth. His Grace, the owner, calls it shantung. He tells me it was woven from the cocoons of wild silkworms on the left bank of the Yangtze."

"But we digress," the Colonel spoke to the M.O. "Have you forgotten what we talked about on the way down?"

"No, I haven't. Colonel Quilter remarked on the train that a knee-trembler in a doorway is rather rare these days."

"Lovers nowadays enjoy better conditions than in my youth," the Colonel told them. "And it's all been achieved without the help of trade unions."

"A knee-trembler is an exciting and beautiful thing." MacGeoch turned poetic. "It isn't at all to be compared with grappling between sheets."

"I know it's a cold night, but the M.O. has prescribed something better than Bovril to warm the blood," the Colonel told them. "You are each to have a knee-trembler in the porch, and I want nothing less than a bull's eye from every man jack of you. The M.O. will report to me all failures and near misses. For complete failures I shall prescribe nothing less than Field Punishment No. 1. And those of you who only tickle the fourchette will have to perform three times in full battle dress in the Fowler position, followed each time by two tablespoonfuls of Fowler's solution."

"Are you to have a knee-trembler too?" Garlick asked him.

"Yes, Lance-corporal."

"And if you miss, who will prescribe the punishment? Who in other words will punish the punisher?"

"I shall be the arbiter of that," said the M.O. "But to set your mind at ease I can tell you that a failure by the Colonel is inconceivable."

"What drawers are you wearing, M.O.?" the Colonel asked.

"My usual scanties. Shot silk, the ones you so kindly sent me for Christmas."

"No good," said the Colonel. "Especially on a brass monkey night like this. For a true knee-trembler you need nothing less than camiknickers. Can you raise a pair, Major?"

"No, sir."

"Keating? What about you?"

"I'm afraid not, sir."

"No one to step into the breach? Then we'll have to make do with an old pair of pink winceyettes from my personal collection. They're not A-one for the purpose, but at least they're real Blighty, not bloody French."

"They're even better than camiknickers," MacGeoch enthused. "For a knee-trembler on a cold night, you need a knicker with a long leg."

"One thing, gentlemen," said the Colonel. "Those pink

winceyettes you're about to enjoy are special. They were given me thirty years ago by the wife of a retired Field Marshal. They're real cock-cosies, let me tell you. So be careful, I want them back in good working order. I don't mind a stain or two—that's unavoidable, even among officers and gentlemen—but I don't want the elastic strained or the fabric damaged."

Miss Dingles got into the Colonel's winceyettes while the four officers watched in admiration.

"They're rather big," she said.

"They're perfect," MacGeoch told her.

"It's your figure that's perfect," the Colonel said. "You don't have the Field Marshal's wife's embonpoint, and that is not a criticism, I do assure you."

"Come on, Captain." She turned to Keating.

It was dark and cold in the porch, but the warmth of her breath excited him. He knew she had the answer to his question, but the question, he suddenly realised, would have to wait.

"What shall we talk about? I promise not to tell the Colonel."

"I've never had a knee-trembler. They weren't the fashion in Cork. There was always more than enough hay to lie on."

"So you want to see what it's like?"

"It might be a good wheeze." He lifted her dress.

"No, you mustn't pull them down. You must come up through the leg."

"But the leg is at least ten inches!"

"It's the Colonel who made the rules. It's got to be what he calls a 'knicker-leg job.' Otherwise I'll have to report you."

Keating tried and tried but his penis seemed to have lost all sense of direction. After ten minutes the M.O. giggled and told him to relax, that she herself would pilot the gentleman through.

At her touch he lost contact with the ground. He was seated in a great birdlike plane, soaring heavenwards with irresistible ease, the naked air hostess on his lap anticipating his every fantasy, the fluid lubrication providing a lower coefficient of friction than any he had experienced in Ireland. When it came to engineering, these Anglo-Saxons could teach the Celts a thing or two. Even their womenfolk had an instinctive knowledge of how to reduce power loss in the bearing.

For a long time they glided through pure blue sky with nothing but red earth below. Then the "No Smoking" sign began flashing. They were losing altitude, his ears were popping, and the captain was telling them the local time, that the weather was humid, that they would be landing in approximately five minutes. After the captain had spoken the steward advised them to stow all hand luggage under the seats, not in the aisles or near the exits, and suddenly the wheels touched the tarmac.

"Did you like it?" she asked when they had taxied to a stop.

"It was most extraordinary. I had a kind of hallucination that made me realise it was happening to me a long time ago, if you see what I mean. I thought I took off from Melbourne in an aircraft bound for Kuala Lumpur. I had never been to either place before."

"I liked it too. The Joule effect was most pleasing as we touched down." She gave him a warm kiss on the cheek.

"I have a question to ask you," he said.

"I hope it's about air travel." She laughed.

"On second thoughts, it can wait." The lightness of her laugh deterred him.

After Quilter, MacGeoch and Garlick had had their knee-tremblers, the M.O. gave the Colonel back his winceyettes and reported four bull's eyes. The Colonel, delighted at the marksmanship, opened a celebratory bottle of brandy, and they all went into the lounge, where the M.O. entertained them with a string of erotic anecdotes and tantalising glimpses of her intermammary cleft.

"I must be getting back. It's already gone twelve." She looked at her watch.

"Why don't you stay the night?" the Colonel suggested. "We promise to let you rest."

"I'd really love to, but I have an appointment with a bishop in the morning."

"You mock us." The Colonel laughed.

"Not at all."

"Anglican or Roman Catholic?" Keating enquired.

"Neither. He's Irish."

"But it's the middle of Lent!" Keating could not suppress disbelief.

"He's a man of simple tastes. There's nothing he likes better than a cream cracker and a glass of Perrier water."

"If you have a date with a bishop, even an Irish bishop, you mustn't disappoint him. And it is only fitting that you should be driven to him by an Irish jarvey. Keating, you can take my car."

Keating never realised that the M.O. had too much to drink until she tried to get to her feet. He helped her into the car, and she slumped back in the seat with her head against his shoulder. He drove carefully in case he should be stopped and breathalysed, but he was already at Elephant and Castle before she woke from her slumber.

"The funniest things always happen at 'Foxgloves,'" she told him.

"The Colonel is full of invention," he tried to encourage her.

She laughed, or rather choked, against the back of her hand, then pulled forward her horse's tail and put the tip to her lips. After a little while she laughed again, this time so immoderately that her laugh ended with a snore. Keating looked down at her, but she was still wide awake.

"You and I, we've got our little secret," she said.

"What secret?"

"That the first time we did nothing."

"Oh, that."

"I shall never tell the others."

"They might be amused."

"Not the Colonel. He wouldn't understand the complexity of self-denial. He's a straightforward man himself, but he goes to great lengths to justify what he does."

She laughed again, her chin going up and down uncontrollably as if it were not the laughter of good humour but of personal compulsion.

"The strangest thing the Colonel ever asked me to do was to grip him firmly while he was inside me so that he couldn't get out."

"And did you?"

"I wasn't able. A woman can't contract her vulva just like that."

"I wonder what he was up to."

"Without coming out, he rotated very slowly until we were bum to bum, facing in opposite directions. I thought it the oddest thing, so I asked him if he were having a good time. And do you know what he said? 'I'm just trying to prove a theory I have about the fox.'"

She sucked the tip of her horse's tail and snored deeply into the palm of her hand.

"The Colonel is a man of striking originality." He laughed heartily to make her tell more.

"I'm not joking. He told me that mating foxes stay locked together after the act for up to half-an-hour. But, as if that wasn't enough, he put a leather strap round us both and asked me to fall off the bed with him onto the mattress he'd placed on the floor. We landed facing east and west, and I asked him what theory he was trying to prove just then. 'Oh,' he said, 'it's just that I once surprised two mating foxes and they tumbled down a railway embankment in fright still tail to tail.'"

"He has a vivid imagination."

"I never tell tales out of school, but I think he's just a little bit kinky. He once asked if he could urinate on my shoulder."

"On the strap of your bra?"

"No, on my bare skin. And he said he'd like to do it because in mating the dog fox scent-marks the vixen."

"Did you let him?"

"No, I drew the line for the first and only time. He took it in good part. He's really a lovely man. It's a pity he's such a misogynist, but if he tells the truth about his ex-wife, she made him what he is. He once confided to me that she treated him like a teaser. She would allow him to stimulate her, and then she'd chuck him out and reach orgasm on her own."

"Manually?"

"So he said."

She directed him down Piccadilly into White Horse Street and Shepherd Market where she lived.

"Come in for a nightcap."

"I'm very tired. I should be getting back, but I'd like to call on you sometime when you're not too busy."

He took down her phone number and leant over and kissed her.

"Tell me about the Irish bishop," he said.

"Why do you want to know?"

"Because he's Irish. I thought all Irish bishops were killjoys."

"But you can kill everyone else's joy and still preserve your own. He isn't much like a bishop really. He's more like a farmer, heavy and red-faced and not very sophisticated. He comes over once a year, usually during Lent, and he gives me two hundred pounds for two hours of my time and a hot tip for the Grand National."

"Is he a generalist or a specialist in bed?"

"A generalist who wouldn't stoop to specialisation."

"You disappoint me."

"What did you expect?"

"I thought he might wish for fellatio."

"That, I find, is an Anglican foible."

"But he must come to you for something he fails to find in his housekeeper."

"How perceptive of you. He once said he comes to me for insight into the nature of those who must try to live by his pastorals."

"Will you promise me something?"

"Anything short of allowing you to pee on my shoulder."

"I'd like to know what he fancies for the Grand National."

"I'll ring you," she said. And with a hearty laugh she banged the car door.

11

As he drove back alone, he could not put the Colonel from his thoughts. The M.O.'s revelations troubled him, and he was unable to say precisely why. After all she had not told him anything new. He was already aware that the Colonel was a phantasist. So many of the things he talked about never came to anything—the radio-tagging of foxes, the book on cooking for the rising man, his ambition to make the goose into a more potent symbol than the fox. But the Colonel was not the only one whose evidence was unreliable. MacGeoch would believe black was white on the Colonel's say-so, and Garlick was so critical of everything that he could not see the hair for the nits. Yet Garlick probably came closest to the truth. His eye, however jaundiced, was essentially the eye of sanity and common sense. Keating longed for a coign of vantage from which he could observe objectively and without preconception, and Ann Ede was aware of his longing.

"I think you're in danger," she told him the week before.

"My life?"

"No, your soul. You're an innocent here, and the knowledge you seek is the abnegation of innocence. Here all men are guilty, and all who sup with them sup at their peril. The reten-

---

174

tion of innocence is the only breastplate in a society which puts mere knowingness above self-knowledge. Furthermore, you concern yourself exclusively with the particularity of here and now, when you should be seeking truths that are universal and immutable. So forget suburban man. He does not inhabit the world of the spirit but the world of mechanics; money, not passion or idealism, spins the skein in which he is entangled."

He smiled at the thought that Ann Ede, whose evidence was as suspect as Quilter's, Garlick's or MacGeoch's, should set herself up as his unpaid counsellor. Was there anyone who was not deceived by his own sleight and craft, anyone who saw life as it was, not as he wished it to be?

He swung into the driveway, aware of disappointment and physical exhaustion now that he was home. The evening had yielded nothing. He had failed to speak openly to Jilly Dingles; the Wistwood Fox could sleep soundly for another while. He switched on the light in the garage and saw a young woman sitting on the freezer with her back to the wall. Her long hair covered her face and neck. Her left shoe had fallen to the floor. The sickening knowledge that she was dead gave him a sensation of freefall that seemed to lift his stomach into his chest. He looked round to see if anyone was watching from the road, closed the door, and grasped her hand. It was barely warm and there was no pulse. He was about to place his hand over her heart when he retched in panic. He picked up a sheet of paper that lay beside her, a photocopy of an article from *The Cornhill Magazine* for January 1863 with one paragraph marked in red:

Women are seldom garotted; and their exemption is due, perhaps, to some last spark of manly and generous feeling which even a garotter may cherish. There are other motives, to be sure . . . The *pomum Adami* in a woman's throat is so small that it is difficult to choke her on the safest principles of the garotte, and in fact it is safest altogether to allow her to go unmolested.

In the margin by the paragraph, scrawled in red, was the word "Tee-hee," followed by three exclamation marks.

His first impulse was to get in the car and drive off, but as he reopened the garage door he realised that he had nowhere to go.

"If you do a flit, you'll be suspect number one," he told himself. "And if the body is found here, you'll be interrogated and your statement checked with the Irish police. Either way, you're in trouble."

The others had less to hide, he was the one who had most to lose. He decided to have a drink to steady his nerves and to give himself time to think. The others were in bed, or seemed to be in bed. The orderly room, the mess and the cookhouse were in darkness. He stole upstairs and got out the bottle of Scotch he kept in the wardrobe. He poured himself a bumper and crossed the landing to the Ooja-cum-Pivvy for a dash of water. The lavatory bowl was still empty but someone had left the plug in the washbasin which was full of frothy water that smelt of lemon shampoo.

He lay on his bed, sipping the Scotch and rereading the paragraph from *The Cornhill Magazine,* but coherent thought escaped him. He read the rest of the article on "the science of garotting and housebreaking," stopping at:

> His throat is fully offered to his assailant, who instantly embraces it with his left arm, the bone just above the wrist being pressed against the "apple" of the throat.

Each word made a signal but the complete sentence was mute. He poured himself another large Scotch, and as he drank the dregs he knew that he must dispose of the body if he wanted to keep the police off his tail. He would hide it in a neighbour's garage, or better still in the woods. It was after three. He had just three hours before light.

He went downstairs and entered the garage by the back door, but when he turned on the light the body was gone. He opened the freezer and looked at the polythene bags of beef and lamb. He looked at the floor. Her shoe was also gone. Everything had been taken care of. He straightened and breathed a sign of relief.

Once back in his room, he switched off the light and went to bed. Though he was relieved to find the body gone, the mystery of the Wistwood Fox was closer to him and deeper. There were so many questions to which he had no answer. What was the murderer doing with the body in the garage? Had he gone off somewhere? Or had the noise of the car disturbed him? If so, he must know that Keating had seen the body. Who knew? Quilter? MacGeoch? Garlick? Or one of the neighbours? He knew that he should stay awake, but before he could strengthen his resolve he was asleep.

He woke as someone flushed the loo, but he could have sworn that it was not the cistern that woke him. It was half-past four by his watch. He waited behind the bedroom door and came out as the door of the Ooja-cum-Pivvy opened. MacGeoch, hitching up tartan pyjamas, blinked at him.

"When did you get back?" he asked.

"Oh, two hours ago."

"That's strange. I was sure something woke me just now. I thought it was you coming in."

"Something woke me as well," Keating said.

"A cat or a fox maybe." MacGeoch vanished into his room.

In the Ooja-cum-Pivvy he peered into the bowl. The Nocturnal Crapper had struck while he slept. Urinating, he stared at his stubble chin in the mirror and thought it strange that only a moment ago this same mirror reflected MacGeoch's. And he knew that no matter how much he understood about angles of incidence and angles of reflection, it would still seem strange. The cast of his mind was not scientific. It traded, not in certainties, but in mysteries and doubts. And the mysteries were overprinted, one on the other. The Mystery of the Nocturnal Crapper became the Mystery of the Wistwood Fox.

MacGeoch imagined someone had come in, and moreover that the someone was Keating. A reasonable assumption perhaps, but it was the second time he had assumed wrongly. The first was the night he caught him in the mess scoffing Scotch and chips. MacGeoch was devious. It was more than possible that this was his way of deflecting suspicion from himself. He was last out of the Ooja-cum-Pivvy before Keating entered. Did that make him the Nocturnal Crapper? Again there was no certainty, only a hint of shampoo in the immobile air.

MacGeoch said little at breakfast, and what he said only concerned the rejuvenating effect of a knee-trembler on the joints. Keating decided to say nothing about the body in the garage, though he knew that one of the others possibly knew that he knew. The Colonel was busy with *The Times* crossword, but halfway through he folded his paper and turned to Keating: "You know what date it is?"

"The second of March," Keating said.

"And March is the month we buy our goslings."

"You're not serious?" Garlick feigned extreme shock.

"I'm appointing you, Keating, to make preliminary enquiries. We're going to have at least six goslings in the garden, even if it means going to John-o'-Groats to get them."

"I'm looking forward to the eggs," Keating said. "They make the fluffiest of omelettes . . ."

"You forget the droppings." Garlick thrust out a fine-boned jaw.

"We'll simply put them on the flower-beds. Nothing will be wasted, wait and see," said the Colonel.

"I hope Giles Oxbone doesn't mind the hissing and cackling." Garlick tried again.

"Oxbone is a farmer manqué. He'll sleep more soundly

within earshot of agrarian noises." The Colonel rose contemptuously from the table.

When the others had gone, Keating listened to the news, but there was no mention yet of another murder. He knew that he was running a risk, that he should move to a quieter place, but he could not bring himself to leave without Ann Ede. Just before noon she rang to invite him to lunch.

"A ploughman's lunch," she said. "The Bagman's been to Boulogne for a day. He came back laden with wine and cheese."

"Husbands have their uses." He laughed.

"And so do bagmen."

The spread was already laid when he arrived—a bottle of white Burgundy, a long baguette, pickles, tomatoes, Roquefort, Brie and Pont-l'Évêque.

"You heard the news?" she asked. "There's a woman missing, a young housewife from the other side."

"Where will it end? Women are now frightened to move out without a man they can trust. I've noticed it myself. They look at you strangely in the road and in the shops. We're all under suspicion, all tarred with the brush of misogyny."

"If you're a woman, you can't help it. Whenever the Bagman comes home late, I listen to the news first thing in the morning to see if anything's happened."

He couldn't help smiling at her matter-of-fact revelation, which she seemed to offer as she would the salt and pepper.

"Are you ever afraid?" he asked as she filled his glass.

"I'm not a typical woman. I'm not even a typical modern Catholic, if only because I know that my Satan liveth, and that he liveth in particular here in Wistwood. These murders are the thick end of the wedge. Those with eyes to see saw the thin end a long time ago."

"Surely you're wrong. These killings are the work of a

madman, and you'll find one madman even in the most civilized societies, just as you'll find Death even in Arcadia."

"He is mad, I'll grant you, but his madness is only the madness of society writ large. This is a selfish society. Here the best we can achieve is selfishness tempered by decency. But decency, like patriotism, is not enough. The members of the South African government are decent. I'm certain they make loving husbands and fathers and charming companions in the golf club, but the opinions they hold on race are a wart on the face of humanity."

"Here we're a long way from Cape Town."

"In miles but not in sentiment. If you listen carefully on a calm day, you will feel the suburban air tingle with class and racial prejudice. I say so because I know. The Bagman comes back from 'The Fox and Billet' every night with nothing on his lips but dirty jokes about Blacks."

"Dirty jokes don't mean a thing. Men tell them to one another to recover the innocence they felt as schoolboys saying 'shit' for a dare."

"You're not a theologian, Charles. To the theologian the difference between a thought and the deed to which the thought is father is less than microscopic."

"If that's theology, you can have it."

"Charles, there are days when you love me and days when you don't. Be honest and admit you don't love me today."

"I love you less today than yesterday."

"Here, have some more wine for being so truthful. I'm less than perfect today?" She smiled.

"Your body is perfect."

"But not my mind?"

"It forms too many opinions."

"Should women not have opinions?" she teased him.

"I didn't say they shouldn't."

"Then tell me how many opinions you will allow a woman to have."

"As many as she has time to examine." She made him feel distinctly uneasy.

"There's nothing wrong with opinions if they're true."

"Too many make for turbulence. Now and again, as someone said who should know, the heart must pause to breathe, and love itself have rest."

"You don't wish for a woman of our times?"

"You know what I wish for."

"You're a male chauvinist, and not a very cunning one. The Bagman is a chauvinist too, but he hunts in habitats where the vegetation will camouflage his spots."

He was slightly shocked at the crudeness of her conversation. It was not the conversation he would have expected from a devout Catholic in the middle of Lent.

"The Bagman is more successful than you, Charles, because he's more vulgar. He's shamelessly vulgar, as indeed a bagman should be. I once accused him of male chauvinism, and he stuck out his chest and said: 'I'm a reed shaken by every woman whose voice is not soft, gentle and low.' When he said it, I thanked God for granting me the light not to love him."

He was not enjoying the conversation. He could see that she felt the superiority of someone who could quote Scripture on humility till the cows come home. She had religion perhaps where some people have sex—in the head—but this unworthy reflection in no way diminished his desire to go round the table and put both hands down inside her Carmelite girdle.

"Let's have some music." He thought that if she put on a record, he could look at her without having to listen.

They finished the wine and listened to Schubert's great *C-Major Symphony*. At first the bleak March sunlight on the leavings of the feast distracted him. He closed his eyes, but then the open eyes of the murdered woman in the garage stared at him, bloodshot and expressionless, without accusation. He tried to make of his mind a blue Alpine lake reflecting only clear sky, but the dancing figures in the music mocked him like sniggering clowns. He was pleased when it ended and she put the record back in its sleeve.

"That was good," she said. "Oh, the heavenly length of it."

He looked at her to see what she meant, but she looked as if she didn't mean anything.

"It isn't as long as Beethoven's *Ninth*."

"It's only a phrase. I said it because I heard it on the radio the other day. Did you like it?"

"The symphony? Yes, I did."

"It's a work with an extraordinary sense of fulfilment, not a Lenten work, you will agree. It's a work of burgeoning sexuality, and the sexuality is not always audible. It goes underground like a stream in karst country, only to emerge again, clear as crystal, glancing in the light, flowing over clean pebbles as if it had never done anything else. In suggesting wholeness and fulfilment, it conveys the evanescence of all fleshly desire."

And in talking such balls, you suggest to me that it's time I went home, he wanted to say. Instead he said, "I'll see you tomorrow. I must buy some potatoes for the dinner."

"And I shall do a little gardening." She went with him to the door.

On the way to the green grocer's he saw a little girl looking at a big green frog in a toy-shop window. She was the same age as his daughter the year he took her on holiday to Connemara. She had discovered a pond full of tadpoles on the hill, and he took her to see them every day because she wanted to be there at the moment they turned into frogs. Again and again he tried to lift one out of the water in his hand, but each time he opened his fist there was no tadpole on his palm.

"The art of catching tadpoles is to be quiet," he told her sagely.

She bent down and cupped her hands in the water. When she stood up, the water spilled through her fingers, leaving two wriggling tadpoles on her palms. They were dark with transparent tails, rusty specks on their backs and bulging eyes like tiny warts on top of their heads.

"The art of catching tadpoles is to cup both hands," she told him as she put them back in the water.

The following day they found two local boys with jam jars at the pond, and when they had gone she said: "Daddy, let's get a jam jar too and carry the tadpoles to a secret pond where the boys won't find them."

They found another pond in the bog and they filled it with tadpoles when the boys weren't looking. And every day they went to the bog to study them as they grew. Then one day they found the pond filled with green turfs and not a tadpole in sight.

"It was the boys that did it." She tugged at his sleeve and sobbed.

"No, it was a turf cutter, and he didn't realise what he was doing."

At home after the holiday, he would go to her room to tuck her in and she would ask him for a story about a tadpole and a waterfly. It was their secret, because Esther didn't approve of "silly stories witho foundation in fact."

He paused by the toy-shop window to look with the little girl at the frog. It hurt him to think that he would never see his daughter again, either as a girl or as a young woman with a girl of her own. He turned to the little girl and put out his hand.

"Don't touch her. I know what's on your mind."

He looked round to find Mrs. Stooke pointing at him from across the street. Her eyes were wild. She looked ill and haggard, hardly recognisable as the woman who opened the door to him at "Delta."

He fled into Woolworth's and hid in the gardening section with one eye on the entrance. She came in and looked round, and as she made her way towards the confectionery, he escaped out the door. He was breathless and shaken. He went into a green grocer's he'd never been in before and bought three pounds of parsnips before realising that he'd come for potatoes.

This must never be allowed to happen again, he told himself as he crossed the footbridge, remembering how the other shoppers stared at him.

MacGeoch was in the Arsenal, peering through his telescope when he got home.

"I didn't expect to find you here."

"I had an appointment with the dentist, so I came home early. Come here, Keating, and take an eyeful of this."

"I think you should be ashamed of yourself."

"She's in her beige cavalry twills again. It was so dreary during the winter when she wasn't gardening."

"I don't want you looking at her," Keating said.

"Why?"

"Because I'm fond of her."

"Don't be silly, Keating. It's a free country."

"You're treating her like an object. She is a talented and intelligent woman."

"Keating, I do believe you're in love, but that doesn't mean you own her."

"You can look through your telescope at any other woman you fancy, but not Ann Ede."

"Oh, it's Ann Ede, is it? No longer Mrs. Slim-Bum Gardener."

"I must insist you stop looking at her like that."

"The Colonel will not be amused. If there's one thing he can't stand, it's infatuation."

"I'm not infatuated. We're just friends."

"Don't let her fool you, Keating. You know what the Colonel says? You may wish for a juicy steak, but you mustn't befriend the bullock from which you'll cut it."

"I'll befriend whom I like."

"Then you must live with the complications."

Three police vans came down Raleigh Way and stopped opposite.

"They're going to come in here," Keating said.

"No, they're going to search the woods," MacGeoch told him.

Heavy policemen, like rugby players in uniform, poured out of the vans. Front doors opened and housewives came out of the houses. Three police dogs strained at the leash with snouts upraised.

"They mean business," said MacGeoch. "I suppose we should offer to help."

"They're trained for this sort of work. We'd only find ourselves in the way."

"If the Colonel were here, he'd be directing the show."

"I think we may be due another visit from the police," Keating said.

"We've got nothing to hide."

"I don't like it. Though no one says so, we're all under suspicion."

"That's no way for an officer to talk." MacGeoch went down the stairs.

12

A N hour later, as Keating and MacGeoch went into the woods to see what was happening, they met a policeman coming out.

"Any luck, Officer?" MacGeoch asked.

"She was strangled like the others."

"Did you find the body?"

"Yes, at the far end, buried in ferns."

They walked along the bridle path between the trees, avoiding the patches of poached earth with rainwater lodged in hoof marks. After a while they heard voices coming from behind a clump of rhododendrons and they saw a policeman taking measurements on the ground. The body of a young woman lay half-hidden among ferns and a young man in a donkey jacket was taking photographs on one knee. The police had cordoned off a small area with white tape, and three or four of them were going slowly over the ground. The dead woman was lying on her back with rotting leaves in her hair, her knees exposed, and a torn book on her breast. MacGeoch took a notebook from his pocket and jotted down a few sentences.

"What is the book?" he asked one of the policemen.

"It doesn't have a title. All we know is that it reads like a diary."

"Can I see it?"

"I'm afraid not, sir. We mustn't touch anything till the pathologist arrives."

Keating left MacGeoch talking to the police and walked back to the house. He was so sickened by what he had seen that he barely noticed a group of inquisitive neighbours making for the place he had come from. He knocked back two stiff whiskies before tackling the dinner, but as he diced the stewing steak he could not help thinking that he was probably cook and cupbearer to the man who had murdered her. It was the "probably" that vexed him. There was no certainty, only the nagging of "ifs" and "buts," and of conflicting shards of evidence that he could not share with the police without risking interrogation.

The following morning he was awake at half-past six, waiting for the papers to be delivered. He looked through *The Times*, *The Telegraph* and *The Guardian*, but only *The Telegraph* mentioned the coverless book:

> The dead woman's hands were folded over a torn copy of Quaker George Fox's *Journal,* and for good measure the pages were discoloured with what bibliophiles describe as "fox-marks."

This information gave him an inexplicable lift. It was irrelevant information, but for some reason it distanced the act of murder and reduced the weight of the black fug in his mind.

He was expecting a discussion about George Fox and the Society of Friends over breakfast, but the Colonel was more preoccupied with geese.

"Have you made any enquiries yet?" He turned to Keating.

"I asked the butcher where he buys his geese, but he told me he hadn't bought a goose for over fifteen years."

"We're not going to buy geese but goslings."

"I'll ring round today and see what I can find out."

"No need," said the Colonel. "I've heard of a poultry farmer on the other side of Hadlow. You and I, Keating, will drive out to see him at the weekend and try to persuade him to be a friend."

On Saturday the Colonel and Keating breakfasted early and were knocking on the farmer's door by nine. The farmer was a big, soft man in wide-seated trousers, the kind of man who looked as if he would give you the shirt off his back to oblige. However, he was not willing to oblige the Colonel.

"We're starting a little experiment," the Colonel said. "To begin with, just five or six goslings would do."

"If you'd asked me a month ago, I might have been able to help. I only raise as many birds as I think I'll need, you see, and in the last fortnight I've lost ten of the little blighters."

"The fox?" enquired the Colonel.

"No, the raw weather."

"If it's a question of money. . . ." The Colonel paused.

"It's a question of management. If I were to give you the birds, I'd be short myself. You're in this for a hobby, I'm in it for a living."

"Do you know of any other poultry farmer hereabouts?"

"There aren't many of us in these parts, but if you want a hop-farmer. . . ." He scratched the fringe of curly hair above his left ear.

"If you were looking for five or six goslings, where would you go?" Keating asked.

The farmer scratched his fringe again and laughed. He had one big, brown tooth in the front with a big gap beside it. His other teeth were white and noticeably small.

"Come to think of it, I know a man this side of Paddock Wood who might see you right."

He went into the house and made a phone call. Then he walked with them to the gate and gave them a set of directions of such complexity that the Colonel faced the car north instead of south. After seventy minutes and almost as many wrong turnings, they reached their destination, a dilapidated farm with a broken gate, whose owner looked like a clerical worker from the city posing as a farmer to while away the weekend. He had a long face and a beaked nose and trousers which reached up almost to his armpits. The trousers were heavy with bird droppings, but their great weight was supported by a thick leather belt that reminded Keating of a shaft horse's breeching. He listened to the Colonel with his head tilted like a hen's, appearing to give only half his attention to the business in hand while devoting the other half to monetary calculations of a complexity exceeded only by that of the first farmer's directions.

"You have a problem there." He inhaled sharply through his teeth when the Colonel had done.

"But have you got goslings?"

"I've got goslings all right, but only enough for myself. Now, I could sell you six goose eggs and a clucking hen to hatch them."

"Will a hen sit on goose eggs?" The Colonel sounded doubtful.

"If she's broody enough, she'll sit on beach pebbles."

"It seems highly problematical." The Colonel refused to return the farmer's roguish smile.

"I've known hens to hatch duck eggs and then follow the ducklings to the edge of a pond, scolding like starlings as the young 'uns took to the water."

"If it's a question of money . . ." the Colonel put in.

189

"It is a question of money." The farmer spoke seriously. "If I give you six goslings now, I deny myself the income from their eggs and the income from their carcases when they're ready for the table."

"I appreciate that." The Colonel's hooded eye retreated several centimetres into his head.

"I'll sell you six for sixty-three pounds. I can't say fairer than that."

"That's a bit steep. But I'd be prepared to go as far as fifty."

"Sixty-three pounds." The farmer stuck the fingers of both hands down inside his breeching.

"Why sixty-three?" the Colonel asked.

"Because it's the equivalent of sixty guineas in old money. I was a solicitor's clerk, you see, before I took up farming."

"It is not a sound reason for invoking guineas, but I'll not be niggardly—I'll give you sixty pounds."

"Done," said the farmer.

"It's a bargain then," said the Colonel.

"The goslings I'm going to give you are only five days old and still delicate. You'd better keep them in the house for at least a week. If you put them in a three-foot-square box lined with hay and shavings and warmed by a hundred-watt bulb, they'll stay snug as a bug in a rug till they're hardy."

"Are you taking all this in?" the Colonel asked Keating.

"With respect, I know it already."

The farmer put six goslings in a big cardboard box and the Colonel paid for them.

"Now don't forget to keep them warm, and give them plenty of food and water."

"When can we let them loose in the garden?" the Colonel asked.

"When they're three weeks old, if the weather's warm. And don't forget to give them grit for their gizzards. They'll thrive on nice, short grass, if there's enough of it, but you can cut extra greenstuff wherever you find it, and if you bring it to the garden they'll eat it. If you're flush, you could give them a little grain, but it's not economic to feed them on grain. They don't make flesh as easily as a chicken or a turkey."

"We'll have to find a place to house them," Keating said. "If we leave them in the open, the fox is sure to get them."

"Give them enough space, whatever you do. If they're left cooped up too long, they can get cramp or rheumatism in the joints."

"What sort of house do you suggest?" the Colonel asked.

"As it happens, I have an old apex-type house I no longer use. It's got handles so you can move it to fresh ground once in a while, and it's just big enough for six fully grown birds. I'll let you have it for a tenner, seeing that you're stuck."

He showed them the goose house, which was made of wooden slats, and the Colonel agreed to take it, though not until next week because he didn't have enough ready cash. The farmer walked back with them to the gate, the thumbs of both hands hooked inside his breeching. He talked excitedly, as if pleased with the Colonel's conversation, and he shook the Colonel's hand with genuine warmth as they left.

"Now, don't forget the water," he shouted after them. "They like it to drink, and they like it to bathe their heads."

"We shan't tell the others how much we paid for them," the Colonel reminded Keating. "Garlick is the kind of chap who'd never understand."

Keating put the goslings by the radiator in the kitchen and rigged up a light bulb with a wire guard to keep them warm.

"They're such dotes," said the Colonel, stroking a fluffy breast with his forefinger.

"My word, they look like swans already," said Garlick, "and they're not yet, in a manner of speaking, out of nappies."

"Cygnets, not swans, dear Garlick," said MacGeoch. "As gentlemen of the press, we ought to get these things right."

"We'll treat them well, we'll give them a choice of milk and water." Keating filled two saucers.

"Madness, madness." Garlick shook his head. "A woman's been found murdered in the woods, all Wistwood's talking of nothing else, and all you three can do is dote on goslings."

"As usual, you've got it wrong, Garlick." The Colonel was contemptuous. "Wistwoodlanders are not talking of murder. They're talking of the fox, and they'll not talk of murder until it becomes a status symbol, which even in Wistwood is somewhat unlikely."

"You're right, Colonel," said MacGeoch. "Not a word was said about murder on the train all week."

In spite of the goslings, Keating could not ignore the question at the back of his mind. Admittedly, he made every possible effort to ignore it. He dug the garden and painted the guttering and reassembled the goose house, which the Colonel brought back the following weekend, but in the end it seemed to weigh on his mind like an angry sky pressing on a mountain before a storm. If only he had someone to talk to. He crossed the road and knocked on Ann Ede's door.

"Where are you going for Easter?" she asked.

"I'm staying here."

"The Bagman and I are going to Greece. In spite of his bagmanship, he's a confirmed Hellenophile. He simply can't get enough retsina."

"I shall miss you," he said.

"And I shall be sorry to miss the English Easter. Unlike Christmas, it hasn't yet been taken over by the paynims. For them it's just another long weekend, time to dig the garden, go to the seaside or for a picnic, while the real Easter remains unsullied. I find that enormously encouraging, don't you? For once we have something the paynims haven't defiled. For us it's a secret festival, because only we can hear the singing within. And another thing, the Easter liturgy is inexpressibly more glorious than the Christmas liturgy. It has about it something of the purity of the Middle Ages."

"Ann, I wanted to talk to you."

"What about?"

"I don't know yet."

"Well, I haven't got time now. I must finish my painting before we go away. Otherwise the thread of continuity will be lost. You can come up and watch me if you like . . . but you must promise not to talk."

He went back to "Foxgloves" wondering if he should talk to the Colonel, but the Colonel might conceivably be the very man not to talk to. It was a step he could not take lightly, so he spent Easter on a ladder painting the windows in silence. The road below was empty. Now and again, however, a girl on horseback would come by and look up at him. Suburban man was at Margate, Broadstairs or Herne Bay, but a few deviant members of the species pottered about, jacking up their cars, polishing their number plates, or preparing for a family expedition to the municipal dump. For all her fanaticism, he longed for Ann Ede, and as if in answer to his longing a postcard arrived for him before the end of the week. He read it four or five times, lingering over the minute hand, which he realised he was seeing for the first time:

Dear Charles: My guide book has a Who's Who on Mount Olympus, but so far I've seen no gods, only the modern satyr on every side, slim, suntanned, priapic and invariably Teutonic. The ouzo is cloying, the retsina foul. All I can eat with any confidence is souvlakia, but the Bagman makes up for me. He puts at least a kilo of red mullet, which he calls barbouni, in his tote bag every day. Yesterday he ate a plate of sea urchins and promptly called for another. He has a gut of leather, he's as regular as the 8:15 fast to Cannon Street, while I who keep to safe souvlakia have to resort to kaolin. Will justice ever be done? There are times when the Last Trump seems very far away. See you soon, I hope at Massah. Love but no kisses,

Ann

She came back a week later, but he still did not confide in her. She looked clean and suntanned, and she gave him a plate of whelks which filled the house with a sea smell that vanquished her own. The weather was warm for April, so they sat on her patio until it was time for lunch.

One morning, as he talked to her, he was filled with an unaccountable sense of peace, of distance from irritation and perturbation. He lifted his eyes, surprised to find no hills on the horizon. He was sheltered by silver birches. He would sit in their shadow and the sun would not burn him by day. His feeling of security was only transient, however. He sensed in his heart that an invisible net was descending ineluctably on "Foxgloves," and he knew he should flee before he was discovered for a man who was not what he seemed to be.

"It would be nice to drive out to a country pub for a drink one day." She cut his reverie short.

"A good idea."

"The Bagman will be going to a weekend seminar in the middle of May. When he's away, we'll make our own of the Sunday morning."

Her suggestion surprised him because he had the impression that she did not like pubs. However, when the day came, he got a pass from the Colonel and left a cold beef salad on the side-table for lunch. It was a warm morning, full of the scent of cherry and apple blossom, and she drove briskly in stock-inged feet, taking corners with careless ease.

"You drive as if you enjoyed it."

"But are you enjoying it?"

"Tremendously."

"You Irish have the knack of not caring how you ride. The

194

Bagman pretends to be nervous in anything smaller than a Mercedes."

"Where are we going?"

"To a village pub beyond Chelsfield. It will be nice to see green fields and young cabbages."

"And farmers, real farmers," he added.

At Chelsfield they saw two horses grazing, and further on a herd of Friesians, a farm house and a tractor that surprised him into realising that within a half-hour's drive of Wistwood was real countryside with real people doing real work on land with a family history. They stopped in a tiny village full of parked cars, outside an ancient pub looking across a winding river.

"The farmers hereabouts have a taste for swanky cars." He opened the pub door on which was pinned a notice saying "No muddy footwear or backpacks."

"I've seen farmers with muddy boots, but never backpacks." She laughed.

He got her a dry sherry and himself a pint of bitter, and they found a hard wooden seat in a corner under the low, smoke-stained ceiling. The place was packed with lithe young men and their talkative girl friends, and middle-aged men with fat cigars and silent wives who smiled enigmatically, as if they had only one word to say and were determined to keep it till last.

"I love it here on Sunday mornings." She placed her hand on his thigh, as if she had taken it for her own. "The Bagman doesn't agree, though. He prefers 'The Fox and Billet.'"

"I've never been inside it."

"You've missed nothing. I once went in with the Bagman and all I found was a prize collection of capons pretending to be cocks crowing on their dunghills."

"I'm told they do a sumptuous spread on Sunday mornings."

"But not chicken in a basket. I love chicken in a basket. They do it here."

The pressure of her hand on his thigh caused a perceptible tremor in his crotch, giving a pleasurably high reading on the Richter Scale of Magnitude.

"Who comes to eat the chicken in the basket? Surely not the farmers who raised it? Surely a farmer would prefer it on a plate."

"Surely you must know these people aren't farmers."

"They're too pale for farmers," he agreed.

"They're professional men and businessmen, men for whom the Four Last Things are a golden handshake, an index-linked pension, a round of golf and a country cottage."

"Is there any corner of the Home Counties that is not a dormitory of London?"

"Stop grumbling. Is it not the clash of city and country that gives the Home Counties their faint flavour of fantasy?"

"I should like to go to a pub with real farmers."

"Don't be childish. After another drink you'll feel more at ease, and then we'll have chicken in a basket. If you don't like that, you can have pâté and toast."

"A picnic would be nice."

"What a splendid idea! We'll have chicken in a basket to take away."

"What about the basket? Won't the landlord want it back?"

"Now, don't fuss. Just leave everything to me."

After he had bought another drink, he thought it was time to confide in her.

"Do you ever think of these murders? Do they ever keep you awake at night?"

"Only when the Bagman's out late. When he's in the next room, I sleep like a log."

"I think about them every day. They often keep me awake till three in the morning."

"What do you think about?"

"I keep thinking the murderer is close to me like a brother, as if I had some satanic insight into his thoughts."

"You mean you have a theory about who it is?"

"Not a theory," he retreated. "I just feel I understand how the murders came about. I abhor murder, but in my dreams I feel sympathy for the murderer."

"How very Christian of you! Hate the sin but love the sinner."

"If it were that, I shouldn't mind. On the contrary, I sometimes feel I could easily be the murderer myself."

"You have a too tender conscience, that's your trouble."

"I think most men want to murder some woman during their lives. I think all men, in that sense, are guilty."

"You're troubled, Charles. You should delay no longer, you should go to confession."

"But I have nothing to confess."

"Nonsense."

"I have nothing to confess that a priest has power to absolve."

"You overestimate your capacity for originality. To a confessor everything is old hat. It's all been done before."

"A priest can only absolve a sinner with a firm purpose of amendment. He is powerless if the sinner refuses to acknowledge the possibility of grace."

"Come to Mass with me next Sunday, Charles. If you do, you will not be alone. You will be surrounded by guiltier men, men who have spent the week with their fingers in the muddy pond of commerce, indulging their egos, terrorising office typists. As I sit in the pew beside them, I cannot help marvelling at how I escape contamination. And I think, how wonderful, how Christlike, to worship with guilty men, to be the kid that lies down with the leopard—if only for an hour.

So, come to Mass and listen to the Psalmist with men who are guiltier than you:

> As for man, his days are as grass:
> As a flower of the field, so he flourisheth;
> For the wind passeth over it, and it is gone;
> And the place thereof shall know it no more.

"The power of those words dwarf all human effort. They tell the adulterer that the flesh he craves is already withered, the businessman that profit and loss are equally illusory, and they would say to you that your obsession with your sins is a form of pride, the sin that unseated Lucifer."

"If you thought you knew the murderer, what would you do?"

"Do you know him?"

"No."

"Then why do you ask?"

"It simply interests me."

"I think you're obsessed with evil, Charles. I'll order chicken in a basket for two while you're finishing your drink."

She came back with the food as well as a litre of white wine and two glasses, and they drove farther out into the country until they found a field without animals. Then she spread a rug on the ground, and they ate the chicken and chips and drank the wine while she told him about Greece and the Bagman's superb contempt for anything he couldn't swallow. Sleepy after the meal and the wine, she lay on her back on the rug with her arm over her eyes and her breasts poking like pinnacles through the white cotton of her blouse. He lay on his side, considering the bulge of her breasts, chewing a blade of grass, and calculating the chances of appeasing the erection in his left trouser leg.

He put down his hand and drew it up so that it lay less

uncomfortably against his belly. Then, with unhurried craftiness he surveyed the terrain. Her trousers were tight and creaseless, the mound at her crotch like a dome without a spire. He had never tackled a woman in trousers before, and he had no idea where to start. You couldn't start down at the ankle and put your hand up her calf because of the tightness of the trouser leg, so presumably you had to start at the midriff where the zip was. But where was the zip? It wasn't in the front. Could it conceivably be at the back? And if it was at the back, would he manage to turn her on her belly without making his purpose too obvious?

He thought hard for a moment. She was brought up among sophisticated men who would proceed cautiously from camp one to camp two. Presumably she knew how to deal with such men, but would she know how to deal with a man who skipped camp one and went straight to camp two? He put his hand in his pocket and felt his erection. It had the right degree of stiffness and perpendicularity for the ascent, and moreover weather conditions were good. Visibility was excellent and the wind had fallen to a breeze. He checked his watch and put on his crampons. It was precisely 3:57 P.M. He would start the ascent at four o'clock exactly so that it would be easier to calculate how long it took.

Come to think of it, the crampons are a mistake, he thought. I'll sling them and take the funicular as any gentleman of leisure would.

Still on his side, he moved closer to her and simultaneously kissed the ethereal pappus on her cheek and put his left leg over her groin so that his penis nestled against the smoothness of her thigh.

"What's that?" She woke from her dream with terror on her suntanned face.

With one spring he was astride her, the bulge of his tickler against the bulge of her mound, his chest flattening her breasts, his cocked lips seeking her averted mouth.

"Get off me, you beast."

"Ah, give us a kiss," he pleaded lamely.

"If you don't get down off me this minute, I'll never speak to you again." She threatened with all the impregnability of a woman inside tight cavalry twill trousers.

With as little loss of male dignity as was possible in the circumstances, he abseiled down her thigh, telling himself that though he had lost a battle he would win the war.

"I love you, Ann. It came over me suddenly as you slept."

"How do you know you love me?"

"I get an erection whenever you come near me."

"That's lust, not love."

"And I keep wishing to kiss you in the most unorthodox places."

"Worse than lust. That's perversion."

"Not with me. I'm not really a gross man. I've never entertained a heterodox sexual desire till I met you."

"You should go to confession."

"I'm not giving up. I'm going to keep trying till you consent to make love to me."

"Then you're going about it in a strange way. You attacked me like a bear—"

"I did it out of helplessness."

"Shall I let you in on a secret? I never do it lying down, always standing up."

"Why do you tell me if you don't want me?"

"Because it's useless information, dear Charles, utterly academic." She laughed warmly in his incredulous ear.

On the way back they stopped at a fair in a field near Chelsfield village. He followed her from stall to stall with a pain in his heart, or perhaps near to his heart, which he knew to be ridiculous in a man of thirty-six. She was looking at trinkets and women's clothes and talking to him un-selfconsciously, as if she was his wife. She picked up an orange blouse and held it over her breasts with the afternoon sun on the freckles of her face.

"Do you like it?"

The orange of the blouse seemed to glow through her cheeks, and he asked himself if she was an innocent schoolgirl or a heartless witch.

"It makes you look vaguely Greek, like a merry Greek, in fact."

"I shan't buy it then." She led the way to the car.

A police car was parked outside "Foxgloves" when they got back.

"What's happening?" He fiddled with the safety belt to conceal his sudden panic.

"You'd better find out."

"When does your husband come back?"

"Not till tomorrow."

"If you like, I'll look in on you this evening."

"Okay. But none of your ursine pranks, please."

He got out of the car and looked up longingly at the horse chestnuts in full leaf. Someone was burning twigs in a nearby garden. A woman in a yellow dress was waiting for her poodle to pee against a lamp post. He got out his key and reluctantly opened the door.

"What's going on?" he asked Garlick, who was reading the Sunday papers in the dining-room.

"The police are interviewing MacGeoch."

"Why MacGeoch?"

"They've done the Colonel and myself. They're reinterviewing every man in Wistwood."

"I suppose I'm next."

"I suppose you are," Garlick said without looking up.

The two policemen were sitting on the settee in the lounge

when he entered. One of them smiled and the other said his name, or at least the name by which he chose to be known. They told him they were going over the ground again, turning up every stone, re-examining every shred of evidence, and getting people to remember things they might otherwise overlook.

"It's a time-consuming business," said the one who smiled. "But someone in Wistwood, without knowing it, knows the murderer. Someone, without knowing it, has the evidence we need to crack the case."

They asked him a score of questions, not questions about his past, he was relieved to find, but questions about the people he met and what he himself thought about the murders.

"Why do you think he picks on women?"

"Maybe it's because they're not as strong as men."

"Would you say he hates women?"

"It's very likely."

He decided to seek anonymity in conventional wisdom. What they were looking for was a man who would say something no one else had thought of.

"Why do you think he only attacks women from the other side?"

"I don't really know, but it's possible he may have been jilted by a woman from Wistwood West."

"You don't think he's a snob?"

"It would be taking snobbery rather far."

"Have you wondered why his last victim was found on this side?"

"I've heard the local gossip. I heard she was visiting a man."

"Where would you look for the murderer, in Wistwood East or Wistwood West?"

"In both. A madman could live on either side of the railway."

"Would you confine your investigations to Wistwood?"

"No."

"Why?"

"Because most of the other crimes committed here—burglaries, muggings, etcetera—are done by youngsters who come in from other areas for an evening."

"Why do you think he leaves a trademark on his victims?"

"He probably sees himself as the Wistwood Fox."

"But he had already left a fox-fur and some foxtail before the press gave him his nickname."

"They're jokey references. He may just have a warped sense of humour."

"Have you ever heard anyone talk about the fox here?"

"Since these murders started, many people wonder why this particular trademark."

"Thank you, Mr. Keating." They got up to go.

"Did the spelling test not throw up anything?" he asked.

"It didn't work. All it showed was how few people can spell. In fact only five people in all Wistwood got the complete list right. You will be interested to know that four of them live here at 'Foxgloves.'"

Keating laughed, and the policemen smiled as he led them to the door. When they had gone he went up to his room and poured himself a large whisky. His hands were trembling. His heart was racing. And he kept asking himself what precisely they had hoped to learn from him.

13

As a place of trees, Wistwood found glory in May. In the roads the chestnuts put forth white and pink birthday candles, while in the gardens pink apple blossoms turned white, rowan trees turned cream as cauliflowers, and in the distance the reddish brown of copper beeches wrestled with the deep pink of chestnuts for the right to festoon red brick chimneys. This hosanna to the spring seemed as if it would last forever, but one night in the third week of May a stiff wind covered the pavements in drifts of white and pink.

He got up at six because the murders and murderer were on his mind. As he shaved in the bathroom, the early sun picked out his newly made garden path and a recently full moon, a transparent disc with one side slightly worn, melted into the southern sky. The trees at the back of the garden were a hundred shades of green, with shadows between the branches that increased the three-dimensional effect, making a mere twenty of them into a wood of depth and mystery. From where he stood he could not see even one roof or chimney, and he could only marvel at such a cunningly contrived illusion of rurality, and at the strange chance that had brought him to this place in which nothing was as it seemed.

The Colonel returned late from town the previous night, humming an aria from Verdi as was his wont after three or four hours at his club. He asked for MacGeoch and Garlick, who were already in bed, and commanded Keating to prepare him an omelette à la savoyarde.

"A little heavy for so late an hour?" Keating suggested. "A soufflé, for example, might be more appropriate."

"No. I fell asleep on the train and woke up at Sevenoaks dreaming of an omelette à la savoyarde. . . . There's a bibacity that shapes our ends . . . I could think of nothing else on the next train back."

Keating made him the omelette and bore it into the dining-room on a silver plate, but the Colonel was so deep in poetry that he did not notice. He was reading to himself aloud, and as he read, a tremor of feeling in his voice brought a tear to his sunken eye:

> They shall grow not old, as we that are left grow old:
> Age shall not weary them, nor the years condemn.
> At the going down of the sun and in the morning
> We will remember them.

"Have you ever been moved by poetry, Keating?" he asked as he closed the book.

"Only by nature poetry."

"What about love poetry?"

"No."

"Not even Donne's?"

"His least of all."

"You're silent by preference, Keating. I get the impression that when you speak you do so only out of politeness. Some men speak as if language were a loud hailer, and others speak as if it were a thick layer of cotton wool. These men in their hearts would rather think and be silent. What do you think of when you're silent?"

He looked warily at the Colonel, who was performing a delicate operation on the omelette, holding his knife like a scalpel while he ate with a forceps that seemed too small for his hand. For a moment Keating wondered how far he could go without giving anything away.

"These days I think of the murders."

"Which murders?"

"In Wistwood there is only one set of murders to think of."

"But will thinking stop them?"

"Don't you think about them?"

"I prefer to think of something more amusing. I pay income tax to provide a police force that will do that kind of thinking for me."

"I find it hard to believe that you can shut it all so easily from your mind. I wish I could."

"What's your problem, Captain?"

"I'm pursued by a sense of immanent evil. I can smell it in the aroma of apple blossom, I can see the shape of it in the clouds, and I can see the colour of it—"

"What colour is it?"

"Purple. A deeply luxurious purple."

"And what shape is it?"

"When it has a shape, it looks like a comfortable divan behind heavy drapes."

"I think you need another visit from the M.O. Perhaps we all need a visit from the M.O."

"I wasn't joking," Keating said. "I do have a sense of sharing the murderer's guilt. I have dreamt, for example, that I myself was to blame. . . ."

"Extraordinary."

"If you dream at night that you are the murderer, you can't entirely escape his guilt during the day. You might even come to feel a hideous rapport with the man."

"You've obviously been brooding too much. Perhaps a little

holiday is what you need. Why not go to the seaside for a long weekend?"

"You may be right, but I'm convinced that I'm not the only man who thinks this way."

"I myself don't go in for all this communal guilt. In my view the murderer is guilty and no one else. Your problem, Keating, is that you've been reading too much liberal crap. It's even more insidious than Christianity itself. If you take that bullshit seriously, you'll next be accusing yourself of rapes, muggings, black riots and football hooliganism. Remember, Keating, you owe all those feelings to the feminine side of your nature. It is not the side we seek to encourage in the army."

The Colonel is not so easily drawn, he told himself as he wiped the lather off his ear lobes.

He went downstairs, made some mash for the goslings, and left it by the sink so that the Colonel could feed them personally before going to the office. They were now over two months old and they had grown quite big and hardy. He had wired off the bottom half of the garden, not only as a protection against the fox but to keep the upper half and the patio free of droppings.

He decided to let them out to graze while the dew was still on the grass. Farmer Giles saw him from the window and came down the garden to the fence, his hair still uncombed, his grey stubble unshaven.

"You're only making a bed of nails for yourself." He shook his head. "When those bleeders get bigger, we won't get a wink of sleep at night. They'll be awake and cackling with every fox that pokes his head over the wire."

"They've been good so far."

"You don't seem to mind the mess they make."

"They're not dirty . . . compared with pigs."

"I had a friend who kept geese in Scotland. I know all about their watery droppings. Wait till the weather gets warm. We'll not be able to stand the stink."

"It's only the beginning." Keating laughed. "Within two years every garden in Wistwood East will have its own flock of geese."

"I know one that won't." Farmer Giles puffed his way back to the house.

After breakfast Keating went to the bottom of the garden and sat in what he called his "bothy" between two closely growing conifers. He had made himself a stone seat from broken paving slabs and cut away the intertwining branches close to the ground so that he could sit in comfort, surrounded on all sides by trees, and observe the goslings graze without himself being seen. The secrecy of his seat gave him a kind of boyish pleasure. He pulled out his book of Irish nature poetry and read the poem about the hermit who had a bothy in a wood:

> The doorsteps are of heather,
> The lintel of honeysuckle;
> And wild forest all around
> Drops mast for well-fed swine.

He tried to write a nature poem himself, but by eleven o'clock, thirst and the lack of a rhyme had so defeated him that he rang up Ann Ede and invited her to lunch.

"I've had an inspiration," she said as he opened the door. "We'll both go to Aylesford Priory for a weekend."

"And what shall we do at Aylesford Priory?"

"Meditate, talk to the white friars, go for walks, and eat wholesome home cooking.'"

"Curiously enough, I was thinking of going to the seaside for a couple of days. The sea air would be more bracing than the cloister. Will you come?"

"Only if you promise to come to Aylesford first."

"I'll think about it," he said.

He did think about it, and promised the following week that he would go. It was, he felt, a small price to pay for a weekend with her by the sea. She made the plans. They would drive to Aylesford on the first Saturday of June and after a day and two nights of fasting, prayer and meditation they'd come back on Monday, refreshed, renewed and, she hoped, in a state of grace. She rang him on Saturday morning with the news that her car had broken down and that the Bagman was driving in his to a convention of bagmen in Birmingham.

"We can put it off till next weekend." He felt slightly relieved.

"No, I'm too excited to wait. We'll go by train." She had already made up her mind.

Saturday morning was warm and calm. He got up early to do the shopping, unable to suppress a flutter of excitement in his chest which reminded him of how he used to feel as a schoolboy before a school outing. Shortly after eleven they took a train from Wistwood to Orpington where they were to get another to Paddock Wood, and then to Aylesford.

"You'll like the Priory dining hall," she told him on the platform. "It's the old fifteenth-century pilgrim's hall restored. In a sense we're taking a train back to the Middle Ages. Aren't you excited?" She tugged at his sleeve.

"Watch yourself on him. He's not the lamb he looks."

Keating turned to find a wild-eyed Mrs. Stooke standing behind them. She had aged since he last saw her. The skin of her neck was loose and grey, and her cheeks sagged under an excess of makeup.

"He made a fool of me. Don't let him fool you. He'll tell you he loves you, but all he wants is to drink your water. Don't be shocked. He even knows the word for it—uriposia. Got it in his precious encyclopedia, or so he says."

"She's a raving lunatic." Keating pulled Ann away.

"He's a muff-diver too," she shouted after them. "Keep your legs closed tight or he'll drink your army and navy."

"What is a muff-diver?" Ann asked him when they were out of earshot.

"I have no idea."

"Do you know her?"

"I think I saw her once in the library."

"He'll try to sell you his encyclopedia. He'll show you his F-volume, wait and see, but don't have anything to do with him. It's the worst encyclopedia on the market." Mrs. Stooke had caught up with them again.

Luckily, their train came in. He pushed Ann through the door and found a seat on the far side. He was breathless and shaken, but he smiled at Ann as they pulled out of the station.

"She should be locked up in the nearest loony bin," he said.

"She sounded as if she had meant every word. She obviously confused you with someone else."

"Another bagman." He laughed. "A seller of inferior encyclopedias."

The sun shone on trees and houses, and on gardens aflame with lupins, purple and pink. Below them a line of cars glided like mechanical toys along a ribbon of motorway, and farther on a field sloped with fallen apple blossom like white daisies in the grass. He opened a window for coolness and remembered cold mornings in Lent as he grew up in Cork. He was a mass server, shivering in a frozen surplice as his stomach folded over emptiness, seeking to grasp at the food he had not eaten. High requiem masses were the worst. They lasted well over an hour, and they always seemed to be held in frost—in a cold church with cold earth in the graveyard and cold priests chanting. Fasting from the previous midnight, he would bow low at the *Confiteor* and cast a sidelong glance at the black chasubles of the deacon and subdeacons while his body stiffened against the prod of icicles in his belly. Little did he know then that as a man his whole vocation would be the recovery of the knowledge of death he so took for granted as an altar boy.

"Are you happy?" she asked him.

"More or less."

"A frown passed over your forehead, as if you'd had a sudden pain."

"It was only a memory. A memory of childhood."

"What would you wish for, to be completely happy?"

"To live with you on what you Anglo-Saxons, in less prosaic days, called a twisla."

"A twisla? Never heard of it."

"On a tongue of land in a river fork."

"It's a bizarre wish."

"And what do you wish for?"

"To live in a wood in springtime in the Middle Ages, or at least in an age before the ice of negative experience burnt the heart of humanity. In such a wood and at such a time, the love of God would augment the love of nature and the love of nature would glorify God."

"Strangely enough, I've often wished for something similar, the coenobitic life of early Christian Ireland, when solitary monks had birds and animals for friends and saw in the beauty of nature the radiant face of God."

"One thing we must remember. We share a faith, you and I, though one of us is no longer a practitioner."

"More accurate to say that we share a respect for lives in which the senses are not the only doors of experience."

They walked from the station to the Priory and spent a blissful hour strolling in the grounds. Though they were only two hours from Wistwood, the murders and the murderer seemed far away. He walked with her through a soaring nave of trees, while her thoughts danced among the shafts of sunlight that pierced the leaf-roof above them. She was no longer merely the sum of her opinions. She was a caring and enriching woman, and there was nothing he wanted more than a daughter from her womb. He grasped her hand and asked some god somewhere to make her think him worthy of her, but she pulled away, telling him that she had come to be quiet.

He left her to meditate and nipped down to the village for a pint of bitter in "The Little Gem." It was half dark inside but the sun was shining on the clematis by the door, casting spangles on the blouse of a girl across from him. He looked up at the pair of hames above the lintel, hearing the voice of the Colonel and the sycophantic laughter of MacGeoch.

"If there's one thing better than a goose, it's a goose and duck," the Colonel said.

"And if there's one thing better than being goosed, it's being ducked." The Major split his sides.

He had escaped from the obliquities of "Foxgloves" into the world of the Four Last Things, and now, though Ann Ede would not agree, he was enjoying the third, or at least enjoying a foretaste.

"Have you had a look round?" she asked him the following morning.

"I've been to the gents. Very impressive."

"They get lots of pilgrims. The faithful come in busloads on retreat."

"I deduced as much. In the gents I counted thirty-two urinals, six handbasins, four loos, and two warm-air hand driers."

"Is that all you've got out of it?"

"I can't help noticing. I'm a journalist."

"There's only one cure for you: confession. You mustn't leave here without going."

"But I didn't come to go."

"You came to find peace."

"No, I came to be with you."

"If I'd known that, I wouldn't have let you come. I'm certain, however, that you're not telling yourself the truth. Your trouble is that you don't trust yourself enough to achieve what you truly desire. There are two men inside you. One is intuitive and open to all experience, a man who senses the flesh in the spirit and the spirit in the flesh, and who knows that for him the only true and authentic experience is his own. The other is clever and worldly-wise. He rejects the materialism of his contemporaries but he cannot forget their possessions. He has read philosophies of reduction and negation and rejected them too, but he is worried by the thought that someone may have written them out of experience. Charles, you are too much put upon by other lives. Forget them for one weekend. Remember that even the best is only responding to the pull of personal compulsion. If you are to be judged by your actions, let them be actions that are authentic to you, performed according to the glimmer of light that is your own."

"One thing I know: I didn't come here to be classified." He laughed to end the conversation.

Nevertheless, he knelt beside her that afternoon in the Priory chapel, while one of the friars heard confessions. She went first, and came back and squeezed his hand. Then he entered the dark confessional and carefully closed the door. As he waited, the whispers of the penitent on the other side and then the priest's softly spoken absolution filled him with a premonition of impossibility. The window slid open and the large ear of the confessor on the other side of the grille seemed to demand a confession of such enormity that it might cause even Herod himself to regret the inadequacy of his iniquities.

"Bless me, Father," he lisped the familiar opening formula, then stopped because he couldn't remember what came next.

"How long since your last confession?"

"A long time, Father."

"Judging by the way you're going about it, I would say it

was before Vatican Two. That was in 1962, twenty years ago."

"No, it isn't that long. I went to confession in 1970."

"And what have you been up to since then?"

"Much badness and little good."

"Be more specific, my child."

Keating told him his most grievous sin, which must remain secret since the seal of the confessional is not to be broken.

"Any other sins?" The priest inclined a floppy ear.

"The remainder are small beer by comparison."

"You are obliged to confess all your mortal sins, my son."

He recited a list of sins so exhaustive that he could only marvel at such unremitting application in the cause of Satan. He felt that he should have given the past more thought before entering the confessional, but he couldn't retreat now.

"Are you sorry for all these transgressions?"

"I'm sorry for most of them."

"But most is not enough. Are you willing to put matters right?"

"I can't put matters right."

"Then you can't be said to have a firm purpose of amendment."

"I knew what that meant before Vatican Two. What does it mean now?"

"The confessional is a place for contrition, not flippancy."

"I'm genuinely at a loss, Father."

"Having a firm purpose of amendment means having a willingness to make amends, where possible, and a firm resolve not to sin again."

"Then I haven't got a firm purpose of amendment."

"And I cannot give you absolution. The confessor's power to absolve sin is limited only by the penitent's lack of true sorrow."

"I might find a less strict priest."

"Even if you did find a priest willing to give you absolution, his words, without your sorrow, would only be an empty formula. Go away, my child, and pray for God's mercy and the grace to live by the light of your conscience. Pray for single-mindedness in the pursuit of truth, and pray for me because I too need prayer."

He returned to the pew and Ann grasped his hand.

"What penance did he give you?" she asked as they emerged into the afternoon sun.

"Six Our Fathers and six Hail Marys," he lied.

"You got off lightly." She laughed excitedly. "I'm so pleased that I helped, if only in a small way, to bring you back."

He was up before her the following morning and he went to the first mass in the chapel. It was refreshing to hear the words of Isaiah again followed by the poetry of the Psalms. He had not seen the inside of a church for over ten years. He felt excited and at the same time ill at ease, as if he were the wedding guest without a wedding garment. There was so much that was wonderful in what she believed, and so much that he could only reject. It was a pity you couldn't choose the bits you liked and forget about the rest. You had to swallow it hook, line and sinker or not at all. He regretted that he was unable to receive Communion, and, when she assumed later that he had, he could not bring himself to disillusion her.

Monday was gusty and dry. They caught a train in mid-morning and sat alone in the sunlit compartment without saying much. Now and again she would look at him and smile, but he didn't want to speak in case he should disperse the aureole of numinous excitement that surrounded her. He felt excited himself. He couldn't believe that he was returning to the worldly concerns of "Foxgloves." He seemed to have been away so long.

"Are you pleased you came?" she asked, after they'd changed at Paddock Wood.

"Yes, I am."

"What have you come away with?"

"A sense of spaciousness within myself. Before I went, I had the feeling that I was at the mercy of every suburban Tom, Dick and Harry. Whatever is inside me was becoming moss-grown."

"You mean your soul?"

"Something like that. Whatever it is, it's now clean like a bone on a shore—scoured by wind, sand and seawater."

"For me it was different. I was drowning in a disused canal. I've been pulled out and I'm standing on the towpath with the sun on my shoulders."

"If we can keep the world at arm's length even till we get to Orpington, we'll have achieved something."

She suddenly turned, caught his head between her hands, and sucked the breath from between his lips with a kiss. He put his hand between her knees and felt the gloss of her copper-coloured, copper-bottomed, fifteen-denier tights.

"Not there," she said, taking his hand and putting it over her left breast.

"It was a hungry kiss." He laughed.

"It was a Christian kiss. I thought I heard the truth on your lips for a change, and I wished to taste it."

He kissed her on the lips again and she responded as if he had a veritable monopoly of the truth. She was like an autumn crabapple that's been seasoned in a haystack, hard and sweet-smelling with a hint of sourness overcome. Kissing her was like saying boo to Newton and his law of gravity. A gust of perfumed wind lifted him like a feather high over a hill. He floated and soared and dived and then floated upwards again. The train stopped and they both looked out of the window. They seemed to be in the middle of nowhere, opposite a stand

216

of chestnuts decked out in cone-shaped blossoms. The wind was ruffling the leaves, making the cones bob up and down like riders on horseback. She caught his hand and led him out of the carriage to the toilet at the end. He locked the door. The train started again. She kicked off her shoes and pulled off her tights, which she stuffed like a handkerchief into his breast pocket.

He put her standing against the door, but the swaying of the train made negotiation difficult. He pulled down his trousers and sat on the lavatory seat. She lowered herself gently into position, filling him with a succession of sensations so heavenly that he visualised a sky of exploding fireworks replacing one another endlessly.

The train wobbled over points. He was in a small boat, rowing through a cutting against the current, with a bank of high reeds on both sides. The cutting was narrow and airless and the only sound was the lisp of the water in the reed stumps and the faint rustle of the pennant leaves above them. Suddenly he looked over his shoulder and saw that he'd come to the end of the channel. Unbelievably, it had opened out into a flat, wide lake, full of the dancing sunlight of rejoicement. He shipped the oars and held his breath. He was the only one on the water. A perfumed breeze played in the collar of his open shirt. The sun warmed his shoulders, filling him with the sensation of a greater warmth being cooled. It was a moment of unparalleled perfection. He knew that there was a hamlet on the opposite shore and a wooden jetty where he could put in. He bent over the oars and rowed without looking over his shoulder till the gunwale grazed the black planks and he made fast the painter to one of the rings.

The boat rocked unaccountably. She began sneezing, and with each sneeze she tightened on him below until he thought his whole body would burn with the acceleration of sensation.

217

"I can't believe it. I've committed adultery," she said when it was over.

"Don't think of it like that. For me it was too precious to be given a label."

"At least it was with another Catholic."

"Does that matter?"

"Of course it matters." She laughed. "The coupling of paynims is as significant as the coupling of hamsters."

They returned to their compartment and she sat with her head on his shoulder until they arrived at Orpington. He held her hand and looked out of the window, filled with a sense of sunlight on calm water.

14

"I HAD what you might call a timely idea as I woke up this
morning," the Colonel said when Keating had served the
after-dinner coffee.

"What was that?" MacGeoch affected immediate interest.

"We shall hold a waygoose on August twenty-fourth to
which we shall invite the cream of Wistwood West to meet the
cream of Wistwood East."

"What is a waygoose?" Keating enquired.

"Traditionally, it was an annual beanfeast given by a master
printer to his journeymen round Saint Bartholomew's Day to
mark the beginning of the season of working by candle light.
He not only filled them with good food and strong drink but
he also gave them pocket money to spend at the alehouse. I
suppose we could give the Westmen a fiver each to spend at
'The Fox and Billet' on the way home."

"What right have we to hold a waygoose?" Garlick demanded.

"I know we're not master printers," the Colonel told him.
"We're one better, however. We're the master journalists who
write the words that keep the master printers in business."

"I seem to remember that a printer's annual staff outing is

properly called a 'wayzgoose,' not a 'waygoose.'" Garlick could not help indulging in a little nit-picking.

"Westmen, I'm sure, may call it a 'wayzgoose,' but Eastmen prefer the older, more established form. What I'm really saying, my dear Lance-corporal, is that your spiritual home is the West."

"Am I right in thinking that we shall give them roast goose for supper?" Keating asked.

"You are indeed, Captain, though not for the reason you think. There is no historical evidence to support the belief that goose was the *pièce de résistance* at a master printer's waygoose. However, as our geese will be fat by Saint Bartholomew's Day, we shall take the opportunity of introducing our fellow Wistwoodlanders to a dish which most of them have heard about but few have tasted. So, you see, my dear Keating, how much depends on your culinary skills. The purpose of our waygoose will be to send Eastmen home determined to raise a flock of geese next year in their gardens and to send Westmen home with a better appreciation of the mode of life to which their betters would like to be accustomed."

"Well put, Colonel," said MacGeoch. "What you are really saying is that we at 'Foxgloves' have a duty to both East and West."

"The French have a word for it," said the Colonel. "*Noblesse oblige.*"

"You oversimplify East and West." Garlick spoke directly to the Colonel. "I know at least one Westman who always has goose at Michaelmas and at least one other who has goose at Christmas. Just as I know several Eastmen who are on this side only by virtue of their income from second-hand car dealing, and who disgrace us all by their preference for meat vindaloo and sweet and sour pork. If you wish to impress the gentrified upstarts we are condemned to live with here, you should forget about goose and get Keating to reheat their favourite nosh from the Chinese take-away."

"If you think so highly of the West, you should go west," the Colonel almost spat at him. "If there's one thing I can't stand, Lance-jack, it's disaffection."

Life at "Foxgloves" became more unpredictable every day. First it was the fox, then the goose. And now it was the way-goose. What, he asked himself, would it be tomorrow? He made up his mind that he must escape while he was still in touch with reality, though at times he saw more truth in the Colonel's fantasy world than in any "real" world he had so far encountered here. It was the Colonel's truth, not Keating's, however. What the Colonel did was to take certain representative parts and make them stand for the whole. They did not transcend the whole, but they were bolder, more striking, and they worked on the imagination in a way the whole could not. In this he was not original. He was merely applying to life a principle of journalism, though not necessarily of the best.

The following morning Ann Ede invited him to lunch.

"It will be a cold lunch," she said. "Beef salad with more salad than beef, because the Bagman invited another bagman to dinner last night and between them they did for nearly two pounds of sirloin. I took the opportunity of telling them both, when they had finished, that they were not so much good bagmen as good pokemen."

He bought a litre of plonk and poured it with such sleight that she drank more than half of it without noticing. Then, when they had eaten, and she had become giggly, he confided to her that what he desired most was to lie naked beside her in the white-covered bed upstairs.

"Why naked?" she asked. "I've never lain naked with a man in my life."

"I want to feel the polish of your skin."

221

"You're turning me into what a fortnight ago I would have called a very wicked woman."

"Surely you don't think it's more sinful naked."

"If it's more pleasurable, it's more sinful. Just as the greatest moral good is to be derived from overcoming the greatest temptation."

"It's more natural naked, and therefore less sinful."

"I suppose there's one way to find out." She giggled as she led the way upstairs.

He was right about her skin. It was smoothly silken all over, with not one mole or goose pimple on her back or bottom. Her bottom in particular was like satin, and it was warm too, the antithesis of the arctic waste of fatty tissue which was Esther's, and the cold mahogany veneer of Mrs. Stooke's. Of all the bottoms his hands had cupped, there was only one that might stand comparison for form and texture, that of Jilly Dingles, which had acquired a kind of gloss finish from the hours she spent on her back each day in the practice of her much maligned profession.

As he kissed her, he was pleasurably aware of the gentle pressure of her full tummy against his own, and then of the whiteness of her room, which gave his delight a surrealist tinge, as if he were making love to her on a tropical oasis in a landscape of snow. She kissed him first smoothly and then suckingly, and up from under the sheet came the scent of wet seaweed, transporting him briskly from the tropical oasis to a temperate island in a boat with a large triangular sail and a canoe-like outrigger, from which he watched the dizzying surface of glinting seawater pass smoothly underneath him like a flight of swallows.

"It's time," she whispered, getting up with the sheet about her shoulders.

She leant against the wall, and when he embraced her again she put the sheet over both their heads and clung to him, pressing down so insistently on the root of his penis that at first he thought he'd lose his balance. Being inside the sheet with her increased his sense of secrecy and of angels treading carefully so as not to intrude on the music of a waterfall somewhere in the background. But however carefully they trod, he still could not catch each note. He strained every nerve to listen, but the music was fitful and remote, not of this world or at least not for ears grown accustomed to the noise of engines revving. When they finished, he wanted to start all over again, but the music had ceased, the last note like the ping of a raindrop on an upturned bucket. He felt disappointed with himself, as if his knowledge of the Wistwood fox had coarsened his ear.

"We'll lie down again for a while." She opened the sheet to the light of suburban day.

"I thought you were making fun of me when you said you made love standing up."

"It's because of what my doctor calls an anatomical irregularity. I can do it lying down, but I enjoy it better in the perpendicular."

"Why didn't you sneeze?"

"You didn't make me."

"Oh."

"Don't worry, Charles. You'll improve with perpendicular practice."

They lay in silence under the sheet with their legs entwined.

"I'm pleased you didn't make a dash for the bathroom," she said after a while.

"Did you expect me to?"

"The Bagman always does, at least he did when I knew him in that particular way. After 'extricating' himself, to use his carefully disinfected English, he would sprint across the landing and the next thing you'd hear was the sound of running water, vigorous soaping and furious scrubbing. He's one of those men who are kinky about cleanliness and never clean. I found it positively insulting. It's the woman who should wash, not the man."

"Perhaps we should both wash."

"We shall, but not yet. After sex, I like to lie close to my man and resavour in imagination that which at its best is not an everyday occurrence. There, put your other arm round me and pretend you still want me."

"But I do . . . in a manner of speaking."

"Don't be dishonest. The man spurns the woman in the very moment of ejaculation. That's why the Bagman must do his lavabo bit and get back to his proper sphere of giving positive direction to the firm's manufacturing and distributing facilities. He's a walking paradox. Though the typing pool and the typists are never far from his thoughts, he knows that he has yet to discover a position that is consonant with his over-blown sense of gravitas. Do you think sex absurd?"

"I think it's like the fox, very fugacious."

"You don't feel that if we were meant to do it, we'd be better at it?"

"But I *am* good at it!"

"You impossible male chauvinist. That's surely for me, not you, to say."

He told her he was going for a pee and not to get up, that he would be back. In the bathroom he ran the water quietly so that she wouldn't hear, then he retracted his foreskin equally soundlessly and washed himself with a miniature bar of her subtly scented, lilac-coloured soap.

"I'll suffer agonies of guilt for this," she said when he came back.

After the lovemaking he had expected her to talk of murder, but instead she wanted to talk about herself. Rightly or wrongly, he felt that life here should be about murder, because murder was the ultimate in one-upmanship, but life went on as if the murders had happened in Manchuria and not in everyone's back garden. He looked at her incredulously. He simply did not expect to see her where she was.

"Only a very jealous God would deny you a little innocent pleasure after a good lunch," he said.

"No need to pretend, Charles. You know and I know what I mean. I can't help feeling trapped. The Bagman and I haven't had sex together for over three years. I felt I was drying up. I felt like a sapless twig, thin and brittle, ready to break. And that gave me guilt feelings of a different kind. I kept remembering something that happened to me in Crete when I was a girl of sixteen on holiday with my father. We were staying in Heraklion, and I used to go down to the harbour every evening before dinner to watch the fishing boats coming in and the fishermen mending their nets. One evening I saw a superb young man with powerful thighs coming up out of the sea. His wet hair shone in the low sunlight, and as he came towards me I noticed a terrible fluttering inside his swimming trunks, which excited me beyond anything else I could remember. He stood before me, put his hand down inside his trunks, and drew out a wriggling fish the size of a mackerel. Then he put down his harpoon gun and offered me the dying fish without a smile. I refused, but I went back to the harbour other evenings and saw him again and again. He took me to a beach east of Heraklion on his motorbike. I don't know what it was called, but the airport lay to the northwest of it and you could see the jets in silhouette as they taxied into position for take-off like big, black ants against the sky. I shall never forget their thunder coming across the water to the beach, as he lay stretched beside me with his leg against mine and the thick hair, like hackles when it dried, tickling my thigh. As the light began to fail, he began to kiss me. I became excited because it was my first kiss off a real stranger. The thunder of the jets seemed to come up out of the sea and shake my bones, but unaccountably I turned my head away. He got up and stood angrily before me, the black hair like thick fur on his chest. 'All you English the same,' he shouted. Too much worry, not enough bouzouki.' In the last three years, living with a man I couldn't allow near me, I often thought the Greek may have been right, that I didn't have enough bouzouki, that there was something lacking in me as a woman."

"Surely not."

"I felt guilty for having denied myself sex, and now I feel guilty for the opposite reason."

"I should like to prove to you that it is possible to stop worrying and love the bouzouki—or at least the harp. . . . If, as the Pope claims, there's no erection after the general resurrection, should we not make the best of our opportunities now?"

"It's a pity you have no sense of the sacred, Charles. To you, and, I suspect, most men, one ejaculation is more or less like another. All you want is more of the same. Another intromission, to be followed, after a bit of jiggling about, by yet another climax. I, on the other hand, feel renewed. For the next three days I shall be content to bask in the afterglow and remember. But it's strange that someone as life-soiled as you could give me a glimpse of an experience I had never before associated with the temporal."

". . . and God fulfils himself in many ways."

"There you go again. The unearned cynicism of journalism."

"But my greatest problem is that I can't find a job as a journalist."

"I want you to forget about journalism, to be a man of noble mind. Journalists, like admen and politicians, are in the business of buttonholing. They must attract your attention immediately or not at all. They may enquire about the truth, but they never have time to wait for an answer. At 'Foxgloves' you're among journalists. When have you last heard the truth there?"

"I'm sick of 'Foxgloves.' I want to go away and start a new life in a new place with you. Ann, will you come?"

"Where to?"

"I don't know yet. But you can't stay here with the Bagman, who is also in the business of buttonholing. If you do, you'll dry up inside. You'll lose what's left of your sense of innocence and joy."

"But living with you would be living in sin. There's a difference between taking one or two bites of the apple and consuming it to the rotten core. Imagine being in sin twenty-four hours a day, seven days a week, and fifty-two weeks of the year."

"I shan't try to persuade you. You must decide for yourself. But I'd like you to think about it. We are all singing birds. It is only by singing that we discover ourselves, and in discovering ourselves glorify our Maker. We can sing only out of our hearts and souls, and if we deny their nature and deny them joy, how can we glorify anything? We become dead things, fingers of dried afterbirth on a thorn bush flapping in the wind."

"It seems to me that you are now trying to persuade yourself." She jumped out of bed and picked up her bra from a chair.

"My father used to say that there are two types of women: those who put on their knickers first and those who put on their bra first. I once overheard him say in a pub that women who put on their bra first are better in bed."

"I suppose it raised a laugh."

"I think he meant it seriously."

"Well, it's a lot of nonsense. All practical women start with their bra."

"Were you practical enough to take precautions?"

227

"No need. My doctor says I'm sterile."

"Doctors aren't always right."

"This one is so convinced he's right that he's never once tried to prove otherwise."

He laughed at her flippancy to cover the keen stab of disappointment he felt at the news. He had so wanted a daughter from her, a fair-haired girl with freckles who would never grow older than nine. Without knowing it, he had foreshadowed the future, but the future was going to cheat him out of his dream.

As he said goodbye in the doorway, Mrs. Stooke passed the house without seeing him. She was looking up at the windows of "Foxgloves" with a mad, unwavering stare, her head shaking with every step as if her back and shoulders were rigid wood. His eyes followed the hunched shoulders and the wide-apart trouser legs that did not touch as she walked, and he recalled the bird of prey that terrified him once at Chilham Castle on a Sunday.

"Isn't that the woman we saw at Orpington?"

"I think you're right." He trembled at an unexpected attack of pins and needles behind the knees.

He went home slightly shaken. The discovery that Ann could not have children and his narrow escape from Mrs. Stooke had cracked the calm with which he began the day. He sat for a long time in the kitchen looking out at the spiky, green chestnuts that had replaced the white and pink blossoms of a fortnight ago. Then he made a pot of coffee, but after the first sip he poured it down the sink and went out to mow the lawn, or rather that part of the lawn that wasn't under geese. The mower, which needed sharpening, was chewing rather than cutting, but he didn't care. He went over it again with the clippers, kneeling down to pluck the odd tuft with his fingers. When he had finished, he felt better. He felt pleased with himself for being the kind of man who never did anything he wasn't prepared to do well.

"Absolutely splendid, Keating. Not a whisker standing. The geese couldn't have done it better." The Colonel, red-faced in loud tweeds, appeared on the patio.

"You're back early."

"I had a heavy lunch. I decided, since I wasn't doing much good at the office, that I might help you choose the dinner menu."

"I thought I might treat you to Irish stew."

"Dammit, Keating, it isn't Saint Patrick's Day."

"But it's thirteenth June, Yeats's birthday."

"The last time I had Irish stew was after the war in India, and it gave me the worst Jimmy Britts in the history of the Raj."

"Jimmy Britts?"

"The shits, Keating, the shits."

"My Irish stew is rather special, thick and creamy, not just a few forlorn neck chops swimming in consommé."

"I have a bone to pick with you." Giles Oxbone poked a bristly turnip head over the fence.

"Pick it then," said the Colonel. "I'm listening."

"It's those confounded geese of yours. I don't get a wink of sleep some nights till morning."

"If you're suffering from insomnia, I can recommend a hot toddy before retiring. Or if you're a teetotaller, a cup of hot chocolate."

"I'm not suffering from insomnia. I'm suffering from the cackling of your bloody geese."

"My only criticism of my geese," said the Colonel, "is that their necks are not as long or as gracefully curved as a swan's."

"If they don't stop their cackling, it wouldn't surprise me if someone stretched their necks to meet your specifications."

229

"On the other hand, a goose walks better than a swan. Its legs are longer, you see, and set closer to the middle of its body."

"It's obvious that a fox is disturbing them at night. I've spoken to Berkeley next door and he can't sleep either."

"They're better than any burglar alarm," said the Colonel. "Remember the sacred geese in the Capitol and how they warned the Romans that the Gauls were coming."

"Now, look here, Goossens—"

"I'm Quilter, Peter Quilter, I'll have you know."

"I'm not to be made fun of. Either you get rid of your silly birds or—"

"Silly birds! *Au contraire,* they're more intelligent than most humans, as many a fowler knows. And they're more faithful than most wives. Did you know that domestic geese keep their mates for life and that the female lines her nest with down from her very breast?"

"I'm not interested in your fucking geese. I don't like the sound of them and I don't like the smell of them. If they're not gone by tomorrow, I shall write to the Borough Health Officer—who incidentally is a member of my club."

"I shall not be threatened," the Colonel shouted as he retreated to the house.

That evening the Colonel held a council of war in the orderly room.

"We are assembled as officers in an emergency," he said. "Oxbone means business. We must find a way of forestalling him."

"He's a bloody liar," MacGeoch said. "I sleep in one of the back bedrooms and I never hear a peep."

"I don't altogether agree," Garlick said. "Over the past month I've been dreaming a lot about geese, which means that they disturb me in my sleep without actually waking me."

"He's got Berkeley on his side," said the Colonel. "And Berkeley, we must remember, is a solicitor's clerk."

"My advice," said Keating, "is to turn a blind eye. My own feeling is that he was just letting off steam. He complained to me before and nothing came of it."

"He is a threat to our plan to raise the goose to the status of the fox. If we lose this battle, we've lost the war. But if we win it, he's outgeneralled for ever. Once the goose is established in every garden, the cranks will have to lump it."

They argued until midnight, and finally the Colonel came round to Keating's view that they should sit tight and do nothing.

"I don't like inaction unless it's masterly inaction," he summed up. "On the other hand, I don't want to declare outright war, at least not yet. You should never draw your sword until you're prepared to throw away the scabbard."

After all the talk Keating found it difficult to sleep. He read a few Old Irish nature poems but no image of life under the heavens came to dispel the sense of unease that made both bed and bedroom the width of a coffin. At one he went to the Ooja-cum-Pivvy for a pee. As he contemplated the empty bowl, it occurred to him that the women of Wistwood were safe at least tonight. The moon was almost full, looking down from a vacant sky with a tilted face, as if inclining a confessorial ear to a sin-steeped earth. The lawns were flat and silvery, the trees dark and mysterious. A black cat came through the fence and padded across the grass into the shadow of the opposite fence. Things were happening soundlessly so that sleepers might sleep soundly. For a moment he sensed he was the murderer looking up at the earth-weary moon and cursing her light for making it easier to pick pins than strangle without being seen.

He went back to bed and dreamt of a short, stout girl in

jodhpurs and riding boots, who laughed too heartily and too easily. With every laugh, she lifted her left leg, as if kicking imaginary pebbles, and put her right hand to her crotch, as if to relieve an insistent itch. She was calling to him across a ploughed field but he could not hear a word she said because of the rattle of the harrow. Then he realised that MacGeoch was shouting something about fox and geese outside his door.

He pulled on his dressing gown and followed the others down the stairs.

"I got up the moment I heard the squawking," MacGeoch was saying. "I was just in time to see him slink off with one of them over his shoulder."

"How did he get in through the wire?" Keating asked.

"We'll soon see," said the Colonel, taking a torch from beside the kitchen door.

The wire had come away from one of the posts and there was a space between it and the ground. The door of the goose-house was open with a scattering of feathers on the cropped grass.

"This looks serious. Not a sound inside," said Garlick.

The Colonel shone the torch.

"He's killed every one of them, the fucking bastard," he shouted. "It was your responsibility, Keating, to make sure they were secure."

"The wire was in place when I locked them up for the night."

"Look," said the Colonel, "there's a staple missing. Some bugger will answer for this."

"I'm sure it was all right when I checked it before dinner," Keating said.

"Where is the staple?" MacGeoch got down on his knees to look.

"The staple is in Oxbone's dustbin," said the Colonel.

232

"We'll make a thorough search of the ground in daylight," Keating said.

"First things first." The Colonel assumed his role of C.O. "We'd better salvage what's left of the geese. Otherwise we'll have no entrée for our waygoose."

"Surely you can't give the guests geese that have been killed by the fox." Garlick sounded horrified.

"Yes, we can." The Colonel was firm. "Can't you see the aptness of it, indeed the piquancy?"

"It's more disgusting than piquant."

"Get me a sharp knife from the kitchen, Keating," the Colonel chose to ignore the Lance-corporal.

To Garlick's loudly expressed consternation, the Colonel cut off the heads of the five remaining birds and hung them up by the legs in the garage with a preserving pan underneath to catch the blood drip.

"I think we caught them in time," he said to Keating when they returned to the house. "We'll roast one of them to see if it's up to snuff. If not, we'll make goose pie of the rest. You had better pluck and clean them tomorrow and prepare them for the freezer. Do you know about freezing fresh meat?"

"I've done it before."

"I think it utterly irresponsible to give your guests meat that's been mangled by the fox. Foxes are carriers of rabies and God knows how many other diseases," Garlick said.

"Our guests eat meat vindaloo. Rest assured they're well immunised. Now, what I want you all to do is go to bed and think about our next move. I shall be up at sparrow fart to find out if the fox had a human accomplice. The rest of you can sleep on it. We'll hold another council of war over breakfast."

At breakfast, however, the Colonel was in no mood to take

counsel. He was already convinced that Farmer Giles let in the fox, and he was adamant that he must pay the penalty.

"We'll send him a solicitor's letter," MacGeoch suggested.

"But it's all surmise, there's no evidence," Garlick said.

"Someone pulled out the staple," Keating said.

"Did you see Giles Oxbone do it?" Garlick wanted to know.

"Oxbone knows that the evidence against him is merely circumstantial," said the Colonel. "He's a crafty old bugger. He's so crafty that he knew he could rely on a craftier ally. But I am craftier than either. And I'm willing to wait. Revenge is sweeter tomorrow than today, because you have a day to gloat over it. So we'll say nothing for the moment. We'll talk to him as usual over the fence, and when he enquires about the geese, we'll say the fox took them. He's not called Farmer Giles for nothing, however. His weakness is his pride in his vegetable plot. We'll wait till the tops are a little higher, and then one night we'll clip them level with the ground."

"Nasty!" Garlick drew out the vowel.

"Serves him right," said MacGeoch.

"The beauty of it"—the Colonel laughed—"is that in his heart he'll know who did it, but like us he won't be able to prove a thing."

Keating spent the day plucking and cleaning the birds and getting them ready for the freezer. Though their necks were the worse for toothmarks, the legs and breasts were untouched except for one or two bruises, which careful cooking, he hoped, would camouflage. And if careful cooking failed, there was always, as the Colonel suggested, goose vindaloo.

Contrary to all expectation, the Colonel came home from the office cock-a-hoop in the evening.

"I've had an idea," he announced as he came through the door. "We'll bring forward our waygoose. At the weekend we'll send out invitations for Old Midsummer Day."

"When is it?" MacGeoch wanted to know.

"The sixth of July."

"No one will know that," Garlick said. "They'll all turn up on the twenty-fourth of June."

"Suburban man thinks of himself as a countryman with a foot in town. Seeing Old Midsummer Day on an invitation card will puncture his complacency, give him that little frisson of self-doubt which he experiences all too rarely. A few days later he'll receive a reminder saying that Old Midsummer Day is not, as he thought, Midsummer Day but the sixth of July. If nothing else, it will serve as an intimation that this is no common or garden party."

"Will anyone come to such a party?" Garlick wondered with well-simulated innocence.

"We'll make sure that no one declines by printing 'Please don't bring a bottle' in bold above 'RSVP,'" the Colonel told him.

"Isn't that a little shitty?"

"Suburban man will know not to look a gift horse in the mouth. He's a freebooter in the city during the week; he'll hardly scruple to show himself as a freeloader at the weekend."

"Will you be inviting Farmer Giles?" Keating asked.

"Of course, we shall invite him."

"Then I'll give him the necks," said Keating.

15

O<small>N</small> June eighteenth, the Colonel commanded Keating to cook a dinner of roast beef and Yorkshire pudding to commemorate the victory of the English over the Frogs at Waterloo. Keating cooked the meal with loving care and served a good French claret in a Chianti bottle, thus flattering the Colonel's palate without arousing his Francophobia on this greatest of anniversaries.

"An excellent sirloin, Keating," he commented. "And the Chianti is like no Chianti I've ever tasted. In fact the whole meal is so perfect that I almost wish the Brigadier were here to enjoy it."

After dinner, on the Colonel's suggestion, they eschewed cognac and drank port, which was so insidious in its effect that midnight overtook them while they thought it was still ten o'clock. Though it was late, they gathered round the piano and, to the air of "Under the Bridges of Paris," sang:

> Après la guerre finie,
> Soldat anglais parti;
> Mam'selle Fransay boko pleuray
> Après la guerre finie . . .

Keating, in a vacantly mellow mood, hurried to bed after the singing and tried to imagine Ann Ede naked inside loose silk pyjamas. He was dropping off when a quiet knock on the door roused him. MacGeoch, in tartan pyjamas, looking for a light.

"Can we have a word in private?" he whispered, ignoring the proffered box of matches.

Keating closed the door and pointed to the only chair in the room.

"I've been thinking about the geese," MacGeoch said.

"Not about the fox?"

"I don't think Oxbone did it."

"Then who did it?"

"Someone who wanted the Colonel to fall out with Oxbone."

"I'm sorry," said Keating. "I don't follow."

"Someone at 'Foxgloves,'" MacGeoch whispered as he looked at the keyhole of the door.

"Not me," said Keating. "Not you, because you'd hardly be talking about it if you'd done it. Not the Colonel because he loved those birds. Was it Garlick?"

"What do you think of him?"

"He praises neither God nor man. If there's a fault in life's circuit, he'll find it."

"He often gets up in the middle of the night."

"Is he the Nocturnal Crapper, then?"

"No, that's the Colonel. Garlick's neither big enough nor bountiful enough to deliver himself of such a donation."

"I had made up my mind that the Nocturnal Crapper and the Wistwood Fox were one and the same."

"We delude ourselves in our search for symmetry."

"Forgive me." Keating laughed. "For a time I thought it was you."

"You flatter me."

"If Garlick isn't the Nocturnal Crapper, why does he get up at night? To piddle?"

"Think again."

"That's the only other excretory function I know. Of course, like you, he could get up to have Scotch and chips."

"Has it occurred to you that he might get up to murder?"

"From time to time."

"But you rejected the idea?" MacGeoch smiled too understandingly.

"It has also occurred to me that it could be you."

"Interesting. For a while I was convinced it must be you."

"Have you considered the Colonel?"

"That's treason."

"How do you know it's Garlick?"

"I don't know, but I suspect him."

"It's a serious business. You must have some grounds for suspicion."

"I've heard noises in his room in the small hours."

"That could be Captain Flint saying 'Split infinitives.'"

"No, I heard a step on the stairs at three in the morning. When I came out of my room to investigate, there was no one about but I could see light in his room through the keyhole. Later, in my own room, I heard a noise on the other side of the party wall, and the following day we all heard that a woman had been attacked and almost strangled in the night."

"That was months ago. That was Mrs. Stooke."

"I've been keeping an eye on him since, but he's too crafty. The suspicion is weighing me down. I feel I can't bear it alone any longer."

"Why don't you go to the police?"

"I have nothing concrete to tell them. It isn't an offence to make a noise in your room at three in the morning."

"Have you told the Colonel?"

"I wouldn't dream of telling him. I can just hear what he'd

say. 'You're imagining things, MacGeoch. Kindly keep your nightmares to yourself.' "

"They are nightmares, and I'm certain that you're not the only man in Wistwood who has them."

"I thought we might get together, you and I."

"How?" Keating looked at him to see if he was playing games. If he was, he was not a bad dissembler.

"We could take turns watching at night. All we need is a single piece of evidence. He hasn't struck for several weeks. He's due to strike again. Are you game?"

"When do we start?"

"Not tonight. I'm too sleepy and he's too drunk. I think tomorrow night will do. It's light these mornings at four. If we split the watch between bedtime and morning, we'll only have two hours each."

"But why Garlick?" Keating spoke as if to himself.

"He's a misogynist."

"But so is the Colonel and, to a lesser extent, so are you and I."

"I can only guess."

"And what do you guess?"

"We three are suspicious of women because we've been scarred by them, but I suspect that we spend a lot of our time idealising them in our dreams. We don't hate women. We're just disillusioned because they don't live up to our romantic expectations. We're lonely men, and only a woman made in our own image and likeness will satisfy our starved imaginations. The Freudian concept of transference, which is at the root of romantic love, doesn't work with us. We shan't be happy till we meet a woman who is truly flesh of our flesh, rib of our ribs, as Eve was to Adam. Garlick is different. He was hurt by only one woman, the woman he married. He lacks the imagination to be hurt by the banality of every woman he meets. It is not women he hates but himself. A man who loves himself must also love women—or at least the idea of women."

"I'm surprised that a hardheaded Scotsman could come out with such airy-fairy fiddle-faddle. There isn't a shred of evidence to support one word of what you say."

"There's the evidence of Jilly Dingles. She once confided to me that Garlick does his best to put her off."

"She told me she liked all four of us."

"She told you, but she didn't confide in you. I love the M.O. Don't you?"

"I suppose I do."

"And because we shall never marry her, we love her all the more. She is the perfect woman, at once accessible and inviolable. We three know that and love and respect her for it. Garlick knows it too and resents her for it."

"Did she say how he puts her off?"

"Of course not. Even the coarsest women are made of infinitely finer stuff than the finest men. Any man can easily put any woman off by giving rein to the grossness that makes him a man. Do you ever look at other men's mouths and wonder how any woman can kiss them?"

"All right." Keating smiled. "You've told me about his hatred of women and your own lack of enthusiasm for men. Now tell me why he hates geese."

"I was being serious. I think it's time I went to bed."

After MacGeoch had gone, Keating lay awake for an hour, wishing for sleep. He couldn't make up his mind if MacGeoch was genuine, or if he was trying to avert suspicion from himself and at the same time discover where Keating stood. Before falling asleep, he told himself that he must keep both eyes open. And if he had a third eye for the Colonel, he'd keep that open too.

The second half of June was a time of happiness for Keating. Though he shared the nightly watch with MacGeoch, he seldom thought about the murders because he could think of little except Ann Ede. From morning to night he was enveloped in a cumulus of sexuality like an invisible garment that gave off her aroma whenever he lifted a hand or foot and kept him warm in the knowledge that at last she was his. It was a magic garment that gave him a magical view of the world, as if the very quality of the light had changed, as if everything had become purer, as if rank midsummer leaves had regained the pale green of newly burst buds.

He could not escape for a moment from the physicality of her body, from the warmth, weight and touch of it, inside him and outside him, as if he were carrying her in his arms with a child in her belly, a child which was not just his son but himself. She had made him into flesh of her flesh and rib of her ribs, but he was old enough to know that both flesh and rib must finally return to their owner. For the moment, however, he was content to bask in the heat of her sun and marvel at the sweetness of grapes he had not so long ago condemned as sour.

Off and on he tried to talk to her about the future, but all she wanted was the uncomplicated present.

"The future makes me think thoughts that are painful," she said. "The present is an analgesic that we must keep taking for as long as possible."

At length he decided to take her for a drink on the last Sunday of June to see if he could make her see sense. The day, when it arrived, was warm and dry. After breakfast he sat on the patio reading the more scandalous of the Sunday newspapers and listening to snatches of banal conversation from the neighbours' gardens. A copper beech, framed between two still conifers, flickered as the breeze turned up its leaves like miniature petticoats. Farmer Giles came out in overalls to creosote his oft-creosoted fence. Berkeley, whom the Colonel called "the Bishop," was spiking his lawn, supervised by an overpowering wife who was digging up inoffensive daisies with a table fork.

He looked uncomprehendingly at the three of them and thought he heard a whisper on the breeze:

> I am sick, I must die—
> Lord, have mercy on us!

He looked again and saw a bank of flowers in intensive care with surgeons in gloves stooping over them, repeating to each anaesthetised patient: "I love my garden more than my poodle, and I love my poodle more than my spouse. I am sick, I must die, but . . . simply the thing I am shall make me live."

That was not for him to worry about, however. All he wished for was to go away and take Ann Ede with him, but could he go without acting on the suspicions he was at such pains to ignore? It was possible, even here among the tents of Kedar, to take detachment and inaction too far.

At twelve she drove him to Chislehurst and they sat outside a pub in the shadow of a cedar, opposite a church with a spire that reminded him of St. Germain des Prés. Young men and their girl friends were arriving in sports cars, laughing as if they had yet to discover a limit to life's possibilities. The girls, looking carefree and cool in summer cotton, responded to the confidence of their men, held half-pints of shandy to their slippery lips, and smiled mysteriously at the red roofs across the road and at other young men getting out of other sports cars. They were all younger than Ann Ede. They had smaller waists and flatter tummies, as if they had never tucked into a heaped plate of roast beef, Yorkshire pudding, cauliflower, Brussels sprouts, young carrots and new potatoes. It was impossible to look at them with detachment, without a painful constriction of the chest. He looked at Ann, calmly remote in flimsy cream trimmed with Franciscan brown.

"Unto everyone that hath shall be given, and he shall have abundance; but from him that hath not shall be taken away even that which he hath."

"Why do you quote that at me?"

"To reassure you. You looked like a man who wanted more."

"All I desire is to leave this place and go away with you. I don't care where we go provided we can be alone."

"Where would you like to take me?"

"Somewhere in the country, preferably near a rocky coast, far from tourists and sandy beaches. A place with fields and hedges and farmers on tractors ploughing and harrowing. A place with copses and coverts and foxes that are merely foxes. A place where people remember their neighbours' parents and grandparents. A place with a local history and local heroes, where local life is so rich that those who live it cock a snook at the banalities of politicians, bishops, trade union leaders, half-educated businessmen, and indeed anyone who is ass enough to bray in public."

"There's no such place." She laughed. "Even if there was, you would still have to earn a living! What would you do in the country?"

"I'd find something to do. I was brought up on a farm. I have a good pair of hands."

"As it happens, that isn't the problem. I have a cottage and an acre of ground. I also have some money of my own, or at least enough to keep us in necessaries until we find our feet."

"I wouldn't want to sponge on you. I wouldn't be happy unless I could support you."

"The real problem is not one of logistics, as your Colonel might call it, but one of morality. Can we find true happiness if we live in sin?"

"You can't give your life to a man you no longer love. If you do, you'll shrivel up and the life you have left to offer

God will be a travesty of the variousness and richness of His own creation. If you must maim yourself to retain God's love, then God is a scoundrel."

"But He commands us to maim ourselves. If thine eye offend thee, pluck it out, and cast it from thee."

"What if it is God who offends you? Will you pluck Him out?"

"You say these things because you're a man. Men are more myriad-minded, and therefore more prone to error than women, who by their nature are closer to the single, greatest truth. Sin, which is a betrayal of the truth within us, is therefore more reprehensible in a woman. In other words, I should be putting myself in greater danger than you."

"What nonsense! How can two intelligent people hold this medieval conversation in the latter half of the twentieth century? Look round you. Look at those randy young girls leaning on those randy young men. They've been at it like flies since the day they reached puberty. Do you mean to tell me they're going to burn for it?"

"I wish you wouldn't introduce so many red herrings. As it happens, there's no need. I've already decided to leave the Bagman, not because of your non sequiturs but because I'm not saintly enough to live with him any more. I'm going to move to my cottage in Suffolk before the end of the summer."

"I should like to go with you."

"Come if you like. I've thought about that too. As I see it, there are two truths in my life and they are mutually exclusive. Our love is the lesser truth of the two, but it's the one I've chosen."

"We shall be happy, wait and see. Forget this nonsense about sin. Those young people will tell you that the only sin in the twentieth century is self-denial."

"There is one thing I must ask of you, Charles. Don't try to comfort me, because I refuse to be comforted. And don't try to teach me theology because you know nothing about it. I know what I'm doing, and I'm doing it in full knowledge and with full consent."

"Try to be less tragic, Ann." He placed a hand on her knee.

They drove back in silence. There was something he had meant to ask her, but it slipped his mind. Then, as he carved the Sunday roast in the presence of Quilter, Garlick and Mac-Geoch, it came to him. He wanted to know why she had one rough knee and one smooth.

"We have less than a fortnight to prepare for the way-goose," the Colonel reminded them. "I shall see to the drinks, but I'm making you responsible for the food, Keating, *id est,* goose."

"Very well."

"I want this party to find its way into the lower-middle-class folklore of Wistwood. In other words, I don't want any of you buggering it up. Your aim must not be to enjoy yourselves but to see that the guests get what they come for. You must make every effort to flatter their social aspirations. You must see to it in particular that the Westsiders go away with the feeling that they are coming up in the world. They have never hooked a salmon or shot over the butts, but they will enter enthusiastically into any conversation about fishin' and shootin'. Get that right. A common mistake is to refer to those pursuits as fishing and shooting. Another thing—most of them, especially the younger men, will have been to university, though regrettably not an ancient one. However, you can take it from me that none of them has been educated at university. They have all benefited rather more from the review pages of *The Sunday Times.* In other words they will have heard of Plato's *Republic,* but they will not have read it. So no intellectual pyrotechnics, please. You may talk about the signposts but not about the landscape; remember you are in the company of men who are first and foremost motorists."

"Shouldn't we flatter them just a little?" MacGeoch asked.

"Of course you may flatter, but not fulsomely. The best flattery is self-concealing. It lingers like a hint of perfume in the air after the flatterer has gone, making the flatteree turn and sigh for more. It is as appetising as canapés, as crisp as *crudités*. It is beyond doubt the guerdon, indeed, I may say, the just reward of snobbery. You may use words like 'guerdon' but only sparingly and only in contexts in which the meaning is clear."

"The most subtle form of flattery is to give your interlocutor an occasional opportunity to question the accuracy of your observations." Garlick spoke without a smile, but Keating knew and the Colonel knew that he was ribbing.

"Brilliant, my dear Lance-corporal. You're fast improving." The Colonel spoke as if he too were serious.

"Another ploy is to put them at ease with the odd plebeian phrase, such as 'sweating like a pig,'" MacGeoch said.

"I see what you mean," said the Colonel. "If nothing else, it gives the buggers the opportunity to ask you, 'Does a pig sweat?' Remember that these men by virtue of their jobs are trained to ask all the little questions. They postpone the big question till they arrive in Eastbourne or Bexhill on retirement. But that is to digress. After lunch I shall issue each of you with a copy of the Highway Code."

"Whatever for?" Garlick wrung his napkin in amazement.

"For the waygoose, you fathead. When they've exhausted the fox and gorged themselves on goose, they'll turn to motoring. Needless to say, there will be discussion and argument that can only be settled by reference to the Highway Code. You will be charged with the responsibility of seeing that truth prevails. But don't parade your superior knowledge. Allow the disputants to exhaust themselves. Put in your oar only when they've fired the last shot in their lockers. Note that sentence. If there's one thing they like better than a well-mixed cocktail, it's a well-mixed metaphor."

"A capital idea," said MacGeoch.

"Interesting," said Keating, who could not decide if this was one of the Colonel's jokes.

Garlick said nothing but pretended to look for a thorn in his thumb.

"Flattery is not everything, however," the Colonel continued. "If this waygoose is to live in the folklore of Wistwood, we must arrange for a happening that will seize the eye and kindle whatever imagination there is here."

"I have an idea." MacGeoch waved his napkin like an order paper. "We'll give them something to think about besides patios and house extensions. Now, if I were to go up to Scotland at the weekend and come back with a brace of capercaillie—"

"Is that a species of haggis?" Garlick asked innocently.

"No, Lance-corporal, it's a bird of the coniferous forest, as big as a goose, almost as big as a turkey. It is the largest gallinaceous bird, not only in Scotland but in Europe."

"What we need in Wistwood is a bird unique to silver birch forests." Garlick poked gentle fun.

"But we have two conifers in the garden."

"I don't understand," said the Colonel.

"With a little imagination you can turn two conifers into a coniferous forest," MacGeoch said. "We'll hide the capercaillies behind the conifers, and you will come out on the patio to show someone the action of your new twelve-bore. When you do, I'll release the birds, one after the other, and you will wing them as they rise."

"Wing them? I'll do better than that, by God."

"This is more insane than the fox and goose," Garlick jeered.

"Hold it, Major," said the Colonel. "I smell a fault. It's the middle of the close season, is it not? Capercaillie and wood-cock shooting doesn't begin till September thirtieth."

"Close season, my tickling stick," said MacGeoch. "Who in Wistwood, apart from yourself, is likely to know? Most of them, like our Welsh lance-corporal, couldn't tell the difference between a capercaillie and a caber."

"I could never be party to such an unsportsmanlike act." The Englishman's sense of fair play triumphed over Caledonian fervour. "However, you've given me a better idea. We'll hide a fox in the conifers."

"I thought the fox was *persona non grata* since he garrotted your geese," Garlick remarked.

"You mean you'll shoot him, Colonel?" MacGeoch was still out for blood.

"No, as we're all on the lawn inspecting the roses or whatever, Keating will release him from behind the conifers with a ringing 'Viewhalloo.' For a moment there will be the complete silence of recognition and disbelief."

"Will he mix freely with the guests?" Garlick wondered.

"He will stare at us for a moment and then hightail it over the fence. And Westmen will go home and tell their children that they saw a real live fox at Mr. Quilter's party."

"But where will we get a fox?" Keating asked.

"You will catch him, Captain."

"Where?"

"In the woods, of course."

"You'll need a leg-hold trap," MacGeoch said.

"No," said the Colonel, "we don't want a lame fox at our party. You'd better use a snare. I'll get you some suitable wire from town. If you set it on a foxrun and visit it two or three times a day, there will be no difficulty, I do assure you."

It was a typical suburban summer afternoon, long, dreamy and still. After lunch, Keating slept on the patio, and when he woke at six, people were beginning to emerge from their houses to enjoy the cool of the evening. For a moment he lay immobilised by the memory of the Colonel's bizarre conversation over lunch and MacGeoch's obsessive belief that Garlick was the murderer. He could not bring himself to believe that the Colonel was serious about the waygoose, no more than he could credit that MacGeoch was serious about Garlick. Nevertheless, he shared the nightly watch with the Scotsman, and he knew that if the Colonel came home with a snare, he would humour him by taking it to the woods. He would set it on a foxrun among ferns with the same sense of absurdity he experienced whenever MacGeoch woke him for his watch. Quite simply, his sense of reality was not, and never would be, theirs.

At seven he lit a fire to burn hedge clippings, which Farmer Giles called "brash." Soon another brash fire set up a delicate spiral of blue among the trees of a neighbour's garden and within an hour he counted four more fires with smoke thickening the evening light. A wraith of a moon slowly absorbed the brightness from the sky, and spaces among branches darkened under trees. It was half past nine. The sun had gone down in a pool of gold behind shadowy chimney pots, and he knew that within half an hour the moon would have all the polish of a silver platter. The suburban twilight moved him with memories of the country and of growing up. In the half-light he heard the rustle of girls' dresses which used to fill him with intimations of mysteries that gave daily life the excitement of the unknown. Life was still unknown, but most of the poetry had drained away. He did not wish to wait for the waygoose. He wished to leave for the country with Ann Ede that very night. Excited and breathless, he knocked on her door and told her what they both must do.

"It's impossible," she said. "I promised the cottage for a fortnight to a very dear friend who is not well off and is badly in need of a break. I just couldn't disappoint her now. But

---

249

don't worry. We'll move in as soon as it is vacant in mid-July."

"The following day the Colonel brought home one locking and three free-running snares, and Keating made anchor pegs out of lengths of wood from the shed. He set them in the woods at nightfall and got up at dawn to visit them before the first dog-walker appeared. The Colonel was waiting for him when he got back.

"Any luck?" he enquired.

"No."

"Then you must do something to attract them. What about a lure?"

"I laid down two pounds of lamb chops from the freezer."

"How did you present them?"

"On paper plates. I didn't want them to get dirty in case I should decide later to put them in a stew."

"I'm surprised you didn't serve them on silver."

"Why?"

"You pay excessive deference to Charles James. As a feeder, he's not a connoisseur; he will eat offal as heartily as tournedos Rossini. Take my advice and buy a few pounds of pig's fry, preferably in a state of near putrefaction. Any housewife in the road will be only too pleased to recommend a suitable butcher."

Keating followed the Colonel's advice to the letter, but after a week of effort and early rising he had to report complete failure.

"This is serious," MacGeoch said. "We have only three days left."

"I'm afraid I can't guarantee to catch one," Keating said.

"I'm not so easily defeated. If we can't have a fox, we'll have his faeces." The Colonel banged on the table.

"His faeces?" Garlick made a goose-like hiss.

"Mark my words, the lower-middle class of Wistwood West will come whimpering to my door for the characteristic odour of fresh fox faeces. We'll scour the woods, we'll quarter the railway embankments. If necessary, we'll raid our neighbours' gardens. We shall search in the fields and in the streets, we shall collect them in the hills; we shall not cease till we have enough to prove the presence of a family of foxes in my garden."

"Bravo!" MacGeoch shouted.

"You can't invite civilised people to a party on a lawn strewn with faeces." Keating decided that the Colonel must be teasing him.

"Not faeces, dear boy, but fox faeces. You've been here almost a year, and you're still a greenhorn. If you wish for a job on an up-market Fleet Street newspaper, you'll have to evince a more intimate knowledge of your prospective readers. I shall expect you to go to the woods on the morning of the waygoose and collect them while they're still fresh after the night."

"I wouldn't recognise foxsh from dogsh." Keating still refused to believe the Colonel was in earnest.

"Disgraceful! Where have you been all your life? As every countryman known, fox faeces look like pencil stubs sharpened at both ends." The Colonel looked round the table with the air of a man who is beset by imbeciles.

"The joke has gone far enough," Keating said. "If you want fox shit for your party, you'll have to collect it yourself."

"Treason and mutiny!" shouted Garlick.

The Colonel tapped the table in disbelief.

"Report to the Orderly Room in ten minutes." He rose and left his fellow officers gazing at one another with stark incredulity.

Keating stood on the square of carpet and the Colonel sat down behind his writing desk.

"What's all this then? Refusing to carry out an order!"

"It's an unreasonable order. I refused because I suspected you were only joshing."

"I was never more serious in my life, Captain. As I said, if I can't have a fox, I must have his faeces."

"But you mustn't expect me to collect them."

"Why?"

"I have a keen sense of the ridiculous. Would you collect fox faeces?"

"Yes, on the orders of a brigadier. My natural distaste for the job would soon be dispelled by the satisfaction of doing the wish of a superior officer."

"Even if you disliked the superior officer?"

"I might dislike the officer but I'd still respect the office. Do you mean to say you dislike me?"

"No, I just think it a job for a lance-corporal."

"The Lance-corporal is an ass. If I asked him to collect fox faeces, he'd be sure to slip on them. But all this is by the way. I suspect the real reason you refuse to carry out my order is that you think of fox faeces as more faeces than fox. That, my dear boy, is a failure of philosophy every bit as serious as a failure of imagination. Let your mind dwell on the fox. Let it play with the idea of foxness, and soon you will find yourself responding, as I do, to the richness of the symbolism and the ceremony. You will then bring to the pursuit of fox faeces the magic a poet brings to the marriage of one true word with another."

"I think you exaggerate my capacity for self-delusion."

"I'm deeply disappointed in you, Keating. I don't mind telling you that I've cashiered men for less. However, the eve of our waygoose is no time for disciplinary action. If all goes well—if the civet of goose, the goose terrine, or whatever you propose to give them, makes the right impression—I shall be prepared to overlook this . . ."

"As a matter of fact, I had planned to give them goose ragout à la bonne femme." He tried to bring the Colonel back to earth.

"Excellent, my dear Keating, all is forgiven."

Keating turned on his heel to go.

"One last question, Captain. Do you know why you're standing on a square yard of carpet?"

"Is it because I'm being carpeted?"

"Keating, I'm delighted. You do have a sense of ceremony after all."

Keating went to his room and sat quietly by the window, looking across at the light in Ann Ede's study. The Bagman, he knew, was in "The Fox and Billet," but he did not go to her. Instead he thanked God that a woman who prided herself on her knowledge of theology should still be a blue ribbon ride, that her brains were too multifarious to be confined to her pretty little head. Then he realised that in thinking such a thought he had proved himself unworthy of her. If she loved him, it was simply because she did not know him. With shame and humility, he jumped into bed and slept soundly till the first flutings of the dawn chorus.

When the Colonel and Garlick had gone to work the following morning, MacGeoch came down the stairs.

"Now's our chance," he said to Keating. "For the first time this year, Garlick's left his window open. We can get in."

"It would have been simpler to ask the Colonel for a key."

"We don't want to involve the Colonel. We're capable of dealing with a mere lance-corporal on our own."

MacGeoch got out the ladder from the garage and they both clambered in through the window.

"It stinks in here." MacGeoch sniffed.

"It reminds me of steam in the kitchen on washday when I was a boy."

"Could he have a washing machine in which he washes and rewashes the underclothes of his victims?"

"I know what it is. It's the smell of the bird."

"You're right," MacGeoch said. "It's like the smell you get in pet shops, a stuffy smell that would give a headache to a Barbary ape."

253

"We mustn't disturb anything," Keating said.

"You take that side and I'll take this side." As superior officer, MacGeoch was giving the orders.

They went through the room with a fine-tooth comb but all they discovered was that Garlick was a collector of immemorable mementos. The room was a museum of faded postcards, crumpled letters, scribbled diaries, vases, paperweights, photos, and newspaper cuttings celebrating Welsh rugby. It was the room of a sentimentalist who liked to keep his sentimentality to himself. It was not the room of a murderer who washed and rewashed the underclothes of his victims.

"I feel ashamed," Keating said. "The man's as innocent as we are."

"We've looked at everything except his books. We'll go through them one by one."

They began at each end of the bookcase and looked in each book with the self-conscious stamina of literary biographers who are weary of literature but are still determined to discover the least vagary of their subject's privates. The books were those of a man who kept his favourite schoolbook and added only different editions of the same book over and over again. They were certainly not the books of a man who liked to unwind before sleep with a chapter or two of stylish soft porn.

"I wonder what he sees in *Treasure Island*," MacGeoch said.

"Maybe he likes the pictures."

"Eureka!" shouted the Major. "This isn't *Treasure Island*. It's a stamp album with a false jacket. And look at this. Cloth postage stamps. What, I wonder, would the Attorney-General give for these?"

"What are they?"

"Can't you see? They're the squares he cut from the dresses of the murdered women. Keating, we've solved the crime that failed Scotland Yard. And *The Mirror* will be first with the news."

"How can you be sure they are the squares?"

"There were three murders and one attempted murder. There are three scalloped squares stuck down like stamps and one that's cut straight and labelled 'imperforate.' The imperforate must be from the dress of the woman who survived. He's named the other four after famous postage stamps: Penny Black, Black Jack, Black Beauty and Twopenny Blue."

"We'd better ring the police."

"Not yet." MacGeoch put the stamp album back on the shelf.

"Why?"

"The Colonel wouldn't like it. We must wait till after the waygoose."

"But the waygoose isn't till Saturday."

"If we go to the police now, the Colonel will have to postpone it because it would be overshadowed by Garlick's arrest."

"Surely the waygoose isn't that important."

"It is to the Colonel."

"But if we don't go to the police, he may strike again."

"He only strikes at night, and at night we'll watch him like hawks. We'll go to the police first thing on Sunday morning."

"I don't like it," said Keating.

"Don't worry. He's as good as locked up already."

"You'd better take the evidence with you."

"You're right. If he came to suspect anything, he might just get rid of it."

Keating went to his room to be alone. He was afraid, irresolute and confused. He knew that if Garlick was the murderer, he should go to the police at once. But was Garlick the murderer? He might have been more certain if he himself had found the "stamps." It was just possible that they had been planted in the album by MacGeoch.

255

16

O N the day of the waygoose Keating got up at dawn because there was much to be done in the kitchen. He
planned to devote the morning to preparing asparagus and
Derby canapés, stuffed prunes, shrimp tartlets, dips and dunks
and odd things on sticks. The afternoon he would devote entirely to goose. He had changed his mind about the ragout. He
would give them roast goose with sage and onion stuffing, or
perhaps roast gooseling, since the unfortunate birds were neither geese nor goslings. A roast was simpler to prepare and
less likely to go wrong, and he knew that it was by the goose,
not the savouries, that his reputation as chief cook and bottle
washer at "Foxgloves" would stand or fall.

Though he was soon to be called to higher things, he still
took his cooking seriously. He was quietly determined to go
out in a blaze of glory that would cause the name of Keating to
be remembered when the history of "Foxgloves" came to be
written. Nevertheless, as he cut a slice of pumpernickel into
little squares, he experienced a sudden sense of hopelessness.
Fear of the future flew into his face like a hungry raven croak-
ing "pruk-pruk-pruk" before the day had quite begun.

Yesterday Ann told him that she would like to go to Italy in

September. He said, "What a good idea!" and mentioned Florence and Venice to conceal from her his certain knowledge that it wasn't a good idea at all. He told himself that now he ought to be happy, really happy, for the first time since his arrival in England. He had the love of a woman he loved more than any woman he had ever loved before, and what was more, the love of a woman who was so good and serious that she made him doubt if he himself was sufficiently good and serious. But life was not so simple. The past lurked like an ugly toad in the foreconscious. It did not bite like a wolf or adder. It just lurked without moving a limb, poisoning the present by the venom of its warts and inflating its throat to make its ugliness uglier. That was the threat within. The other threat would come without warning, someone—an Irish detective perhaps—laying a hand on his shoulder, saying, "You're Martin Reddin. I thought you'd gone on ahead."

It was strange to be alive and dead at the same time. He was dead to his wife and only daughter, dead to his ex-colleagues on *The Cork Clarion,* dead to his friends at the golf club, dead to his cronies in Madagan's pub. The people to whom he was dead easily outnumbered those to whom he was alive, just as the past easily outweighed the present. He had thought of it as so much ballast to be thrown overboard when wind and water were favourable, but the past was not the ballast but the ship itself.

He looked out of the window and found himself face to face with a fox. He couldn't say where he had come from. One moment he wasn't there and the very next he was. Just as if he had materialised out of the smooth-streaked lawn. The fox looked at Keating and Keating looked at the fox and held his breath. He had seen foxes in Cork, but this one was smaller and thinner than any he remembered. If you cut off his tail, he wouldn't look much bigger than a cat. The coat was also less rich—paler and shaggier but that was because it was the moulting season. His white bib, prick ears and sensitive snout gave the impression of fastidious daintiness, but the whiskers of the upper lip called to mind a crusty old major who bristled and snapped at anyone who came near.

Suddenly he sniffed the air, and as he sniffed he vanished behind the ivy trellis, the act of sniffing and the act of vanishing one. Keating went out and looked all round, but there was no sign of him anywhere, neither under the trellis nor in the garden next door. It was as if he had gone down into the ground from which he rose, leaving Keating with a sense of his own insubstantiality, as if, like the fox, he were here and at the same time there.

"I saw a fox," he said when the Colonel came down to breakfast.

"Did you catch him?"

"No, before I could blink, he was gone."

"I'm surprised he showed himself to you. Why not me?"

"I have no idea."

"At least it proves he exists, that he isn't just a figment of the communal imagination."

"I was disappointed in him. He looked rather scruffy, not at all suburban, more like a down-at-heel bohemian."

"It's a good omen for the waygoose . . . But, look, Keating, there's no need to slave all day over the cooker. I'll get Mrs. Oxbone and Mrs. Berkeley to come in and give a hand. They can do the odds and sods, so that you'll be free to attend to the more serious business of the goose."

"I'd prefer to do it all myself."

"Some men are born perfectionists." The Colonel laughed and left him.

The morning and afternoon slid by with Keating still in the kitchen. From time to time the Colonel came in to inspect the work, nibble at a prune or tartlet, and enquire further into the apparition of the fox.

"I do not doubt that you saw him," he said, "but I don't warm to your description. He may have been shabby-genteel, but he was not down-at-heel. Down-at-heel conjures up a man who is by nature slovenly, while shabby-genteel brings to mind a rogue who has seen better days. Once a country gentleman perhaps, he is now reduced to the suburbs and to keeping up appearances on a meagre income from dustbins and rubbish dumps as opposed to chickens, lambs and Embden geese."

Keating nodded and said as little as possible. By half-past five his work was done, so he poured himself a glass of white wine and sat on the patio with the Colonel, the Major and the Lance-Corporal. They sat in the shade of the mountain ash, whose berries were yellow, not yet brightening into red. The afternoon sun was warm, the sky clear, and the shadow of the west fence lengthening on the lawn. Keating had worked so hard that his mind was blank. All he was aware of was the gentle tiredness in his legs and the cool wash of the wine against his palate. What he wished for now was to sit quietly for an hour, listening to the idle conversation of his fellow officers and, then, after another glass of wine, knock on Ann Ede's door and climb the stairs behind her to the cool whiteness of her bed. It was the kind of afternoon that could lead to an evening on which that would be the natural thing to do. It was quiet, fragrant and full of enchantment.

At six the first guests arrived, two couples from Wistwood West, who marvelled at the length of the garden and what they called "the velveteen" of the lawn, and took a critical interest in the roses for which they prescribed generous mulching and more regular watering. The first half-hour was difficult, because one of the couples had been to the Chelsea Flower Show in May and had still not recovered from the experience. The Colonel, MacGeoch and Garlick, who wouldn't recognise a daisy from a daffodil, tried to look impressed with their guests' gift of total recall, which was so totalitarian that they could not get a word in edgeways.

Mercifully, the other guests began to arrive, and by seven o'clock the waygoose was well under way. The women in bright dresses glided between the roses, dahlias and begonias, which like themselves were in full and magnificent flower. The men brought the women drinks with a whiff of gravity, because they were men who took themselves seriously, for whom laughter was synonymous with an expansion of the chest and the forgivable excitement of self-importance. Keating listened in vain for the laughter of pure comedy, which is the laughter of love, the laughter of Falstaff, but Shakespeare drew his genius from another England. However, he was pleased to find that not a word was said about the fox and only one or two about motorcars. The Colonel had led him to believe that in suburban conversations the opening gambit was "Have you changed any good wheels lately?" but in this as in many things the Colonel was not a reliable witness.

Keating made an excuse and escaped from the fearsome Mrs. Berkeley who wanted to know why he hadn't tied the daffodils. He escaped into the dining-room where the drinks and savouries were laid out, only to be buttonholed by the Colonel, who looked flushed and even more Colonel-like than usual.

"We'll mess at nine," he said. "Or should I say nosh, given the company?"

"As you wish."

"Is this your first suburban party?"

"Yes."

"Have you noticed that there are no freeloaders round the drinks table?"

"No, I haven't."

"At the average suburban party it's impossible to get next or near the drinks. Too many moths about the candle. Here there's no problem. Why?"

"I have no idea."

"Because there's an abundance of booze. Even the most dedicated freeloaders are clearly convinced that nothing short of a miracle could cause the wine to run out. Here there is no need of your Galilean."

"I must get myself another drink." Keating thought he might escape once more.

"My dear Keating, you've drunk enough plonk. Come upstairs and have a glass of something better with me."

They went into the Brigadier's room and the Colonel produced a bottle from the bottom of the wardrobe.

"As you can see, I'm keeping the good wine for myself. It's a bottle—one of six—I had from the M.O., who had it from a peer of the realm, who had it from a French aristocrat not unconnected with Château Lafitte."

"It's a pity to drink it dishonourably on the q.t."

"Fuck you, Keating. You'd look a gift horse in the mouth, you craven Irishman. Or do you simply refuse alms from Albion?"

"If it's a good wine, I'll drink it."

"A good answer, Keating. The real division is not between East and West but between how and why. We why-men must stick together and say boo now and again to the how-men."

"Are you the Wistwood Fox by any chance?" Keating couldn't believe he'd said it, but having said it he thought it amply made up for the Englishman's patronising conversation.

"Why do you ask?"

"I'm convinced it's one of us. I know it isn't the Captain, so it must be the Colonel, the Major or the Lance-corporal."

"You rate me too highly, Captain."

"You haven't answered my question."

"If you have suspicions, you should go to the police."

"If I did that, he'd get a three-month trial and a sentence of only ten years. Not enough, Colonel."

"What do you want?"

"I want to throttle the bastard with my bare hands. Choke him dry, if you wish to hear the phrase that best describes my feelings."

"Typically Irish. No sense of law and order."

"You still haven't answered my question."

"Your question is laden with irony. I invited you up here to ask you the very same question."

"All women I haven't ridden irritate me more or less, but not enough to give cause for strangulation."

"Keating, you and I are kindred spirits. The Wistwood Fox has still to strangle more women than I've strangled in my dreams. Do you want to choke me dry?'"

"Why did you think it could have been me?"

"You're a man who says less than he could. Your shoulders bear the burden of unspoken thought, but if you spoke, in my view you'd speak through the cooker. You'd simply put arsenic in the soufflé."

"I've chosen the wrong time, I see. We'll talk about this again."

"You disappoint me, Keating. I saw you as a man of metaphors, not metonyms. Shall we now revert to the metaphorical mode and say a word about the goose?"

"The goose is cooked."

"Whose?"

"That is not for me to say."

"You say it isn't you. I say it isn't me. Have you spoken to MacGeoch and Garlick?"

"MacGeoch says it isn't him."

"That's good news. It's ill taking the breeks aff a wild Highlandman. But what about Garlick?"

"Tar-baby ain't sayin' nuthin', en Brer Fox, he lay low."

"Did you ask him?"

"Not in so many words."

"No need. It's him."

"Why is that?"

"You say it's one of us. MacGeoch, you and I have denied it. There's only the Lance-corporal left."

"That's to assume that MacGeoch, you and I are telling the truth."

"We're officers and gentlemen. Need I say more?"

"Then what should we do?"

"If you're convinced you know something, you must go to the police. But let me remind you that you must wait till the last of the guests has gone."

"Would you go to the police?"

"It's your suspicion, not mine."

"I think it wrong to make light of it."

"What did you think of the Lafitte?" the Colonel asked.

"We'll talk about this again tomorrow morning."

"Don't forget, we nosh at nine," the Colonel shouted as Keating went down the stairs.

In the hallway he ran into Ann Ede, who had just arrived.

"You're late," he said.

"I got delayed."

"Where's the Bagman?"

"He wouldn't come. He went off to 'The Fox and Billet' in a huff."

"You told him?"

"He didn't take it as philosophically as I expected. In fact he took it rather badly. I'm afraid he lost his gravitas—he professed his undying love for me."

"That's a bit thick, after the way he's treated you."

"He swore he went to bed with all those typists because he felt I didn't really like sex. He did it for my own good. He said he'd go to any inconvenience rather that subject his wife to something she only endured. I must say I found it very touching."

"You're shaking. Let me get you a drink."

They went out into the garden where MacGeoch, in full chieftain's regalia, was handing round the canapés, making the Highland equivalent of a *pas de chat* every now and then for the entertainment of the Anglo-Saxon ladies who, he believed, loved nothing better than a glimpse of an unbreeked thigh. The Anglo-Saxon ladies seemed strangely unmoved by the glimpse, perhaps because, as Ann Ede said, they had glimpsed this particular thigh on many such occasions before.

"I suppose it's my last suburban party." She smiled at Keating. "In a way I'm sorry to be leaving. I gave nine years of my life here. It's difficult to admit that they've been wasted."

"But surely you enjoyed yourself from time to time."

"I enjoyed the garden and the trees, and the sunsets behind the trees, but they are all things I could have enjoyed better in the country."

"I hope the illusion of rurality doesn't prove more potent than the real thing."

"I'm going to make a fresh start. I just hope it isn't too late."

The setting sun tarried on her neck and face. She was in her cream cotton dress, the one she herself had trimmed with brown, and he wanted to walk with her along a river path under willows when she was nineteen, because it was the girl he loved in her, not the woman. Her face had now begun to harden, to lose the innocence of the rose in May, but it did not matter. He would live with her and love her, and nothing that life could do to her would now change him. Between the lines round her mouth he would discover the girl she once was, the girl he should have met in time, the girl who had yet to be found. He felt the rage of impotence against a stunting history, but he told himself that he was past caring, that life could now do its damnedest.

"You've had a bad time," he said. "Most men are bagmen, but I'm a ploughman. What I start I finish. I've never yet failed in the furrow."

"We might adopt a child, perhaps a boy."

"We'll talk about that tomorrow. I must get up the food."

"I'll give you a hand," she said, following him into the kitchen.

The rosy afterglow behind the trees was taking on a tinge of indigo at the edges as the last stragglers came in from the garden. He was pleased to have Ann beside him and delighted that several of the guests came back for seconds. When they had eaten the goose and nibbled at the cheese, he went upstairs, glad that his work was done. The Colonel came out of the Ooja-cum-Pivvy and placed a hand on his shoulder.

"First class, Keating. I refer to the goose. It couldn't have been better. In a word, a jolly good show."

"I'm pleased you liked it."

"If I have a cavil, it's about the guests. Not a word was said about the waygoose. There's a conspiracy of silence. It's as if they'd been invited to a common or garden party."

"Most reprehensible."

"The most absurd thing I heard was a Westman trying to tell Oxbone that last October he'd seen a fox blackberrying in Blackbrook Lane. 'He was standing on his hind legs,' he said, 'picking them with ladylike delicacy.' I couldn't help laughing. Blackbrook Lane! As if a fox would stoop so low!"

The Colonel went down the stairs and Keating heard a voice in the hallway that made him retreat to his room.

"Sorry I'm so late. I was visiting a friend in north London . . . I waited for a train at Charing Cross for an hour."

"Good to see you, Sarah. You must be in need of a drink."

He knew the Colonel was guiding Mrs. Stooke into the dining-room.

He lay on the bed, wondering what he should do. It had not occurred to him that she would be among the guests, and he knew that if she saw him, she was bound to make a scene. He looked up at the ceiling and realised that he was tipsy from the way the vermiculated patterns above him crawled and turned. He seemed to be inside a barrel vault which ran into a groin vault with a barely visible ocellus. The ocellus turned into an oculus from which poured, not light, but stench and darkness. And he lay on his back beneath the oculus, now a *mal occhio,* and knew from the rustling all round him that he was inside an enormous crinoline worn by an Amazonian Mrs. Stooke. No higher than Gulliver, he got to his feet and tried to push the two mighty pillars apart before the evil eye above should shrivel him up. He pushed until he sweated and the evil eye closed and the groin vault above turned back into the vermiculated plaster of the bedroom ceiling. He did not relax immediately, however. He held his breath as if only an effort of will could keep the ceiling as it was and the thin wallpaper of life from cracking under his gaze to reveal the horrors painted by shrieking demons underneath.

If you look into the eye of the sun for more than a second, you'll go blind. And if you look into the depth of your heart for more than a second, you'll go mad, he told himself. Better to run lightly so that the twig will not break under your foot. The best of life is the surface glitter. Watch the noon light on the sea waves and leave the sea floor to sea monsters.

The gravelly voice of Mrs. Stooke obliterated the sea murmur of voices below. They came up the stairs, she and Ann, and stood together outside the Ooja-cum-Pivvy.

"I've seen you again with Charles Keating. He's up to no good. He came to my door to sell me an encyclopedia, but it was not encyclopedias that was on his mind."

"Charles doesn't sell encyclopedias." Ann Ede released a jet of contempt.

"Not for a living, only to get into the houses of the women he fancies. The encyclopedia downstairs in the dining-room is his bait. If he tries to interest you in the F-volume, don't think, as I did, that the F is an accident. He's utterly depraved. He begins innocently enough with a bit of firkytoodling— have you ever heard him use the word?"

"Of course not."

"Has he ever told you he's frugivorous?"

"Frugivorous? Never heard of it."

"'Frugivorous means fruit-eating,' he'll say. 'There's nothing I'd like better than to eat your breasts.'"

"What nonsense!"

"Firkytoodling is what he calls the preliminaries. Are you sure you haven't heard the word? And are you sure he hasn't told you how to deodorise his stink-finger?"

"I'm certain, Mrs. Stooke. And now, if you don't mind, I should like to use the loo."

"He's the dirtiest lover I've ever had. I blush to think of the things he made me do and the things he made me say while I was doing them."

Ann banged the door of the loo in her face. Mrs. Stooke waited on the landing, and Keating watched in dazzled disbelief through the keyhole of his bedroom door. He held his breath, at once afraid and excited, as if his very life depended on a game of hide and seek. Ann came out of the loo and he saw rather than heard Mrs. Stooke's strangled laugh, as a wren sees a barn owl by day, a flash of buff with white underparts and a grapple of metallic claws.

"A word from the wise," she said to Ann. "Eau de Cologne is no good. For his precious stink-finger only a one percent formaldehyde solution will do."

Ann went down the stairs and Mrs. Stooke went into the

loo. Keating waited for a few seconds, then followed Ann into the lounge.

"Where have you been? I thought you'd gone home." He pressed the palm of his hand against her elbow.

"Have you ever heard of firkytoodling?"

"No, why do you ask?"

"Do you know the word 'frugivorous'?"

"I have heard it applied to certain birds who feed on fruit—our feathered fruitarians, you might say."

"Would you apply it to a man?"

"Not on fruit alone . . ."

"That woman is here, the woman who shouted at you on the way to Aylesford."

"If she sees me here, she'll make a scene."

"She's a foul-mouthed frump. You wouldn't believe the things she said to me. I couldn't find the words to stop her, I felt so smeared, so utterly defiled."

"Let's go out on the patio," he said.

They walked to the bottom of the garden and round behind the conifers, and he put her sitting on the hidden seat where he sometimes read his book of poetry. The night was full of stars and the perfume of flowers cooled by dew. Through the dense branches he could see the light from the french windows, the vague pattern of the trellis on the lawn, and a man and woman with their heads together in the kitchen. He sat beside her and placed a hand on her knee, recalling a summer afternoon by an Irish river and the sparkle of the water enlivening the leaves of the willows with dots that ran to and fro—a magic irroration. Then he had that, but not Ann. Now he had Ann, but not that. Never the time and the place and the floozie all together.

"It's lovely and cool here." He felt guilty for having called her a floozie in his thoughts.

"Why is that woman so obsessed with you, Charles?"

"Perhaps she thinks I'm handsome."

"You've met her before?"

"I spoke to her once in the library, that's all."

"She's convinced you came to her door to sell her an encyclopedia."

"The suburbs are the last place to sell encyclopedias. Here it would be impossible to find one man, let alone one woman, who doesn't know it all."

"She said you showed her the F-volume."

"You don't have to be Freud to see what's on *her* mind. I'm afraid I'm old-fashioned. I always thought women's fantasies were a little more romantic, more to do with Flowers than Goose and Duck."

"Tell the truth, Charles. Have you been to bed with her?"

"Of course not." He laughed. "But I'll bet I know who has."

"Who?"

"The Bagman."

"You're teasing now, but I can't help feeling that though she's cracked she's also very sane."

"She should be locked up. If I'd known the Colonel was going to invite her, I would have asked him to think again."

"She seems to be sane with everyone except you and me."

"Let's forget about her. Just think, in a week we'll be together in the country, away from all this sham."

"Charles, have you ever been dishonest in your relationship with a woman?"

"How can I answer such a question? If I say no, you won't believe me; and if I say yes, you may well turn your back on me."

"I could never blame you for telling the truth."

"The answer is yes."

"Was she a woman you loved?"

"Yes."

269

"You couldn't have loved her, because love, as Saint Paul says, rejoices in the truth."

"Perhaps I was just addicted to her."

"I couldn't bear to think that you could lie to me. For my soul's sake, and in spite of the Bagman, I need to believe that men aren't by nature insincere."

He tried to kiss her on the neck but she told him to stop.

"I need to believe as well that I'm not just something you tuck into—like a dish of strawberries and cream. No, don't. I realise I'm rotten company this evening, but I can't help it. I'm very tired, that's all."

"These waygooses are hard on finely tuned nerves." He laughed.

"I'm going in to say goodbye to my host. You wait here for a while. I'll see you in the hallway before I go."

From behind the trellis he watched her talking to the Colonel in the kitchen. The Colonel had his hand on the small of her back, and Keating knew from the droop of his eye that he lacked the courage to put it on her bottom. In the dining-room, MacGeoch was showing Mrs. Stooke his encyclopedia, his black hair like a hawk's hood over his skull. The hawk bent over the owl, fingering a silk headband, and Keating adjusted the crotch of his trousers because of his erection, which came, not from the fetishism of the silk headband, but from the memory of Ann Ede's bottom rising against his groin.

He went round the house and out through the side gate and waited for her in the drive with a heaviness in his chest which did not come from the goose and a taste in his mouth which did not come from the claret. Should he tell her the truth, and, if he did, would she be Christian enough to forgive him? It was a simple story, but had he the gift to make it sound inevitable and true? He could paint a reasonably convincing picture of Esther, of how he first loved the girl in her because he did not know the woman, of how she tried to deny him the comfort of his daughter at bedtime when his daughter's love was the only love left to him, and of how she made light of his soufflés because they were lighter than her own.

He could understand her jealousy of his cooking, but he would never understand why she wanted to deny him his daughter. Though Isabella was only eight at the time, Esther said that she was already a woman, that he must not lie beside her in bed, that he must not fondle her, that she herself had been fondled by a father who thought girls were rosebuds, not little women. He was not a man for the hammer and tongs, so he listened without comment and took his daughter swimming twice a week instead. Swimming with her kept him sane and gave him the feeling that in the water they shared an element that both Esther and her horse merely jumped. And it was in the water that The Plan came to him like a gift from a fairy godmother.

He spent four years of unobtrusive preparation, establishing new routines, going for a swim in the sea every day, sometimes even after dark. He insured himself for £100,000, and to pay the premiums he gave up smoking and drinking and his membership of the golf club which was his only lifeline to the sane world of male companionship. His reformed character failed to impress Esther, who told him that the ideal husband was not necessarily a man who neither smoked nor drank but a man who supported his wife, like his country, right or wrong. He assured her that he had no intention of dying for either and went quietly about his business until it was time for his last swim.

He took every care to cover his tracks. On a starless night at high water he parked his car above the beach, piled his clothes on a rock, and walked down to the sea carrying a plastic bag containing the second-hand jacket and trousers he bought at a jumble sale over a year ago and hid behind the cistern on the loft. He swam across the inlet to the opposite shore, then dressed and set off over the hill for Cork. Everything went as planned. He took the ferry to Pembroke, and no one even looked his way. They probably searched the bay for his body, and when they did not find it they decided that the ebbing tide had carried it out to sea. After a decent interval he would be pronounced dead, and Esther would get her £100,000, which was ten times more than she deserved. In the meantime, his bank manager, a middling golfer but a staunch friend, would let her have a loan until she got things sorted out.

That was the story, or rather the bare bones of the story. For Ann he would have to flesh it out, make her see the desperation that made him act as he did, make her realise that sometimes in life we have no choice, that sometimes we must sin to survive.

For what seemed a long time, he sat under the horse chestnut in the front garden, waiting for her to come out, wondering if he would find the courage to tell her all. The Bagman came home from "The Fox and Billet" and disappeared into the darkened house, and somehow he knew that the struggle for Ann had hardly begun. She had once told him that as a girl she dreamed of a man who would carry her off her feet. The Bagman was not such a man, and Keating knew that neither was he. If he carried her off, it would not be in triumph but by dint of failure and in the knowledge that both he and she had made greater compacts with greater expectations. The Bagman came out of the house again and knocked on the heavy baronial door of "Foxgloves" without noticing Keating in the shadow of the tree. MacGeoch let him in, and Keating suddenly found himself immobilised by the fear of immobility. Mrs. Stooke was holding him to the ground and the Bagman was laughing at his obvious impotence. Ann came out of the porch and looked at him with cutting objectivity.

"It's Mrs. Stooke you deserve, not me," she said. "But you don't deserve her half as much as she deserves you."

He sprang to his feet and went round the house through the side gate. He looked in the kitchen, diningroom and hall, but

Ann wasn't there. He went into the orderly room to find the Colonel slumped in an armchair with Captain Scott's journal on his knee.

"Another glass of Lafitte, Captain?" The Colonel was drinking alone.

"No, thank you."

"I'm weary of my waygoose. In spite of the haute cuisine, it's a fucking great flop."

"On the contrary, it's going with a swing."

"Listen to the conversation! I came in here to read Scott. In a minute I shall tell them to go home."

"You can't do that."

"Tipsy conversation should be like forked lightning, darting here and there, touching the merest commonplace with the glint of poetry. All I've heard tonight is prose."

"Have you seen Ann Ede?" Keating turned to go.

"She said good-night half an hour ago, but shortly afterwards Bill arrived and said she wasn't home. I don't blame her, married to that ass. And he's not just an ass, he's a pedantic ass. Thinks no one knows anything about the fox except himself. Tried to convince me that he could tell from the footprints of a fox walking in snow that the forefeet are larger than the hind feet."

"I once saw foxprints on dewy grass, but I didn't notice any difference."

"Of course not. When a fox is walking or trotting, my dear Keating, you can't distinguish between the marks of the fore and hind paws, because they both land in the same place. You can only tell the difference when he's cantering or galloping. What a gaffe! It's like saying the best movement of Schubert's *Unfinished Symphony* is the third, or that the Derby is run at Doncaster."

"I hope you told him so."

"I did better. I let him know that in a canter the hind paws

273

fall behind the forepaws, whereas in a gallop the hind feet land ahead of the forefeet."

"I'm going to announce the news to the assembled guests."

In the hallway the hawk-headed MacGeoch caught his sleeve.

"Only another three hours."

"What are you talking about?" Keating asked.

"Garlick. As soon as the last guest is gone, we'll go to the police."

"You've been talking to the Colonel?"

"He told me you'd told him. It was not cricket. You should have let him enjoy his waygoose in peace."

Keating went upstairs, but the Ooja-cum-Pivvy was empty and Ann Ede was not where he had hoped to find her—sitting on his bed reading his only book. He went downstairs again and out into the garden. A brazen-faced moon hung in the south. He did not remember seeing it an hour ago, and he wondered if it had come out from behind a cloud. But there was no cloud, only a bottomless pool of blue in which floated a thousand unblinking stars. The indefinable scent of an unknown flower stopped him. He turned his nose as if to the breeze, but there was no breeze, only erratic eddies of thick-scented air. He knelt and ran the palm of his hand over the grass, sweeping the dew like raindrops off a cat's back. The grass was cool to the touch and rank from geese droppings that had melted slowly among matted roots. His head swam. He got to his feet, struggling for the scent of lupins on the brink of a sewer. But there was no sewer, just as there was no cloud and no breeze.

Standing in the shadow of the conifers, he looked towards the glow of London. A man and a woman crossed the patio to the trellis. He sidled round behind the trees, and knew at once from the chill shiver along his spine that she was dead. She was sitting on the seat with her back to the tree, like the woman on the freezer with her back to the wall. He sat beside her, holding her, kissing her face and neck through the strands of her tousled hair. He put his hand on her right knee, then on her left, and a bag of stinking ichor burst in his chest and rose like a riptide that threatened to drown his breathing. She had lost her shoes and stockings. He felt the roughness of her left knee and the smoothness of her right, and as he saw her again in the garden kneeling on her left, a wild cry choked him and tears burnt his blinded eyes. He had known it all before when he was twelve and his mother came out of hospital in a coffin.

That time he blamed his father who had walked out on them the year before. Now he could only blame himself. The first time his world was his mother, and in a moment his world was gone, nothing left but the pain of loss and a grief that could not be assuaged. In the garden, when they brought her back, the clay was steaming in the morning sun and droplets of night rain ran into the folds of lettuce leaves. A neighbour's wife who smelt of snuff hugged him to her drooping breasts, and he told her that he never wanted to be hugged again. Everything had changed since the previous evening. The talk people made round the coffin was alien and far away, and the breakfast of bacon and eggs, which a neighbour cooked, could have been fish and chips because he couldn't taste it on his tongue. Though it was May, the cold got into him, and at school he gave up games and buried himself in books. It was a cold that never quite left him, though he learnt to forget it for weeks on end after his daughter began to talk.

Ann Ede brought him self-forgetfulness and something approaching love. He had begun to feel the warmth of life again, the ebbing of self-hatred and an awakening of compassion which one day might give birth to kindness, even love. If she did not love him fully, it was because his love for her was flawed. Flawed love was the only love he was capable of giving, and flawed love was the only love he knew how to receive. From her it would have been more than enough, however. Now he would not demand even that, if not demanding could bring her back.

He kissed her rough knee and then her smooth knee and lifted her tenderly off the seat. She was heavier than he expected. He staggered against the tree and sat down again with her on his knee. He felt weak in his limbs and cold in his heart. It seemed to him that a crowbar had fallen on his head.

"Don't leave me, Ann," he whispered into her hair. "Don't leave me in this dry place without rivers of water. Take me with you to where you've gone. Take me with you, because without you there's no hiding place from the wind."

He did not put into words what he must do, but he knew that he had come to the end of a road with a hole in the centre and a pile of gravel at the side. He carried her up the garden, barely knowing where he was going. He had stopped weeping because he had stopped feeling. He was frozen over like a bucket of water left out on a night in winter. He crossed the patio to the french windows, the light now sharp after the shadows. The conversation stopped as he entered, and he looked from face to face.

"She's dead," he said. Her head was on his shoulder, with her legs and arms dangling.

"She's dead," he said, "and I'm to blame."

Mrs. Stooke came forward, as if to kiss him. The Bagman took the dead-weight off his arms, and the Colonel's knife came out of Mrs. Stooke's handbag.

"I knew it," she shouted. "You evil-minded sex maniac."

In panic he stepped back against the table. A chair fell behind him. There was a shout of horror, then another, and a murderous raven, red, not black, flew straight into his upturned face.

17

"I miss Keating most in the mornings," the Colonel lamented over breakfast. Garlick had left to catch an early train, and the Colonel and the Major were alone.

"I still find it difficult to accept." The Colonel poured the last of the coffee.

"He was guilty all right," said MacGeoch. "The murders started the day after he arrived . . . I've been thinking of something one of the detectives said. He remarked that Martin Reddin lived an exemplary life. It was only when he became Charles Keating that he lost touch with reality."

"Like the rest of us, he was not meant to live twice."

"He was a rotten journalist—in spite of all your tutelage. I read his piece about the Wistwood Indians. Very contrived."

"A rotten journalist may be, but a cook who couldn't spoil the broth if he tried. His lamb noisettes would have excited the envy of Brillat-Savarin."

"I think he missed his vocation. With a better accent, he'd have made a perfect gentleman's gentleman."

"He once told me why he liked cooking." The Colonel spoke more to himself than the Major. "When he was eighteen, he went to see his uncle, who was curing a pig he'd just killed.

He put a live eel in the tub with the pickle and told Keating—surely it can't be Reddin?—that if the eel died, the pickle would be too strong, but if it lived it would be too weak.'

"I don't see the connection with cooking." The Major evinced the kind of Caledonian self-confidence that he normally reserved for Burns Night and rowdy Saturdays when Scotland played England at Wembley.

"It's a connection that would not have been lost on Brillat-Savarin."

MacGeoch heaped a square inch of toast with an enormous dollop of marmalade and, after swallowing the choice morsel, licked his thumb and finally the corners of his moustache.

"Unfortunately he had no sense of humour. He took the fox and the goose too seriously."

"I do believe he never once twigged that we were only joshing." The Colonel laughed.

"He was out of his depth here."

"Perhaps he believed in the existence of an irreducible commodity called the truth. We, as journalists, know that there are only angles. . . . If he had wished to live in Utopia, we might have been able to help him. Unfortunately, his ambition was to live in Arcady."

"How right you are, Colonel. He longed for the fox and goose, but not for the fox that eats the goose." MacGeoch spoke with the relish of a man in rude health who feels it his duty to show an interest in lesser men's infirmities.

"I'm going to see Sarah Stooke this evening," the Colonel said after a while.

"What will happen to her? I wonder."

"They'll keep her under sedation in the hospital for another while. When she recovers, there will be a trial and she'll get off. What I want to know is where she got my knife."

"I saw Mrs. Gardener yesterday—I suppose I should now

call her Mrs. Ede. She told me that Bill is taking her to Greece for a rest cure."

"Now, she was luckier than Keating, she managed to live twice."

"I shall never forget the look of disbelief on Bill's face when she gave a moan. 'She's still alive,' someone said, but he never moved a muscle. I could see what he was thinking. The Icewoman, as he calls her, had risen again to replague him."

"Icewoman or not, she had the hots for Keating. I caught them redfooted on the stairs one morning after elevenses."

"And Keating was so infatuated that he turned monopolist, ticked me off, he did, for gazing at her herring-boned bum through my telescope."

"Why do you think he kept those cloth 'stamps' in his room?"

"Actually, he didn't. It was I who put them there." Mac-Geoch smiled like a clever schoolboy.

"What?"

"About a fortnight before he died, he and I came to suspect Garlick—or at least I did. We both searched his room and found the cloth squares in a stamp album. When Keating confessed, I realised that he must have planted them to incriminate the Lance-corporal and deflect suspicion from himself. So I did the sensible thing, I hid them in his poetry book before the police arrived."

"But did Keating confess?"

"He said he was to blame."

"He could have meant that he had failed to protect her. If he suspected Garlick, he would naturally have felt remorse. And if he loved her, as you say, why should he kill her?"

"Yet each man kills the thing he loves . . ."

"Crap, Captain. Or Wilde at his worst, which is the same thing."

"He was the Wistwood Fox all right, and it was I who brought him to the furrier."

"I think you went too far."

"How?"

"You tampered with the evidence."

"It shortened the investigation. If the police had found the 'stamps' in my room, they might have been confused. As it happened, they found them in Keating's, and in a trice they had solved the mystery."

"When you and Keating came to suspect Garlick, why didn't you report to me?"

"It was coming up to the waygoose. I thought you had enough on your mind already."

The Colonel said nothing for a moment.

"Has it occurred to you that the 'stamps' you found in Garlick's room could have been Garlick's?"

"Where's the evidence? Why hasn't he struck again?" Mac-Geoch spoke directly, but his certainty may have concealed self-questioning.

"If you think about it, Garlick fits the bill better than Keating. He's cack-handed for a start. Three out of five, a failure rate of one in three. And he's still obsessed with his ex-wife, whom he sees in every woman, including our own M.O. He said to her once that in divorce there's no decree absolute. 'Behold, I am with you always,' was how he put it."

"If it's Garlick, how do you account for the foxprints—the fox-fur, the foxtail and *Foxe's Martyrs*? He never contributed an iota to our fantasies about the fox."

"I have a theory that the foxprints were meant to lead to me."

A clatter in the hallway announced the arrival of the post, which MacGeoch went to collect.

"From Johannesburg, no less." He handed an airmail letter to the Colonel.

"My godfathers! The Brigadier's coming back for a month. We're to meet him at Heathrow next Saturday."

"Complications, complications!"

"And I had arranged for the M.O. to conduct a short-arm inspection that evening."

"The Brigadier won't like it." MacGeoch spoke seriously.

"I know. He's not a man for an impromptu firkytoodle, as Keating used to call it. I'll have to ask her to come instead on Friday."

"About Garlick . . ."

"Yes," said the Colonel.

"You'd started a train of thought."

"We simply can't have a scandal while the Brigadier's here. We must wait till he's returned to his precious gold fields. If necessary, we'll have to keep Garlick under surveillance ourselves. After all, he could be innocent. We can't act against him without being sure."

"You're right, of course," MacGeoch sounded relieved.

"However, I intend giving him a month's notice tomorrow. When he's off our hands, we can drop a hint to the police that he might be worth watching. I know it's an imperfect solution, but we live in an imperfect society."

"Problem solved." MacGeoch got up from the table. "All that remains, I suppose, is to find a new Welshman and a new Irishman."

"We'll discuss it over a preprandial drink in 'The Fox and Billet' this evening."

"Why not."

"That reminds me. I discovered something yesterday that may amuse you, Major. I was dipping into a book on olde Englishe pub names and I came across 'The Fox and Billet.' You'll never believe what it means."

"Try me."

"'Billet' in that context means fox faeces, not a piece of fire-wood as I had so innocently assumed."

The Englishman looked the Scotsman in the eye, and the Scotsman's eye lit up at the thrill of it. For a moment there was silence. Then the Scotsman inflated his already rotund tummy and laughed with the relief of unexpected relaxation.

"Now," he said, "we know everything, Colonel."